DEATH IN GOOD TIME

JO ALLEN

Copyright Declaration

Author Copyright Jennifer Young 2023
Cover Art: Mary Jane Baker

This book is licensed for your personal enjoyment and may not be resold or given away.

This story is a work of fiction. The characters are figments of my imagination and any resemblance to anyone living or dead is entirely coincidental.
Some of the locations used are real. Some are invented.

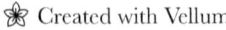 Created with Vellum

FOREWORD

All of the characters in this book are figments of my imagination and bear no resemblance to anyone alive or dead.

The same can't be said for the locations. Many are real but others are not. As always, I've taken several liberties with geography, mainly because I have a superstitious dread of setting a murder in a real building without the express permission of the homeowner, but also because I didn't want to accidentally refer to a real character in a real place or property. I have, for example, taken inspiration from the beautiful church of St Michael at Glassonby for the Capel family's private chapel, but it is not the same place. And although you might take a reasonable guess at where Capel Lodge and other places *might* be, you won't be able to place them exactly on the map.

Although I've taken these liberties with the details I've tried to remain true to the overwhelming and inspiring beauty of the Cumbrian landscape. I hope the many fans of the Lake District will understand, and can find it in their hearts to forgive me for these deliberate mistakes.

FOREWORD

I should also note that the story of Capel Castle and the paintings from the National Gallery is fiction — but based very loosely on fact. For that I have to thank Caroline Shenton, whose book, *National Treasures*, introduced me to this fascinating story.

ONE

Lady Frances Capel had been bolshie, bad-tempered, confrontational and both emotionally and financially mean, but she had been aristocracy (the daughter of an Earl, no less, a cut even above the usual county set) and so everybody who was anybody turned up at her funeral.

A number of people with no claim to be anybody found themselves there, too. Despite her legendary meanness, Lady Frances had fulfilled her social obligations with regular donations to a small but select number of local charities, whose representatives had sat at the back of the church and tagged along behind the distant family for the mile or so back to Capel Lodge for the funeral tea.

'What a life, eh?' Adam Fleetwood muttered as he disengaged himself from the throng in the ballroom and stepped onto the terrace for a discreet and welcome cigarette. 'What a bloody life.' Not that he'd ever considered himself a socialist — he had far too keen an interest in material wealth for that — but there was something about the Lodge, at least a dozen times the size of his own rented flat even without the extensive grounds with their enviable views of the River Eden and the Lakeland hills beyond, that ruffled up a sense of injustice, even in would-be upwardly-mobile Adam.

It was a pleasant summer afternoon, a relief to be outside. The ballroom had been designed for parties, not wakes; the musty black clothing of the mourners, much of it looking as if it had been kept in the back of a wardrobe for half a century, somehow sucked the light out of it. The big room had been stuffy and stale, heavy with the camphorated smell of mothballs. Adam's own funeral suit, a hasty discount purchase from a local department store, was too heavy for the occasion. His body prickled with sweat.

Mindful of the proprieties, he stepped off the terrace and strolled to the side of the house where he was out of sight. Only then did he thrust a finger behind his black tie and tweak his top button free, keeping a wary eye out for anyone who might attempt to talk to him. A door stood open in a creeper-covered wall, giving him a glimpse of a kitchen garden; he hovered near it, ready to escape if someone came out to engage him in conversation, and carried on doing what he did so well — watching. A man and woman had sneaked out onto the terrace, though he knew neither of them and nor — judging by their age and stiffness, the way they stood in silence like a couple who had been married for too long — did he want to. He looked elsewhere. At the side of the house one of the undertakers, who should surely have left by now, was standing next to the sleek black funeral car that had brought Lady Frances's closest relative from the family chapel, and looked at her watch.

Adam allowed himself a sly smile. Her boss must have accepted the invitation that etiquette had demanded the family should extend, and be making the most of what the Capel cellars had to offer. A shame for his underling, probably deputed to stay sober, keep out of the way and be ready to drive home at the drop of a funeral hat, and she was looking most frustrated about it.

As he watched, her patience ran out and she walked briskly towards the terrace to approach the two mourners on the terrace. Neither of them had much help to offer, or so it seemed, because she turned away with the slightest shrug after only a few words, scanning the grounds before leaving the couple to their fossilised silence and beginning to walk purposefully along the path towards him.

If she'd been older or plainer, the kind of character funerals always seemed to bring out into the open, Adam might have dodged deep into the refuge of the kitchen garden a few yards behind him, but he was always susceptible to a good-looking young woman and so he allowed himself the luxury of standing and watching her. Black drained colour from most people but not this tall, striking blonde, whose cheeks were pink with fresh air and concern. He dropped the cigarette among a clump of white agapanthus and thrust his hands into his pockets in an attempt to seem casual.

'Excuse me,' she said, slowing and snatching a look beyond him, to the far reaches of the garden. 'I don't suppose you've seen—'

'The undertaker?' Adam smiled at her. Yes, a very attractive woman indeed, and younger than the black made her seem. About his age, maybe, late thirties or perhaps a little younger — and no wedding ring.

'You have, then?'

'I deduced.'

'Oh,' she said, sounding slightly vexed. 'Then you haven't.'

'He'd popped in to the wake for a drink, had he?' He couldn't resist letting her know he was a step ahead.

'What are you?' the woman asked, with an edge to her voice. 'A policeman?'

As if. Adam almost laughed at that, but he decided against disarming her with the truth. *I'm an ex-convict.* It was the opposite answer to the one she'd expect, and it would almost have been worth it, but not quite. He had too much invested in going straight. 'No, but I could see you were waiting for someone and I guessed he'd have been invited in.' That was how you did it in country areas. The minister, the solicitor, the undertaker, the doctor, all invited along to the raise a glass to the departed.

'Yes, but he doesn't normally stay any longer than the decent minimum. We do have other things to do. Anyway, he's not there. I thought he might have stepped out for some fresh air. His heart isn't that great.' Her look was more anxious, now.

'Is he your dad?' asked Adam, still seeking to impress. Everyone knew the undertaker in question; Duncan's was a family firm of long local standing, and this girl was young enough to be his daughter.

'Yes. If I was a regular employee he wouldn't get away with leaving me standing around.' She was getting irritated now, not looking at Adam but alternating between checking her watch and scanning the terrace in case he should appear.

'We could look in the walled garden,' he suggested. Someone as attractive as this deserved a little of his time and effort and might, as a result, think well of him. 'You must be Miss Duncan, then.'

DEATH IN GOOD TIME

'Yes, I'm Rose.'

'I'm Adam Fleetwood.'

'Lovely to meet you, Adam, but if you don't mind—'

The door into the garden was only half-open, so he pushed it wide and led the way through. Half a dozen peacock butterflies rose from a buddleia bush as they passed and cavorted in a kaleidoscopic vortex before subsiding onto the purple cones of flowers. 'Maybe he just stepped in here.'

'I can't think why. He went to the wake to show face.'

And to drum up some future business, no doubt, pressing the flesh of the old and those with ageing relatives. 'If you can't find someone in the obvious places, the less obvious ones are the best alternative.'

'This certainly isn't obvious.'

Amused by her waspishness, he followed her along a weed-free gravel path edged with lavender. He was so concerned with looking at her shapely, black-stockinged legs and attractive backside (so neatly defined by her closely-fitting black skirt) that he was taken by surprise when she started to run.

'Oh God!' she cried, her voice pitched high with apprehension. 'Dad!'

She veered along the path, past the point where the lavender gave way to a froth of carrot tops and a forest of rainbow-stalked chard, as fast as her two-inch heels allowed her on the uneven ground. Following at a more stately pace, Adam took a second longer to see what she'd seen — a figure in black, face down on the path.

She'd said he'd a dodgy heart. 'Is he alive, Rose?' he asked, as he reached her. 'Shall I run back to the house and see if I can find a doctor?'

She was down on her knees beside him, shaking him. 'Dad! Dad! Speak to me! It's Rose! Can you hear me?' She looked up at Adam. 'Help me turn him over. At least we can make him comfortable. And then, yes. A doctor.'

Adam didn't move. He'd seen the crucial detail she'd missed. As she shook her father's dead body — and Adam didn't have to go any closer to know that he was dead — he'd spotted a dark mark like engine oil, a thick liquid sunk into the gravel.

'I don't think you should touch him,' he said.

She saw it then, stopped trying to move her father's body, though she lifted his hand and felt for a pulse before, defeated, laying it down on the path and getting to her feet.

'He's been there a while.' Even on his good days, when he felt relatively at ease with the world that he held had been unjust to him, Adam was cynical and short on patience. Today his own gentleness surprised him.

'Are you sure you aren't a policeman?' She got out her phone. Her self-possession was remarkable, but the pink had gone from her cheeks and the attractiveness had gone with it. She was parchment-white, now, and the black made her look suddenly as old as that couple on the terrace. 'There was a woman superintendent here. But she went back to the office after the service.'

Bastards the lot of them, the police. But he didn't say it, just thought about how obvious it was that the blood from the dead man had had time to soak into the ground and lose its ruby richness. 'No.'

'I'll call them,' she said, suddenly decisive, 'and you can run up to the Lodge and fetch the doctor. And I mean *run*.'

He did run, but he paused to look back as he reached the gate and saw that she'd dropped back to her knees beside her father and was dabbing her eyes as she spoke into the phone.

Christ, Adam thought as he walked rapidly across the terrace trying not to make eye contact with the couple in black, that was all he needed. Going straight was hard enough without drawing the attention of the police to himself. He paused on the edge of the ballroom, scanning the press of people, the mass of musty black. There was the woman who had inherited Lady Frances's money, lucky cow, and half a dozen catering staff circulating in white aprons with drinks and sandwiches. And thank God, there was the woman GP from Penrith who he'd overheard bragging at the graveside about how it had been her privilege to attend on Lady Frances in her final illness. He edged along the room towards her, taking care not to get sucked into a random conversation. She was engaged in a heated debate with someone about golf and waving a glass of orange juice in the air to make a point, and it took him a moment to catch her eye (she was about the same age as Rose, perhaps, but not half as good-looking) but when she did, she disengaged herself immediately.

'What's wrong?' she demanded, turning her back on her companion and slapping the glass down on what was surely a priceless antique table.

Adam must look as shocked as he felt. He prided himself on his insouciance but this was different. There was no way on Earth the man's death was an accident and he was barely beginning to process the implications. 'It's Mr Duncan. The undertaker.'

'Oh dear. Old Roger's a walking heart attack. I've been warning him about his diet for years.' She seemed to have no qualms about patient confidentiality. 'Where is he?'

'He's outside in the kitchen garden. And I don't think it's his heart.'

'An accident, then? I'd better get down there and put him back together.' She strode out through the doors and seemed to know where she was going.

'It must be.' She'd find out the truth soon enough. He

hung back to let her go ahead and then changed his mind and stopped following her, turning back to the house.

On the terrace, his colleague Geri Foster was peering down the garden towards them with the acute look of someone cheated of her rights. She, like him, always needed to know what was going on.

'What's the matter, Adam?' she asked. 'You look like you've had the telegram. *All is discovered. Fly at once.*'

'It's not the done thing to be cheerful at a funeral, Geri.' He hung back and let the doctor disappear into the walled garden. 'Didn't your parents teach you that?'

'You know damn well my eccentric upbringing never had any time for social ritual. What is it?'

He took a deep breath. Geri was older than he was and through her highly unconventional upbringing had mustered more life experience than anyone had any right to. It meant you couldn't hide anything from her, but it meant, too, that her threshold of belief, even for the incredible, was high. 'Someone's murdered the undertaker. In the kitchen garden.' Like a game of Cluedo, only he didn't know what the murder weapon was, or who had wielded it. 'I found him. I have to get out of here.'

'For God's sake,' she said crisply. 'It wasn't you, was it?'

He knew her well enough to trust her. 'Of course it wasn't, but you know what it's like. An old lag like me, right on the spot.' He was far too strong in his self-belief ever to fall prey to fear, but even he knew this one didn't look good. He might not have been inside for murder, but a violent assault marred his criminal record and a revenge fantasy over a former friend simmered in his heart. 'You know it's not the first time I—'

'You didn't kill the last dead body you found. You didn't kill this one. It'll be fine.'

'No.' But Adam was engaged in a long-time feud with

a local detective, the troubles between them always of his own making, intended to provoke a response which never came. Because his enemy (he thought that wasn't too dramatic a way of putting it) hadn't previously reacted to him in any way it didn't mean he wouldn't. 'But he's going to try and pin it on me, isn't he? Jude Satterthwaite, I mean.' It would be so typical of the man, with his monumental patience, waiting and waiting until Adam made one false step too many, or just got unlucky.

'He'd bloody well better not,' said Geri, outraged.

'I have to get away.' He shuffled a few urgent steps away from the building. 'I'll be the first person they—'

'Yes, that would make everything look great, wouldn't it? It's way too late for that. You found a dead body, the doctor knows it. She'll know it's murder by now. You'd have to kill her and you'd probably have to kill me, too, and I'm obviously not going out of anyone's sight as a precaution.'

Knowing Geri, he judged that was a joke. 'The man's daughter knows. She found him.'

'Does she? Oh God.' Geri, who was tough as old boots most of the time, and had a difficult relationship with her parents, nevertheless showed a sudden sympathetic side. 'Dear, oh dear. The poor woman.'

'At least we're already dressed in black,' he said with a shrug.

She smothered a laugh, and then straightened up. 'The doctor's coming back. Shush.'

'I thought you'd done a runner,' said the GP, hurrying past him and scowling. 'Rose said you were there when she found him.'

'I'd seen enough. I'm squeamish.' Maybe the woman knew who he was, and if she did she'd be like everyone else, bound to give more weight to his crimes rather than his rehabilitation. 'I thought I'd leave it to the professionals.'

'You'll be dealing with them soon enough. She says there's a posse of police on their way here right now. And you'll be the first one they want to talk to,' she said, and shouldered her way through the crowded room.

TWO

Sitting at his desk at the police headquarters in Penrith, Jude Satterthwaite found himself spending far more time than necessary dwelling on the problem of Adam Fleetwood. He scowled, annoyed at himself.

'Trouble at t'mill?' asked his colleague, DI Chris Dodd, looking up at precisely the right moment to catch the scowl from the other side of their shared office.

Doddsy always knew. He and Jude and been mates for a long time. 'No. Not yet.'

'What's this, then? A premonition? That's a dangerous route for a hard-boiled copper to go down.' Seeming to have reached a break in whatever he'd been doing, Doddsy pushed his chair back a few inches and reached for his coffee, sitting back in the expectation of some gossip.

'Not a premonition. A prediction. That's much safer.' These days every time Jude had dealings with Adam, even at a distance, there was a dark sub-current, a threat of trouble. By now he was used to it, because the two of them had been friends years before and had come to know each other far too well, but today it troubled him more than usual. This time, Adam had unwittingly landed him in a difficult position with his boss, something that would have delighted him if he'd known. 'It's the Capel funeral today.'

'Today?' said Doddsy, checking his watch. 'Wasn't there some talk about you going? That was what Faye said.'

'I was supposed to go.' That had been the plan. Someone had been required to turn up at Frances Capel's funeral because she'd been a significant figure in the community and had supported various charitable causes associated with the police alongside her other small, but numerous, philanthropies. But when it came to it everyone had something in their diary that couldn't be changed, and the unwelcome responsibility had trickled down through the ranks until it had landed at Superintendent level. Faye Scanlon, Jude and Doddsy's mutual boss, had taken one look at the email and passed it down a rank further to Jude.

'Supposed to? From what Faye said, it sounded like a done deal, no negotiation.'

Faye was always definite, about everything. Jude had come to understand it as a defence mechanism against her deep insecurity. He looked at his watch. It was three o'clock, and the mourners would have made their way to Capel Lodge by now. Faye would be half way back to the office if she wasn't there already. 'I'd agreed.' Reluctantly, but he had. 'But something came up last night and I told Faye I couldn't go. So she had to.'

Doddsy let out a long whistle of admiration. Faye was notoriously closed to any kind of argument once her mind was made up. 'Brave. You must have had a good reason, if she let you off. And it can't have been work because there's nothing right now you couldn't put off, and not even you can predict the next emergency.'

'That's what she thought.' Thank God, Faye had accepted his objections, though not without dispute, and he knew there'd be a price to pay later. It would be filed away in her mind for the next time something came up that he really didn't want to do, and then she wouldn't let him off the hook. She never forgot or forgave a perceived slight to her authority. He waited a moment to see if Doddsy was prepared to offer a guess, but nothing was forthcoming. 'Apparently the late Lady Capel left a sum of money to a local mental health charity, so naturally they'd be sending along a couple of their representatives to pay their respects.'

'Ah.' Doddsy understood. 'Your old friend Mr Fleetwood, eh? Isn't he their brand ambassador, or whatever fancy title they give their fundraisers these days? And the feisty Ms Foster, too?'

'Got it in one.'

'It's just as well you found out.' Doddsy was familiar with Jude's fall-out with Adam Fleetwood, and aware of all its ramifications. 'Did someone tip you off?'

'It's my detailed network of local informants,' said Jude, and laughed. He prided himself on knowing pretty much everything of interest to him that was going on in his patch but this particular titbit had nearly slipped past him. He was lucky to have picked it up in a chance encounter with his ex-girlfriend, in time to avoid the potential embarrassment. 'Becca,' he added, for clarification, and spared a thought for his ex-lover. *Your mum said you'll be going to the Capel funeral,* she'd said, swinging her handbag and avoiding meeting his eye when they'd bumped into one another outside his mother's cottage the previous evening. *You'll need to watch out. You'll bump into Adam.*

That had been enough. He'd gone straight to Faye first thing that morning and told her he wasn't going.

Doddsy was fully *au fait* with the saga of Jude's relationship with Becca, too, or most of it. 'It's just as well the two of you are still speaking.'

'You know me, Doddsy. I'm always civil.' There was no excuse not to be. He and Becca had been apart for years, long enough to get over the feelings of bitterness and betrayal. Adam had had a part to play in that, as well. 'As I would have been if I'd turned up at the funeral and bumped into him there.' He'd have sneaked in at the back just before the funeral party arrived, made sure they'd realised who he was as the congregation filed past at the end of the service, stood on the edge of the circle of mourners for the commitment and left as soon as was decent, avoiding any contact whatsoever with his erstwhile friend. Knowing how long to stay and when to leave was a useful tool in the detective's skill set. 'But the same can't be said for him, and I don't think Faye — or anyone else — would have forgiven me if there'd been a scene at the Capel funeral, even if it wasn't my making.'

'Did you tell her why?'

'Not in great detail.' He thought, on reflection, that Faye had let him off lightly. Maybe he'd been convincing, or maybe she'd half-fancied going along and rubbing shoulders with the great and the good after all. It didn't matter. He'd been spared an awkward encounter and had the added bonus of having not lost the guts of a working day to other people's expectations.

Then his phone rang.

Even in his hurry, Jude remembered to knock on Faye Scanlon's office door, but he didn't hang around to wait for her to answer. 'Faye, hi. Good funeral?'

She was kicking off patent black heels and swapping them for flats as he entered. Faye loved bright colours and he couldn't remember ever having seen her in all black before; even on sombre occasions she made a point of accentuating her outfit with a silk scarf or bold statement jewellery.

'Are they ever?' She got up, slipped off the severe black jacket she'd been wearing, hung it on a hook behind the door and swapped it for a royal blue linen one that had been gathering creases on the back of her chair. 'I couldn't get away from there quickly enough. It goes against all my principles having to pay respects to the dead aristocracy just because of what they were born, and I had a dozen other things to do.'

'Did you go along to the wake?' he asked, as she gestured him to a chair.

She lifted an eyebrow as she slid into her seat, but no more. The two of them shared a mutual respect although they'd never be friends, and they'd become used to one another's foibles. 'No. I left after they'd carted the coffin off to the crypt.'

'A crypt? The rich really are different, aren't they? Was the undertaker there?'

'Of course. The place was crawling with them, at least half a dozen. The usual severe lot, along with a rather attractive young woman who seemed to be second-in-command. Why do you ask?'

'It might turn out to be a pity you didn't stay a little longer.'

She picked up the patent shoes and thrust them into a plastic bag, which she placed on the desk. 'New shoes on the table mean a death they say, so this seems appropriate.' In their job, they couldn't afford to be superstitious.

'Maybe not the death you're thinking of,' he said, dryly.

That got her attention. 'Why? What's happened?'

'Ashleigh just called me. She's down at Capel Lodge right now. They found the undertaker dead in the walled garden. He'd been shot.'

'My God.' Faye sat bolt upright. 'Not Roger Duncan? Surely not?' Everyone locally knew of Duncan's undertakers. 'Shot?'

'That's pretty much all I know right now,' he said, before she could ask, 'but I thought you ought to know. Given the circumstances.'

'From the way you're talking, I don't imagine you think he shot himself. You'd better get on and find out what happened. Damn. This is going to be one of those cases that's all over the press, I can tell. I'm not doing any media for it. I was there. It would look a bit awkward. You'll have to take that on, and for God's sake don't ask me to do anything public facing. But equally, make sure you keep me informed of everything. Why the hell couldn't he get himself killed somewhere a little less high-profile?'

'Faye.' He'd known this would be difficult. 'I don't think I should take this on.'

She glowered at him. 'This too? You've suddenly become very choosy about what you do and what you don't do.'

'It's for the same reason I didn't feel able to go to the funeral in the first place. I explained. It's because of Adam Fleetwood.'

Faye's expression tripped from interest to irritation. 'A funeral is one thing. I was prepared to indulge you. A murder investigation is a different matter. I could accept — just — that you didn't want to put yourself in an awkward position with someone you sent to prison—'

'I had nothing to do with him going to prison.' Adam blamed him for it, so he might as well have done, but it was important not to let the myth take hold. 'This is a bit different. He found the body.'

'Is there any suggestion that he did it?'

He shrugged. 'I've told you all I know.' Adam had found a body before and proved guiltless, but it hadn't looked good for him and Jude had come in for a lot of flak over it from people he cared about. Not that he'd ever let that influence his actions, but public confidence was important to them all.

'I appreciate the delicacy of the situation.' Faye removed the bag with the shoes from her desk as if, after all, they'd brought bad luck. 'Regardless, I want you to take charge of the investigation. We aren't exactly awash with manpower and even if we were we can't spend our lives avoiding members of the criminal fraternity who have a grudge against us. They'd love that. And yes, I appreciate the background to this particular case and that he tries to make life difficult for you. But we all know that, and we can factor that in to how we handle the case.'

It was so much more complicated than a grudge borne by a law-breaker against a law-enforcer. So much of Jude's life had once been tied up with Adam's; so much of it, at a distance, still was. They walked the same streets, their parents lived in the same village, they had slept with the same woman. Even now, Adam's long-term friendship with Jude's much-younger brother sometimes felt both malicious and manipulative. 'Yes.'

'Then you'll be quite happy to take it on. And besides, who better? You're the one with the local knowledge, aren't you?'

Jude knew the area around Capel Lodge very well, better than any of the other detectives in the team and far better than Faye, who was a relatively recent arrival in the area and rarely keen to get involved in anything outside the office. 'Fair point.'

'Good. We're agreed, then. And if Fleetwood does try anything, let me know. I'll have your back.'

'Appreciated,' he said, dryly.

She gave him a sharp look, as if she suspected him of subversive thinking, and he responded with a meek nod as he got to his feet. So, he'd be involved in the Capel funeral after all, in a manner of speaking. There would be a horde of witnesses with statements to give, stories to unpick, alibis to break. If it hadn't been for Adam he might even have been looking forward to it, because what detective wouldn't be tempted to unravel the intriguing mystery about who had shot the undertaker at a funeral?

THREE

Detective Sergeant Ashleigh O'Halloran, supervising the scene at Capel Lodge and fully aware of the sequence of events that had led to Faye's attendance at the funeral rather than Jude's, made a particular point of looking out for Adam Fleetwood. Jude's gloomy and irreverent text (*Faye's making me take it on, Adam or no Adam*) had caused her to reassess how she approached this particular matter. Normally she would have spoken to whomever had been unlucky enough to discover the body herself, but Adam was a loose cannon, always ready to allege harassment while harassing the police himself. Ashleigh's own status as Jude's personal as well as professional partner made things a little more difficult and, as a result, she had no intention of dealing with him directly.

The matter was further complicated by the presence of Geri Foster. Adam's brand of trouble was cast very much in the mould of guerrilla warfare, a constant drip of anonymous and malicious tip-offs, words whispered in the darkness, but Geri was a warrior. Her unconventional upbringing had bred a disregard for any authority, and the higher the rank the more her aggression escalated. Her mission was to challenge — anyone, over anything, with reason or without. She, too, was best left to the junior constables in the first instance; any necessary follow up could be done later, when there was a chance she would have calmed down.

Thankfully, Geri hadn't been on the scene. She was making sure she was at the heart of the matter, though, sitting in close conversation with Adam, the two of them together in a corner of the ballroom like a pair of elderly chaperones at a Regency ball. One of the uniformed officers who'd arrived before Ashleigh had lined up all the potential witnesses and was taking their details and a quick statement from each of them before letting them go, but Adam and Geri, their statements presumably already taken, sat a little way apart from them and watched.

The mourners made a phalanx of black in the bright room, a mass of shocked humanity buzzing with outrage and excitement. Ashleigh headed for Tyrone Garner, the constable in charge of this particular task, who had found himself a barely-suitable antique table and a ridiculously small chair and was sitting there like a teacher at a parents' evening.

'Everything okay, Tyrone?' she asked him, as one person shuffled off and the next slid along the row to take her place.

'All in order.' He lowered his voice and stood up, turning his back on the waiting mourners. 'I'm pretty sure we'll be able to rule most of them out when we've cross-checked their statements, but with this many people there's bound to be a few without anyone to vouch for them.'

One of them, depending on what they later learned

about the time of death, might easily be Adam, but that was a problem for another time and, hopefully, another detective. 'Good. We'll get back to them as soon as possible, unless something comes up in one of the statements. I'll deal with that, if you think it's significant. Can you keep on with this and let me know when you're done?'

'Can do.' He, too, was fully aware of the difficulties of having Adam there; he, too, took a sidelong look across the room. 'I've spoken to—' He nodded in that direction.

'He found Mr Duncan, didn't he?' From a safe distance, Ashleigh allowed herself a longer look at Adam, whose arms were folded, his expression set in mutinous fury. Spoiling for a fight, then. Great. 'Have you spoken to him yet?'

'Aye, taken a detailed statement and told him he can go, but he said something about making the most of the food and not letting it go to waste.' Tyrone, who could take a joke, clearly disapproved of this level of black humour. 'He was with the poor man's daughter. Rose Duncan. She's a partner in the undertaking business. She's over there.'

Ashleigh took a look across the room to a tall, blonde woman in stiffly formal black clothing who sat bolt upright on a high-backed chair by the window, staring across the lawn to the buzz of activity around the walled garden. Her expression was blank.

'Right. I'll have a quick word with her later. First I need to talk to whoever's in charge. Assuming someone is.'

'Not you, Boss?' said Tyrone, cheekily, and grinned at her.

She smiled back at him, a very quick smile because of the seriousness of the situation. 'I meant whoever's hosting the funeral. Jude said Lady Frances didn't have any children but someone must have inherited. And while I'm sure she left instructions for the funeral and the wake, someone has to host it, don't they?' She wasn't well enough up on the doings of the aristocracy to know that kind of etiquette.

'Right.' He smiled again. Tyrone almost always smiled. She supposed it was because he was so young and so optimistic; he was such a proficient copper that it felt like he'd been in the force for decades. It was always a refreshing surprise to find him so lacking in cynicism. 'There's a great-niece, multiple times removed or whatever. I put her in the library, through that door over there and across the corridor. I thought you'd want to get the background from her, about who was here and why and so on.'

'Okay. I'll have a word with her and then speak to Rose Duncan.'

'I've said Miss Duncan can go home, too, but she wanted to wait a bit, recover herself. But you might want to catch her sooner rather than later, in case she changes her mind.'

'Good idea. I'll do that now.' She left him to the next in the long line of black-clad interviewees and crossed the room to the door Tyrone had indicated, taking a line that passed close to Rose. As she did so the undertaker's daughter turned away from the window towards her.

'Miss Duncan?' Ashleigh stopped beside her. 'No need to stand up. I wanted to offer you my condolences on the loss of your father.'

'Thank you,' said Rose, and stood despite Ashleigh's stricture. Her outfit was dishevelled, with dust on her skirt and jacket and a brown smear of dried blood on her white blouse.

'I'm Detective Sergeant Ashleigh O'Halloran, the officer in charge. I wanted to reassure you that we're doing everything possible to find out what happened to your father, and we'll be in touch with you throughout the investigation.'

Rose reached into her pocket for a large white handkerchief with which she dabbed discreetly at her eyes. 'PC Garner said something about a family liaison officer.'

'Yes, we'll be assigning you an FLO to assist you.'

'Thank you. I saw you out in the grounds earlier, I think. Is that right?'

'Yes, just checking that everything possible is being done.' Ashleigh took a quick look out and was reassured. The grounds were swarming with police officers and more blue lights flashed up the drive as she spoke; a team of white-suited forensic investigators were already at work in the garden. Roger Duncan couldn't have been dead that long and there was every chance they'd arrived in time to capture some crucial evidence, whether the killer had made their escape or merely slipped back to mingle in the ballroom.

'Sergeant O'Halloran.' A male voice, bolshie and loud. 'Leave Miss Duncan alone. Can't you see she's—'

With a sigh, Ashleigh turned away. 'Thank you, Mr Fleetwood. I know my job.'

'It's all right, Adam,' said Rose, in a voice that quivered a little. 'It really is.'

Adam positioned himself in the very small gap between Ashleigh and the undertaker's daughter, forcing both to take a step back. 'Rose. I'm not having the police intimidate you after what just happened to you.' His first was clenched around the stem of a wine glass and his cheeks were scarlet in his otherwise pale face.

'We try not to be intimidating,' said Ashleigh, mildly, but even as she aimed to divert Adam's aggression she was intrigued. 'You know each other?'

'Now you're interrogating me. I've already given my

statement. But yes, we do know each other. We met out there in the bloody kitchen garden.'

Out of the corner of her eye, Ashleigh saw Geri Foster surging across the room to join in the fray. 'I understand it must have been a shock for you, too,' she said, evenly.

'I know what you people are like. You're going to try and set me up for it, just like you did before.'

Adam's recollection of events had curdled with time. 'As always, we'll aim—'

'I think I will go home just now, after all,' said Rose, putting the handkerchief back in her pocket. 'I'll need to tell the rest of the staff what's happened. I'll need to let them know the police will be wanting to speak to them, like the constable said. And then there are two funerals we have to do tomorrow and we just…I can't—'

'You definitely need to get home.' Adam's voice had softened perceptibly. 'Look, I'll—'

'You can't, Adam.' Geri made it across the room and tweaked the glass out of Adam's hand. 'You'll still be under the limit after just one glass, I know, but better to be safe than sorry. I'll take you,' she said to Rose, 'as I'm not drinking, and I'll take you, too, Adam, since you probably need to get out of here before you give Sergeant O'Halloran an excuse to arrest you.'

That was Geri Foster all over, probing, pressing, trying to shock in much the same way as Adam himself. No wonder the two of them got on so well. And yet Geri, who was forthright and never felt sorry for herself, and who at least had the excuse of unworldly parents who refused to accept societal norms, was somehow a rather more sympathetic character than bolshie, self-pitying Adam.

Nevertheless, she was glad to see the back of both of them, though she'd have welcomed the chance to form a clearer impression of Rose. She allowed herself a moment to watch as the trio crossed the room towards the uniformed constable who checked off their names at the door and directed them out through the bowels of the building, and then she turned towards the library.

FOUR

The library was small and dark, with square casement windows set in walls four feet thick. The front of Capel Lodge was Victorian and far more grand than its name suggested, but walking into the library was like entering a different age. This part of the building was the original, cold even in the summertime, facing northwards to the hills and the Debatable Lands. Two of the walls were lined with bookcases; a quick glance suggested that Lady Frances's tastes — or more likely those of her immediate ancestors — were eclectic, encompassing everything from modern paperbacks right the way through to dusty old volumes that had never been opened. Gaps on the shelving suggested some of them had been taken out and never replaced, either lost or sold, but the spaces they had left contained a peculiar selection of *objets d'art* — tiny porcelain figurines, rococo photo frames, a gilt teapot. The walls on either side of the window were cluttered with dingy paintings of past generations of Capels, along with timid watercolours that must have occupied the time of genteel female relatives, and an oddly dissonant print of Dalí's *The Empress*.

But it was the fourth wall that caught Ashleigh's attention. Above the carved stone fireplace hung an armoury of antique weapons — daggers and swords with long, wicked blades and basket hilts, muskets and blackened pistols. She gave them a long look. *Wouldn't swear to it on a quick look*, the GP who'd examined the body had said, *but I'd say he'd been shot*.

The public-facing Capel Lodge might be open and welcoming, at least today, but the rear peered nervously towards the horizon for possible danger and rattled with ghosts. That wall of death would be the first place to look for the murder weapon.

She turned to the room's occupants. Two women, one with snow-white hair forced into a severe cut and swollen ankles crammed into black shoes, the other some twenty years or so younger and inexpensively neat, had been sitting in front of the window, and both got to their feet as she came in.

'Are you the detective in charge?' asked the younger of the two, stepping forward.

Crossing the room, Ashleigh produced her warrant card, introduced herself and murmured through the formalities — condolences on the loss of Lady Frances, shock at the violent death of the undertaker, assurances that everything possible was being done.

'I'm Emma Capel,' said the woman, seeming to gather her wits, 'and this is Irene Jenkins. Irene was Frances's... well, I suppose you were her friend, weren't you?'

'Lady Frances always referred to me as her companion.' Irene Jenkins spoke with a refined Welsh accent, maintained a respectful distance behind Emma, and kept her eyes on the worn but probably valuable carpet.

'I always got the impression you were much more than that,' said Emma Capel with a warm smile.

Ashleigh, aware of the pressure of time, added a polite reminder of the reason for her visit.

'Of course. You'll need to talk to everyone, won't you but really, I don't even know—'

'Shall I ask Carly to fetch you and Sergeant O'Halloran some tea?' asked Irene, turning to the door.

'Would you mind? Thank you, Irene, you're an absolute treasure. Do have a seat, Sergeant O'Halloran.' Emma sank back into her deep leather chair with what was almost relief. 'I'm sorry. I'm just a bit rabbit-in-the-headlights right now. First Frances dying, then the funeral and now this.'

'It must be hard, losing a close relative.' Ashleigh sat down, the chair conveniently located so that she could see the door and keep half an eye on what was going on outside without having to take her focus off Emma.

'No, not at all. I mean, I don't mean it the way it sounded.' Emma became pink and flustered. 'But I never thought my life would take this turn, and certainly never so quickly. I didn't really know Frances very well. She was just a distant relative, a cousin of some kind, and I'd met her a few times in my life, at family weddings and so on. She was an only child and never married, and it turned out there weren't any male heirs. There had been one, I think, but he was a bit of an adrenaline junkie and was killed skiing off-piste in the Andes or something, but although I suppose I knew I'd inherit I never thought about it until she died. My own personal life was in a bit of turmoil, you see. I lost my mother last year and then my husband upped and left me after twenty-five years, and our son has just gone to a job in New York and couldn't even get leave to come today, so this has all…'

She ground to a halt as the door opened and a woman in black entered. 'Tea, Miss Capel? Sergeant?'

'It's Emma, Carly, please. Let's not be formal,' said Emma, and waved a helpless hand in front of her face.

'Of course, Miss Capel,' said the woman, her face expressionless, and placed a tray with a china tea set and what looked like home-made biscuits in front of them.

'Honestly,' said Emma, in some frustration when the woman had withdrawn, 'I don't know what century Frances thought she was living in. It was all *yes your ladyship* and *no your ladyship* and *of course your ladyship*. All forelock-tugging and obligation, and absurd levels of gratitude for cast-offs, and she didn't even have the courtesy to call these poor people by their names. Even Irene, for God's sake, and she'd been with Frances for bloody decades. I don't think poor Carly has been here much longer than a year or so and you'd think she's young enough to expect to be treated a bit more informally, but no. She seems to have bought into it like the rest of them.' She sat back and sighed.

'Shall I pour?' asked Ashleigh, amused. Emma clearly wasn't one for the aristocracy.

'Would you mind? I'm sorry, I sound crotchety, but really.' Emma fanned herself with her hand. 'Do you know, even when I did briefly wonder if I might inherit it never occurred to me that I'd inherit the staff as well. Servants? Me? I've never even had a cleaner and of course I really don't need or want them, but I can't just sack them because their livelihoods depend on me. Honestly, with all the problems I had in my life I never thought I'd end up wrestling this kind of moral dilemma.'

Emma's background seemed interesting but probably not relevant, and even then this wasn't an appropriate time to go into the matter further. Making a note to contact the solicitor and establish the exact terms of Lady Frances's will, Ashleigh poured two cups of pale tea and handed one over to Emma, declining a biscuit. The china cups were so fine that the sunlight shone through them and the level of the tea inside was visible. 'I hate to add to your difficulties by asking you about what happened.'

'I don't know.' Emma frowned at the tea and sipped at it with a look that bordered on disgust. 'Frances has been gone for a couple of weeks, that's all, and as soon as I heard of course I came up. Not because I give a damn about the money, even if I can't deny that it's a godsend for my current situation though I daresay it'll cause me as many problems as it solves when my husband finds out. But there's basic respect, isn't there, and I had to come up and deal with the solicitors and the undertakers and, God help me, the *servants*, and so it's all been a bit of a whirl.'

'You're staying here?'

'God, no. This place is so cold and stiff. And dark! I decided to stay at the George in Penrith and ease myself into things a bit. I left it to Irene to do the organising of the catering and so on because she knows how these things are done. All I did was I sign everything off with Wilf Hamley — he's Frances's solicitor — and agree to everything Roger Duncan said Frances had wanted for the funeral, and the I just turned up to meet and greet, as it were.'

'You didn't know Mr Duncan at all?'

'I met him once, that was all. Apparently Frances had told him beforehand exactly what she wanted done, so I just signed it off. He seemed such a nice man, and everyone speaks well of him. Poor man. So awful. But I can't in all honesty say I know anything more about him.' She set the cup down carefully and helped herself to a biscuit.

'What did you do today, Ms Capel?'

'As you'd expect. Got up, had my breakfast at the hotel. Went into the town centre to get new black tights because I'd forgotten them. Killed time for a bit, because the funeral wasn't until one o'clock. Then I came here about half an hour before the hearse arrived. Irene and I went in the car, and Roger was in the front, with one of his employees driving. His daughter — poor girl — was already at the church, I suppose, making sure everything was in order there. It was a fairly desultory procession, with so few family, and personally I'd have skipped it, but those were the instructions. From the church we came straight back here.'

There had been no mention of an interment. 'Was Lady Frances buried or cremated?' asked Ashleigh.

'Nothing so common. The coffin was taken down into the family vault.' Emma's lip curled. 'Roger Duncan supervised that. I just went to the door and shook hands with everyone and left him to it. Then we came back here.'

'Did you see Mr Duncan after that?'

'No, although of course I'd invited him to join us at the wake. but if he was here I didn't get a chance to speak to him. There were so many people — which is odd, because I always got the impression that Frances was pretty standoffish and didn't have any real friends locally.' She rubbed her chin reflectively, a fish out of water in this strange world of etiquette.

Frances had had so many people at her funeral because she was aristocracy and everyone wanted to be seen, or to see inside the house, and certainly to get a taste of what was bound to be an exceptional spread. Even Ashleigh, brought up in suburbia and a stranger to the customs of the countryside, knew that. 'When did you find out what had happened to him?'

'I'd been standing over in that corner of the ballroom,

by the big portrait of Frances, the whole time. People kept coming up to me, people I didn't know. Then one of the mourners came up and said she was a doctor and that someone had found a dead body in the garden. My initial reaction was that someone must have been taken ill, and then she said no, that it was the undertaker and it didn't look like an accident and that she'd called the police. And after that all hell broke loose.'

From there, Ashleigh knew the story. 'Are you familiar with Capel Lodge?'

'No. I haven't been here for years. Not since I was a kid.' Emma cast a look round the room. 'I know what you're thinking. About these bloody guns.' She nodded at the display on the wall.

Ashleigh said nothing, but nodded and let her witness carry on.

'I hate guns. These are antiques, of course, and I've always assumed they weren't capable of being fired, but maybe they are. I wouldn't have had them around the place for sure. Horrid things.'

'I expect they're collectors' items.'

'I wouldn't even sell them, even though they belong to me. I'd just get rid of them, even if I don't sell the place, which I expect I will,' said Emma, and shook her head. 'Honestly, I'm assuming the police are going to seize them and take them off my hands, and if you don't I'll just get the whole lot melted down before anyone else gets killed.'

FIVE

'Irene Jenkins,' said Lady Frances's companion (or, as Emma would have it, friend) when Emma had gone back to flounder about in the strange social circle of which she found herself the reluctant queen, and the housekeeper had slipped in and removed the tray of tea and biscuits. Refreshments, it appeared, were only for those at a certain level in the hierarchy. She offered her hand, as if it were a social occasion. 'Please let me know how I can help.' She smiled shyly as she spoke, a woman who now stood revealed as even more elderly than she'd first appeared, as delicate as a Victorian porcelain doll.

'It's routine inquiries at this stage,' said Ashleigh, taking careful note of how capable this woman seemed, despite the frailty of her appearance, 'after what happened to Mr Duncan.'

'So terrible,' agreed Irene, taking a seat in the chair Emma had vacated and picking what looked like a dog or cat hair off her sleeve. 'It was such a shock. To think such a thing could happen at Lady Frances's funeral! But I've already explained to your police constable that I was in

JO ALLEN

the ballroom the whole time, except perhaps for a moment when I nipped out to see if everything was all right in the kitchen, with Carly being in sole charge of things there.'

'Yes, I understand that. But I understand you've been at Capel Lodge for a long time and might be the person who can explain some of the background.'

Some people might have looked gratified at this, but Irene Jenkins merely took it as her due. 'That's right, though I can't see how it's relevant. Lady Frances loved Capel Lodge but it was remote from the rest of her life and didn't spend a lot of time here as she grew older. She preferred to stay in her London flat.'

A London flat. If that had come to Emma Capel, too, she'd be a very lucky woman, so much so that it would have been worth digging deeper into the will and Emma's inheritance. 'I see.'

'Yes. She continued to come up here for a few weeks in the summer, and whenever she felt the need for a break from London. When she was here she never socialised, though she did feel strong ties to the area and contributed extensively to local charities. And you can see from the attendance today that she was widely admired.' Irene said it with a straight face, as if she believed it.

'She died here, I believe?'

'She came here knowing she was dying, yes. After she had passed, I took charge of all the arrangements until Miss Capel arrived, and then carried out Lady Frances's instructions. When we were here it was always I who dealt with the staff and the tradesmen.'

Ashleigh had already formed a negative opinion of the late Lady Frances; this hint at snobbish stand-offishness confirmed it. 'So you'll know the local community well?'

'I would say I do. Yes.'

DEATH IN GOOD TIME

'Good. May I ask if you know, or had heard, anything about the cause of Mr Duncan's death?'

Irene bowed her white head in a gesture of appropriate respect. 'Dr Askew said he was shot.'

'That's how it seems, although we won't know for certain until the post-mortem is complete. But as I'm currently working on that assumption, I'd like to ask you about this gun collection.' Ashleigh nodded to the pistols, muskets and daggers which studded the wall, the array of weapons forming a pattern that was dense yet strangely incomplete.

'It belonged to Lady Frances's grandfather, the seventh Earl Capel.' Irene stared at the wall, intently. 'He was an avid collector and interested in almost everything. A true polymath. Lady Frances inherited the weapons along with everything else, but I don't think she ever liked them.'

'I'm asking because it looks to me as if some might be missing. Not that I know anything about guns or how to show them or anything, but the display looks a little unbalanced to me.'

Irene got to her feet (levering herself up with some difficulty in the first sign of the infirmity of age) and crossed to the display. Ashleigh followed, keeping close to Irene as she'd been trained to do when an unknown quantity approached the array of deadly weaponry, only to laugh at herself. Irene was no threat; indeed, she seemed reluctant to approach too closely.

'You are right,' said Irene, with a degree of uncertainty. 'It does look unbalanced.'

Ashleigh went closer. There were tell-tale marks on the crumbling plaster, pairs of holes where hooks or other fixings might have been. 'Here, perhaps?'

Irene felt for the glasses that hung on a chain around her neck and peered through them. 'Oh dear. And yet that

that doesn't surprise me. Before her death Lady Frances had been disposing of a number of personal items.'

'Including these weapons?'

'I'm afraid Lady Frances wasn't very discriminating in her later years.' Irene's face crinkled in disapproval.

Still instinctively keeping an eye on her companion, Ashleigh got out her phone. 'May I take photographs?'

'Yes, of course. But don't you send in the search teams, like on the telly?'

'We'll be asking Miss Capel if we can have a look around the property, of course.' Ashleigh snapped a few photos to catch the weapons as they appeared. Emma Capel had been mightily relieved to be told the weapons would be removed, forensically tested and then disposed of, and Ashleigh herself had heaved a sigh of relief that the items would soon be out of harm's way. The blades of the knives had been filed down, making them far less fearsome than they appeared, though still capable of causing damage, but it hadn't been a knife that had killed Roger Duncan. 'Were the guns in working order, Miss Jenkins?'

'I'm afraid I know nothing about firearms. I have no idea whether they've been made safe, or even whether they still have bullets in them. I always assumed not.' Her face took on an expression of consternation as she, like Ashleigh, contemplated the prospect of a wall of fully-primed guns open to any passer-by.

'And you say Lady Frances might have given some of these items away?'

'I can't say for certain. She gave a number of things away in the last few months, sometimes on a whim and sometimes with some thought. Not just the guns, but books and jewellery and other items, too, not always appropriately.' Irene let the glasses fall and folded her lips together. 'There was a book of spells that she insisted the vicar should have. Spirituality and the occult were some of her grandfather's interests, and she had a very keen sense of humour, though I believe the vicar was a little embarrassed. Though in fact it could have been a lot worse. I believe the Earl had a collection of — shall we say picturesque? — Victorian photographs that would have been quite embarrassing if Lady Frances had passed them on.' She went pink.

Thank God it didn't seem as though Ashleigh would be required to look at Victorian pornography. 'Were the collections catalogued at all? It would be useful to know what's missing, even if we don't know where the items have gone.'

Irene's face creased once more into an anxious frown. 'I'm sure things used to be catalogued in the seventh Earl's day, but Lady Frances herself disposed of things rather than acquiring more. Earl Capel died at least forty years ago so if there is a catalogue it won't be digitised and I really couldn't tell you where it might be. It might even be in Castell Capel. That's the family home in Wales.'

'That's no problem, Miss Jenkins.' With Emma Capel's permission, which would surely be forthcoming, they would get someone on to tracking down the catalogue if it existed. The bullet which had killed Roger Duncan would be a clue in itself. 'Who has access to this room?' There was no lock on the door.

Irene Jenkins looked baffled. 'Well, the household of course, but there aren't many of us. Myself. Lady Frances, obviously. Carly, and now Miss Capel. The cleaners. That's really all. There's a local firm of gardeners who does the grounds but they're never in the house.'

'Okay. Someone will have to speak with all of them, so if you could supply me with their details that would help.' Ashleigh looked around her. For all its eclectic contents, the room had a slightly sterile sense to it, like a waiting room. There was a pile of magazines on a side table and a bunch of roses in a tall glass vase, beginning to wilt in the heat. 'Anyone else?'

'No, not since Lady Frances died.'

'And before she died?'

'Oh.' Still worried, Irene touched her forehead and the frown deepened. 'A lot of people, actually, including Mr Duncan himself, and his daughter. Lady Frances was ill for some months and she saw a number of people, tying up loose ends. Not just business people, but there were others who came to pay their respects. I made it my habit to bring them in here until Lady Frances was ready to come to speak to them, which could sometimes be several minutes. She was a little slow on her feet latterly, even before she took to her bed.'

'Okay. And they would be entirely alone in here?'

'Carly would come and bring them a cup of tea,' said Irene, in a voice that quivered, 'but there were so many of them. Dear me, I don't know how many there might have been and I don't even know if I have a record of them all. Some people phoned ahead but some called in passing. Lady Frances was never a very clubbable woman but she was well-respected and when it became known she was dying, people made it their business to call by. The charities and so on. I can write down the ones I know.'

The charities would have had an interest, Ashleigh thought cynically, in reminding Lady Frances of their existence and of her munificence, hoping that she might make a late decision to reconsider the dispositions of her will. Maybe she had, but that didn't mean any of these over-eager visitors had taken a gun from the wall and later used it to kill the undertaker. 'Did you know Mr Duncan well, Miss Jenkins?'

'Only in passing. I would call his office if Lady Frances needed to speak to him, though I was as likely to speak to his receptionist as I was to the man himself, and I would go down to greet him when he called. Beyond that, no, though of course I knew of his excellent reputation locally.'

'As a businessman or as an individual?'

'Both, I think. I certainly never heard a bad word spoken about the man and Lady Frances would have had no hesitation in removing her business from him if she thought he wasn't above reproach in any way.'

'Thank you,' said Ashleigh, suppressing her sigh as she thought of the long list, probably incomplete, of people who would have been left alone in this grim little armoury for long enough to lift a weapon from the wall and conceal it in a bag, a briefcase, or even a pocket, on top of those who might have found themselves with a serviceable weapon as a result of Frances Capel's eccentricity. 'I'll leave you just now, as I know you have many other things to do. But I'd be grateful if you could let me have that list as soon as possible.'

'I can do it now,' said Irene, opening a drawer in a side table and extracting a notepad and a mechanical pencil, 'if you just give me five minutes.'

'Thank you. I'll be outside in the garden, or in the ballroom. If you can't find me, you can give the list to any of the other officers. I'll be sending someone in to remove these guns. Ms Capel is aware.'

She let herself out and went out onto the terrace. Adam was standing with Geri and Rose Duncan at one end of it; despite the conversation earlier, it appeared they had decided not to leave. Avoiding the risk of eye contact, because Geri Foster disliked her and Adam's calculated hatred of Jude was always to be treated carefully and was often manifested towards her as his partner and colleague, Ashleigh walked past them to the end of the terrace and, out of earshot, called her boss.

'This is shaping up to be a bit of a nightmare,' she said, when she'd outlined the progress of the case to date. 'If it turns out the man was killed by one of the guns that seems to have disappeared from the study, then it could have disappeared at any point over the last several weeks, and it could have either been taken without permission or given as a gift by Lady Frances. But we don't even know for certain that they weren't removed years ago. We simply have no idea.'

'We can find out if they were loaded, though.' Jude, at least, sounded a little more optimistic. 'If they weren't then they'd have to get the ammunition from somewhere and at least we might be able to get a lead there. I take it no-one raised a fuss about us removing them?'

'The opposite. Emma Capel seemed delighted to get shot of them, so to speak.'

Geri Foster, she noted, was watching her with intent and looked to be about to approach her, so she closed the call down and, on a whim, decided to face any questions the woman might have head on, rather than avoid them and risk an undignified pursuit. As she walked down the terrace the three of them stilled as they watched her — Adam with suspicion and fury, Geri with interest and Rose with obvious apprehension. Poor Rose, clinging on to the scene of the crime, unable to let go.

'Miss Duncan,' she said, her voice heavy with sympathy. 'Is there anything we can do for you?'

'No,' said Rose, and her smile was a reaction to the kindness, because there was really nothing to smile about. 'I've been told I can go. But it's so hard just to leave Dad, even though there's nothing I can do for him. Isn't that odd? I just feel he still needs me.'

'I think you should go home, Rose.' Adam pushed himself forward and glared at Ashleigh. 'Geri and I will look after you. We need to get you away from these people. They aren't on your side.'

'Don't be silly,' said Rose, almost amused. 'Of course they are. But thank you. I think I will go home now.' She shuffled a few steps towards the end of the patio. 'I was here with Dad a fortnight ago, talking to Miss Jenkins about the funeral. It just seems so—'

'So strange,' said Geri, filling in for her. 'Yes. I know what you mean.'

'Were you here, too, Ms Foster?'

'Adam and I came to visit Lady Frances a couple of weeks before she died. She wanted to tell us about the bequest she would be leaving to the charity. Though I have to say, she made it sound as if it would be rather more than it was. Still, she got what she wanted. Gratitude,' said Geri Foster, with a snort of disgust, and turned her back.

SIX

'Come and put your feet up, petal.' Carly pulled out one of the chairs at the kitchen table and waved Irene towards it. 'You've done enough running around. Settle down and have a brew. And something to eat, as well. Old Frances might have been tight as a duck's backside, but she certainly didn't sell herself short when she'd gone. We'll be eating this stuff for weeks.'

Irene sighed, biting back the reproof that came to her lips. The housekeeper was always dutifully respectful in front of her employer but roguishly otherwise in private, but her heart was in the right place, and anyway she was right. It had been a long day and the tasty morsels left over from the wake were deliciously tempting. 'I don't think I want anything to eat.'

'Yes you do.' Carly placed two plates on the table and then began decanting canapés from the large silver salvers covered with clingfilm which contained the broken meats from the wake onto a third, larger plate. 'Here. I need something, too.'

'But there's all the clearing up to do—' The catering staff who had been brought in for the occasion had been sent home, their work incomplete, and the kitchen was stacked with plates and glasses and napkins, bowls of crisps, stacks of curled sandwiches, a lifetime of crumbled sausage rolls. For a moment Irene was so overwhelmed she feared tears.

'It'll take me half an hour.' As the kettle clicked off, Carly poured the boiling water into the small brown teapot she kept for those little tête-à-têtes she and Irene used to have over meal plans and other domestic affairs, and set it on the table. The plate of canapés swiftly followed and then she, too, pulled up a chair and sat down. 'There you go, darling. It's been a bugger of a day. A bugger of a few weeks, for you. And look, these won't keep. You be kind to yourself.'

How did you do that? Self-pity had no benefits that Irene could see. 'I'll be fine.' But the selection of nibbles that Carly had placed in front of her did look tempting. She stretched out a hand.

'I know you really liked the old girl.' Carly helped herself to a couple of the less tired-looking sandwiches and several delectable cheese and chive scones barely the size of a fifty pence piece. 'You may not be hungry but I could eat a scabby-headed wean, as they say in Glasgow. I've been on my feet all day and not had time to eat, and then that policeman asking me my whereabouts as if I even had second to disappear outside for a fag.'

'Perhaps we should see if the police want some of the food—'

'Put your halo away, Irene. This stuff's far too good for that lot.'

It was. It was all Lady Frances's favourites, no expense

spared. Irene had sat with Carly to go over the menu, at this very table, and had blenched at the expense but the housekeeper seemed quite happy to spend other people's money. 'It really is very good. You did a wonderful job.'

'I didn't make the stuff, though. Just gave the instructions. I'm much better at that than I am at my own job. I was born to be a boss.'

Giving in to temptation, Irene reached out for a delicate sausage and leek roll. Maybe she was hungry after all. 'What will you do now?'

'God knows.' Wiping cream cheese from her long, strong fingers on her apron, Carly reached for the teapot and poured the tea. 'Have a glass or several of that rather nice red that's left when the clearing up's done, that's for sure.'

'I mean, afterwards. I'm not sure Miss Capel…'

'She doesn't give a lot of thought to the little people, does she?' Carly shrugged. 'I heard her talking to that detective. *The staff. The servants.* Wanting to get rid of us and not a thought for what's going to happen to us.'

It was no surprise that Carly listened at doors. She was that sort. Irene lifted her mug and sipped at her tea. 'I will miss Lady Frances.' The two of them had been together for decades, ever since Lady Frances's father, who had had a bad War, had retreated in his rooms and rarely come out until he died, leaving his anxious wife to spend her time worrying about him and neglecting their daughter. Frances's grandfather, the seventh Earl Capel, had decided that his granddaughter needed female companionship and Irene, nearby, appropriately qualified, a fatherless young woman, had been the obvious choice.

'Of course you will, love. I mean, let's be honest. She was a crashing snob and a bit of a bully, but we're none of us perfect and she was your friend.' She curled her lip as she said that, as if it was the kindest way she could think of to hide the brutality of what she really thought.

Irene picked up a sausage roll, thinking about her employer. It was true that Frances had sometimes behaved badly to her, but that was hardly unexpected; her upbringing had been eccentric, her grandfather autocratic, and her childhood loveless. She had been spoilt and accustomed to unquestioning obedience from everyone but the seventh Earl, even as the world had changed around her. And yet she had been loyal, even in her thoughtlessness, and she had never let Irene down. 'Yes.'

'The people we care about leave a hole, don't they? That's what's happened to you. A big Frances-shaped hole in your life.'

Irene nibbled at the sausage roll. The pastry was meltingly folded, the meat deeply, tastily seasoned, the leeks a reminder of Wales, as Frances would have intended they should be. 'Yes.'

'And it's all right for me, isn't it? I'm not even forty yet. I'm young enough to pack my stuff and bugger off somewhere else if the new boss decides not to keep me on.'

'I'm quite sure Miss Capel will still need you.'

'You think? She doesn't like the place. She doesn't like having servants. She'll keep the swanky flat in London, I bet, and sell the rest of it. I would, especially if the alternative is living in some semi in Wembley or wherever it is she comes from. I'll survive, but what about you, eh, Irene?'

'I will also be fine,' Irene repeated, doggedly, and reached out for a bijou brie and cranberry canapé.

'Did she leave you anything? It's none of my business, I know, but you and me are both in the same boat here. Did she even set you up with a pension? I bet you weren't formally employed, were you? Where are you going to live?'

Irene had been asking herself that ever since she'd heard the contents of Lady Frances's will. 'I expect I will go back to Wales. I have savings.' Not a huge amount, admittedly, but some.

'Right. But didn't she even leave you anything? Looking at all those folk who rolled up at the church there hardly seems a good cause she didn't chuck a tenner to at some point, and I know from what I heard her saying to the solicitor that she left money to most of them, though I bet it wasn't that much.'

This was too much. Irene was tired and averse to any kind of confrontation, but she had standards. 'You shouldn't have been listening at the door.'

'Well, my Lord, I wasn't exactly listening. She was shouting at the poor man as if he was going deaf. I could hardly not hear.'

Shouting had been a habit of their employer, who refused to admit her own hearing loss and so bellowed at everyone in the hope that they would shout in return. 'It's confidential.'

'He could be a town crier, that man. But what about you, Irene? He asked her about you and I didn't hear what he said but I didn't get the impression she left you as much as a button.'

This woman knew too much. Despite the fact that she was well-intentioned — perhaps the more so because of it — Irene was tired of her questions. They came too close to challenging her on her feelings, on how she would cope with Lady Frances's death, on the unquestionably bumpy few months she would have to negotiate before she could settle into retirement. Besides, she was a bad liar and she was committing herself more and more into the mire with every word. More questions would expose her. She had no family, in Wales or elsewhere. Her employer had left her no money. She didn't want to talk about it.

'This isn't about material things,' she said, primly.

'Jesus, Irene, you can't live on patronage when your patron's dead.'

There was no answer to that. Suddenly Irene found herself overtaken by tiredness. 'I think, Carly, I'll go and lie down for an hour or so. The police don't need me any more.'

'I'll clear this lot up, then,' said Carly, cheery and unoffended, 'and then maybe get out for a walk. I had plans for this evening, but they've all gone up in smoke.'

'Just put the perishable things in the fridge,' said Irene, though it really wasn't for her to appropriate Emma Capel's role and issue instructions to the domestic staff, 'and get yourself out for a bit. If you can salvage anything of your evening, at least do that.'

'I doubt I can, but at least I can get out of here and have a think about what I'm going to do next.'

Yes, something Irene herself would need to do. 'You're a very dedicated young woman, and I'm sure Miss Capel will keep you on if she decides to keep the Lodge.'

'Oh, I'm sure she will if she does, but I'm equally sure she'll dispose of it as soon as she can.' Carly stood up and untied her apron, tossing it over the back of the chair.

Irene got to her feet and the two of them filled the huge fridge with cocktail sausages, threw away what couldn't be salvaged and then, when the kitchen was vaguely respectable, she headed upstairs to her room. Outside, the grounds still swarmed with police but most of the mourners had been sent home and Emma Capel's car had gone.

It had been a trying day, and it wasn't over yet. Her

brain ticked over with things she still must do. There were the bills to settle. She must write to Rose Duncan with her condolences. She must speak to Emma Capel about her future, see how long she had left at Capel Lodge. And most of all, she must think about how she would do when she had to leave.

SEVEN

'Okay.' Jude sat back and looked around him, thoughtfully. Roger Duncan's death the previous afternoon had led to an all-too familiar late night and early start; with the morning briefing completed and media concerns dealt with in as bland a way as possible (Faye, true to her word, had kept well away from anything public facing) and, as the process of interviewing and evidence-gathering settled into a steadier pace than the frantic activity of the day before, he had time to sit down with his core team and talk matters through. Ashleigh, who combined intuition with sound common sense and whose uncanny reading of character was invaluable in brainstorming sessions such as this, sat opposite him. Doddsy, to her left, brought practicality and a wealth of experience, while DS Chris Marshall prided himself on the speed with which he could rustle up information that had never made it to the official computer systems.

Today there was an extra chair pulled up at the table: Faye had decided to sit in on this meeting, uninvited. It was a habit of hers and one which, as her junior officer, he couldn't reasonably object to, but he disliked it nonetheless. On the best days it smacked of a suspicion that he couldn't do his job without supervision and today it rankled all the more because of her insistence that he take the lead on a case he had good reason to keep well clear of. Despite her observation, senior investigating officers weren't so thin on the ground that no alternative could be found and she could have delegated it elsewhere. But no, there she was as usual, sitting with her chair pushed back and a frown of concentration on her face, listening and judging. Most of the time he liked her but there was no doubt that her insecurities too often got the upper hand over her professionalism. Both her insistence that he take the case and her presence at the meeting were evidence of that.

Still, there was always a bright side. With Faye in attendance he had every incentive to keep the meeting short.

'Okay,' he said again, and looked around the table. 'We've heard what Ash has to say about the interviews with Emma Capel and Irene Jenkins. We've all had the chance of a quick look at the initial statements from those who were there.' There were enough of those and he himself had only had the chance to flick through them, but there was nothing that stood out. 'Any thoughts? As far as I can tell there are at least sixty people who could have done it, most of them highly respectable. It'll be all but impossible to account for the movements of every one of the mourners for every minute of the wake.' And the person who'd murdered Roger Duncan might not even be among them. It would be a smart move, to commit a crime in so public a place, surrounded by so many possible suspects that the investigation moved slowly and gave the killer, whoever that might be, plenty of time to cover their tracks or disappear.

'You know there's one who stands out,' said Doddsy. 'Like it or not, we have to start with our old friend Adam.'

That, judged Jude who knew Doddsy well, was a deliberate prod in Faye's direction. Doddsy was his friend as well as his colleague and was fully aware of the undercurrents and the difficulties this connection might cause. He was an exemplary officer but that didn't mean he would let his disapproval of their boss's decision remain completely hidden.

The remark hit home. Faye fidgeted. 'I've read his statement. Just because he found the body—'

'It wouldn't be the first time a killer did that,' noted Chris.

'It would be a mistake to focus too closely on one individual just because he has previous.' Faye shot an irritable glance at Jude. It wouldn't be a good look if she had to remove him from the case he'd tried to decline.

'He found the body. And you're right. He has a record. And it's not the first time something like this has happened.'

Adam's record involved dealing drugs and a violent assault upon a police officer who'd tried to arrest him, not to mention a lead role as a suspect in a previous murder investigation where, again, he'd been among the first to discover the body.

'Last time he was innocent,' pointed out Faye.

'I'm not really surprised he was on the scene. Adam finds things because he goes looking for them.' Jude and Adam had been friends at school, had been close for some years after they'd left and until Adam's brush with the supply of controlled substances had reached its natural conclusion and he had laid the blame for it at his former friend's door. *If you don't go looking for trouble, how do you know where it is*, he used to say with a wink. And fair enough:

Jude, too, lived by that mantra though he came at it from a different perspective. 'He has a curious nature. And actually he isn't a planner. He's hot-headed but he knows that you're best to keep out of trouble.'

'We know he's violent.'

'Only when the red mist comes down.' Sometimes, when he thought of how their friendship ended and what it had cost him, Jude found it a struggle to be as fair to Adam Fleetwood as he knew he had to be. 'He's a good guy whose bad side can get the better of him, but I don't think he's capable of murder. Unless it's me.' He laughed, trying to make light of it. 'If I'm ever found dead in suspicious circumstances, you'll know where to start looking.'

'We're obviously considering him,' said Ashleigh, 'but he's only one of so many people and as far as I'm aware he has no connections at all with the Duncans, though I have to say he looked very taken with Rose. If it wasn't for the fact they'd never meet before we might want to look a bit more closely at that, but no. According to both of them that was the first time they'd ever met.'

'What about the undertaker?' said Faye, rather testily. 'I saw him, of course, but only at the church. He kept himself as discreetly in the background as you'd expect, and the last I saw of him he was disappearing into the crypt behind the coffin. Why would anyone want to kill him? I know it's easy to get carried away because there were so many people there who could have done it and — according to Irene Jenkins — so many people who came in and out of the room where the guns were, and it's tempting to think that it's something to do with the funeral but I think we should put that to one side. It's Roger we need to look at.'

Chris Marshall began to raise his hand in a mock salute, then remembered who he was talking to. 'I've made a start on that, but I warn you now. There's nothing that immediately suggests any reason for someone to want to kill him.'

With half an eye on Faye's intense expression, Jude sipped his coffee as Chris reeled off what he'd been able to discover about the undertaker. Roger Duncan, it appeared, had lived a blameless, and by some measures dull, life. He was fifty-five years old when he died, and for thirty-seven of those years he had worked in the family business, taking over when his father had retired ten years earlier. In his mid-twenties he had married a local girl and they had had one daughter, Rose, who had herself followed her father into the business, the fifth generation and the first woman to do so. Two years previously, Mrs Duncan had died of breast cancer and Rose, who had been briefly and unfortunately married to a man who soon got bored with life in the country, had moved back into the family home to take care of both her widowed father and the business. Roger, who had always been keenly aware of the responsibilities and the good name of the family business, seemed blameless. He charged fair prices, made his customers' wishes his priority, and paid his bill on time and without quibbles.

'Undertaking isn't exactly a cut-throat business, is it?' said Jude, when Chris had finished this summary of the victim's professional life. 'I know there are other firms around and I imagine the Capel funeral might have been seen in some circles as a prime piece of business, but Frances was the last of them so there was hardly an opportunity for upselling or follow-on business. And as far as I know Duncans have been burying Capels for generations, so they hardly pulled off a coup to get the job.'

'That's right,' said Ashleigh. 'Irene Jenkins told me there was never any suggestion that anyone else would do it, any more than there was any suggestion that Frances would consider changing anything else — the solicitor, even the garage or the supermarket or the florist they used.'

'Did Rose tell you anything about her father's private life?' he asked. 'I don't imagine she was in much of a state to talk to you about it yesterday. I'm sending Mandy Phillips down as FLO. She can ask.'

It must be Faye's presence that stopped Ashleigh making a face at that. Mandy was brisk and efficient but she was often a little more distant than the job required; Ashleigh herself, who was empathetic to a fault and knew it, always managed to get more out of a witness than her colleague. 'No. Rose was very controlled but not very communicative. I know Mandy's going down later today but I did put in a welfare call to Rose this morning.'

'Is she bearing up?'

'She seemed to be. She was talking about getting on with work. Other people's funerals won't wait, I suppose. And she said she was going to give her dad the best possible send-off.'

Not everyone understood that some people were like that, turning to routine as a shield against tragedy, and there were many who would misinterpret Rose's actions as callous. 'I presume she realises she might have a while to wait before we release the body?' Jude spared a thought for Roger, in the mortuary in Carlisle rather than a chapel of rest surrounded by lilies.

'I imagine so, although we didn't discuss it. It must be strange, burying your own father. But she seemed to want to talk about him and I was quite happy to let her.'

That was why Ashleigh would have been so much better as an FLO than Mandy. It was a pity she too often became emotionally involved with witnesses or victims. In the past that had clouded her judgement. 'Anything interesting?'

'I'm afraid not, or certainly not on the surface. He had a circle of close friends with whom he played golf and went fishing. He'd played in the village cricket team all his adult life. He grew roses. That apart, he lived for the business. That's all.'

'Were any of the friends at the funeral?'

'Wilf Hamley, who happens to be the Capel family solicitor. None of the others.'

Someone would go down to speak to the friends and others who had known Roger well, but it was unlikely much would come from that. Scanning the list of names that Chris presented to him, Jude vaguely recalled some of Roger's friends from his years of minding other people's business in the name of public service, but all he knew of them was that they, like Roger, seemed to have lived blameless lives entirely devoid of drama.

So they must look for other motives for his murder. 'Okay. If it isn't something he did or something he was, then perhaps it was something he knew or something he saw. Is that a possibility?'

'It is. I'm assuming the weapon which killed him came from Capel Lodge but there's every chance that might be wrong. If it's right whoever killed him must either have planned it well in advance, or else they must have somehow managed to get into the library and take a weapon without being seen. I don't see how the latter can have been done, so it has to be the former, and that raises a whole host of questions.'

Faye had been listening intently, and now she shifted in her seat. 'How were those guns allowed to be there anyway? They should be licensed, if they can be used. And if they're licensed they should be locked away.'

'Not licensed,' said Chris, 'but they're antiques.'

'So? The law changed a few years back. Why weren't they licensed? Why did no-one follow that up?'

Jude allowed himself a resigned shrug, and a shameful sense of relief that Faye looked like taking her bad mood out on some other officer rather than himself. 'I'm going to guess no-one at Capel Lodge knew about the change in the law. And if no-one here knew about the guns they can hardly be blamed for not sending out a reminder.' It was easy to see how the Capel collection had slipped through the net. 'It's not the process that bothers me. It's that there are firearms that used to be on that wall that are out in the community, and we don't know exactly how many there are or where they went.'

'There are probably half a dozen,' said Ashleigh into the nervous silence, 'going by the marks on the wall. But there might be more and there might be less.'

'Then I suggest,' said Faye, pushing her chair back and standing up, 'that you assign someone to trying to find out. Now, if you'll excuse me, I have a job to do.'

There was silence for a moment after she'd left, in which Chris raised his eyebrows extravagantly. 'Tracing those guns is going to be a bind. I'm no expert but from the photos I'd say they'll be eighteenth or nineteenth century. It's no surprise they aren't licensed, and for all I know, the ones that are missing have gone to museums.'

Jude looked across at the whiteboard where the paraphernalia of a murder inquiry was already spreading. Roger Duncan was at its centre, a smiling man with a shock of white hair, and the pictures of that array of guns had him shaking his head. 'That's given us lots to think about. Chris, I'm going to leave it to you to see if you can find out where they might have gone. And as for the rest of us, I really, really would like to know if anyone who was at that funeral had a reason to want Roger dead and if so, how long ago that reason might have come about.'

When he got back to his office after the conclusion of that meeting, he found two interesting nuggets among the storm of emails and messages that awaited him. One he'd been expecting — the post-mortem result. And yes, it was as he'd thought: Roger Duncan had been killed by a single bullet fired from what looked, subject to a forensic assessment, like an antique handgun.

He sat for a moment, drumming his fingers on the desk and wondering if that gun was the only one he had to worry about, or if the others would resurface, either in Cumbria or elsewhere, in the hands of organised criminals. Then he turned to the second message.

This one, left on his personal phone, was more intriguing. He hadn't recognised the number but when he listened to the message, it fascinated him. *DCI Satterthwaite? It's Gilbert Foley here. I don't know if you remember me? I have a watch repair workshop down by Shap. Nothing urgent, of course, but I wonder if you could give me a call?*

EIGHT

Gil Foley was a man who shunned the limelight, hated attention and kept as far away as possible from public gatherings. If he hadn't been, he might have done two things differently and even as he waited for Jude Satterthwaite to return his call — and the man would definitely be busy, maybe so much so that he wouldn't get round to it at all, or not until it was too late to be any use — he mused on them, wondered whether they might have been bigger mistakes than he feared.

He should have gone to Lady Frances Capel's funeral. And he should have told Jude Satterthwaite that what he had to say might be important.

Important and *urgent* weren't necessarily the same, that was the problem. Gil was fiercely defensive of his own time and his own privacy and equally aware that other people felt the same way about themselves and their work. Under the circumstances the police's time was way more valuable and their resources way more stretched than anyone else's. *And yet*, he said to himself, *and yet*. He shook his head. Perhaps he should have said more.

Are you afraid of the telephone, his mother had teased him when he had been an intense, bespectacled teenager scowling at the dreaded instrument in the hall, and while he wasn't quite afraid of it in the way she had implied he'd always distrusted the way it stripped any conversation of meaningful context. You couldn't see whether the other person was giving you their full attention, whether they were bored or frowning or concerned. He shook his head. If the truth were told he didn't like speaking to people face to face either (he was notorious for not turning up for appointments when he wasn't in the mood) but it was better than the phone.

When the blasted thing finally did ring he stared at it for ten seconds, letting it tremble on his work bench before he answered it.

'Hello.' He knew he sounded abrupt. He always did.

'Mr Foley?' said the voice at the other end of the phone. 'It's Jude Satterthwaite, returning your call. Yes, of course I remember you. You fixed my mum's clock for her a few years back, and I brought it along to your workshop. But you called me Jude then, and I called you Gil.'

Gil relaxed. He remembered the clock — and Jude Satterthwaite — very clearly indeed, and that was how he'd come to have the detective's personal number, but he hadn't been sure those memories would be reciprocated. 'That was the Victorian carriage clock, wasn't it?'

'Yes, that's right. I didn't think you'd remember.'

It had been the best part of a decade earlier. There had been nothing wrong with the clock but age and Gil, who had been cleaning old clocks for almost half a century, had taken it apart and put it back together in a few hours. He remembered every clock that came across his path, from the tall grandfather clock in Capel Lodge right the way through to the mass-produced modern ones or the cheap old ones that had only sentimental value, a gift from a parent or a child. Jude Satterthwaite's mother's clock, he suspected, would be the latter. 'Was it her mother's?'

'Her grandmother's, I think. It's still going, by the way, and keeping perfect time.'

'Good. Good to hear it.' Gil strayed away from his workbench where he'd been working on a rather fine and expensive wristwatch and peered out of the window. His home, in keeping with his personality, was isolated, an old farm cottage down a track a couple of miles out of Shap village, and his workshop was tucked away in a barn at the back of it. Sometimes he had the radio on for company but mostly, like today, he took comfort from the constant ticking of a dozen different clocks.

'You said you wanted to speak to me?'

'Yes, but it isn't urgent.' *No Gil*, he admonished himself, *tell him it's important*. But he didn't, for fear of sounding foolish.

'Can you tell me what it's about?'

Gil stifled a smile. After all, you could tell things about people on the phone and it was obvious Jude Satterthwaite was used to dealing with people who couldn't, or wouldn't, talk. He could imagine him saying *are you safe to talk right now*, like they did on the telly. He remembered that he'd liked the man. 'I saw it on the news. About what happened up at Capel Lodge. That someone died.'

'That's right. Were you at the funeral?'

Gil knew he should have gone. He'd done more work up at Capel Lodge than many of the freeloaders who'd have turned up. For a moment he stood staring out of the window, remembering how Lady Frances had always insisted he stay for a cup of tea — an act he'd always interpreted as cruel rather than hospitable, as everyone knew how uncomfortable such situations made him. Outside, a white van moved down the lane towards his house. He'd been expecting a delivery but not until that afternoon, but they knew to leave anything on the step and no-one ever bothered him at his workshop.

'I don't like crowds,' he said, a poor excuse because the truth was that he didn't really like people. 'And funerals are bad, everyone fake.' He had no regrets, after all. He was glad to have escaped the occasion, with its stifling, meaningless small talk.

'Yes.' Another pause. 'It was the undertaker who died. Roger Duncan.'

That was a shock. Gil had known Roger when he was much younger and had fooled himself that some kind of social and physical activity would be good for him. He and Roger had played cricket together for a couple of seasons until Gil had found that fishing gave him more peace and a better opportunity to enjoy his own company. 'Really?'

'I'm afraid so.'

'Oh. The thing is, I was up at Capel Lodge a few weeks ago. I go there every year to look at all those clocks Lady Frances had. I did it for her father before her.' And Gil's father had done it before him, and on, and on. 'But last time I was there, there was a clock they wouldn't let me touch.'

'Who wouldn't?'

'Lady Frances. It's a musical clock and it had stopped and I offered to have a look, but she said I wasn't to touch it. That's all.'

'Oh, I see. Good of you to let me know.'

So that was it. Not even important. Just a footnote. 'I didn't think it matters, you know, but it troubled me. I don't like the room it was in, with all those guns in.'

'It was in the library?'

'Yes. It's been there for years.'

'Ah, okay. Tell you what,' said the detective, as the door of the white van slammed shut and a figure made its way to the front door, 'why don't I pop down and see you?'

'Oh, but you must be busy.'

'I'm sure you are, too. But I'll be down your way this evening anyway, calling in on my mum. She's only in Wasby. So it's not exactly out of my way, if you don't mind me not coming down until six-ish.'

'I'll see you at six, then,' said Gil, and waited until he heard the buzz as the line went silent.

He stood for a moment at the window, watching through the curtain of shrubs as the delivery man's head bobbed about in front of the house and then went back to the van, but Gil had had enough unscheduled interaction with other human beings for one day and in any case he had work to do. He left the delivery man to do whatever he needed to do and went back to his workbench, thinking about Capel Lodge and the clock and the detective. The man must think it was important after all, coming down to see him. His stomach contracted at the idea of a visit, of questions and answers, all because of a phone call he so nearly hadn't made.

He never knew quite what to make of Jude Satterthwaite, who came from the village of Wasby just a few miles away, and who had a high profile locally that split the community and amounted almost to notoriety. Though he was never one to gossip, Gil still kept half an ear out for the local chat whenever he found himself in uncomfortable conversation with his customers; talking about other people's business was, after all, so much more comfortable than talking about his own. There had been a definite split when Adam Fleetwood had gone to prison for supplying drugs and some folk said that Jude had turned him in, in revenge for him supplying his younger brother with drugs.

Depending on your view that was enough to make him a hero or a villain, but Gil had heard an alternative account which was that Jude had had nothing to do with it.

Who knew the truth? Not Gil, certainly, though the conversation had done much to form his opinion and shift him towards the pro-Satterthwaite camp. The man had been charming enough when he came along with his mother's old clock, and had known exactly how much conversation to make. And though Gil had never actually met Adam Fleetwood he knew the type — a cocky young lad who'd grown into an arrogant man.

But it was none of his business, and he would come to a final conclusion about Jude Satterthwaite when he'd spoken to him and seen how the man responded to him if he thought he'd wasted his time.

He didn't think Jude thought it was a waste of time. That was the slightly unnerving thing about it. If a man that busy on a murder case had time to drop everything and pretend he was going to be passing on a visit to his mother, he must think there was something worth finding out.

He bent his head over his work and concentrated on the antique wrist watch that lay dismembered upon his work bench. It was a nice piece, though the gears were so worn that it would probably never keep perfect time again, but it was a matter of professional pride to see how good a job he could make of it.

After five minutes he realised the delivery van hadn't lumbered its way up the track back towards the A6. And thirty seconds later he heard the soft click as the door to the workshop opened.

NINE

Jude was later getting away than he'd intended. With luck and light traffic Shap was barely twenty minutes from the police headquarters in Penrith and Gil Foley lived on the near side of it, close enough to Jude's mother to make his claim of convenience sound plausible rather than an excuse. He grinned as he packed his laptop in preparation for an evening's work, not imagining for a moment that Gil would have fallen for it. He might be a man who preferred his own company but he was no fool.

On his way out, he popped his head around the door to the incident room. Ashleigh was sitting at one of the desks in deep conversation with Chris Marshall. Both of them, noting that he had his jacket and his laptop bag, wore expressions of surprise.

'I'm on my way out to speak to someone,' he said, crossing the room 'about this,' as though he needed any justification. He put in more hours than any of them and he'd be working away even after he got home, but the last thing he needed was Faye thinking he was skiving off because she'd put him on a job he didn't want to do.

'Are you looking for an update?' asked Chris. 'I'm still ploughing through stuff on guns and the like. I don't have much to report, except that one of the guns found its way to the local am-dram society, and that one's harmless. They have a member who knows about guns and has more sense than Lady F. He checked.'

That, at least, was a relief. 'It's Ash I wanted a word with.' Briefly, Jude outlined the content of his call with Gil. 'I like him. He's diffident and he's not exactly user-friendly, but he wouldn't have made the call if he didn't think there was something going on and he obviously wasn't relaxed enough to talk about it. He called me rather than anyone else, so I'm going to make that effort for him. But I wanted to ask you, Ash. You were in the library. Did you see a clock?'

'A clock?' She creased her brows. 'Do you know, I don't think I did. At one point I checked the time and I usually try and look at a clock rather than my watch because a watch can look a bit obvious. There were lots of odds and ends — china figurines and so on — but no clock.'

'I think looking at your watch can be pretty useful if people have been going on a bit too long,' said Chris, and laughed.

'This particular clock,' said Jude, checking his own watch because time was speeding past, 'wouldn't help you. It had stopped.'

'Gil's a clockmaker. Couldn't he fix it?'

'Lady Frances wouldn't let him touch it. A clock, in the room where all those guns are, where there's every chance the murder weapon was taken from, which she wouldn't let him touch and which seems now to have disappeared. I'm damned if I know what that's about or whether it's got anything to do with what happened to Roger Duncan, but it's so out of kilter that I want to look into it.' Gil must have recognised that. He wouldn't have called otherwise.

'I can call Irene and check if you like. It may have been moved, or it may have been given away. Lady F seems to have been a bit casual with her possessions in her later days.'

'She was many things but from what I know of her everything she did was deliberate. If she gave away a broken clock, there was a reason for it. Yes, I'd be grateful if you could call and ask, and then let me know. I'll need to head off. I don't want to be late and keep Gil from his pie and chips or whatever he has for his tea.'

'I'll call you when I've spoken to her.'

Jude sat behind a truck for much of the ten-mile journey down the A6, enjoying the summer sunshine. It was June and the long evenings overflowed with soft light, drawing the shadows out to great lengths while barely deepening them to darkness, even at midnight. That evening there was a veil of grey on top of the Pennines and the verges were alight with poppies and Queen Anne's lace. It was such a pity to be thinking of murder, such a pity that Roger Duncan, who had been fond of his garden, would never see the season deepen into the richness of autumn.

His phone pinged with a message as he drew up outside Gil's large, ramshackle house. The place was as well-kept as you might expect of someone with pride in his workmanship and no family or all-consuming outside interests to eat away at his time. Stopping the car he checked his phone and saw that it was as he'd expected. Ashleigh. *Irene no help.*

'When you say *no help*,' he said, calling her because though he was already late Gil was at home, or so the pickup parked outside implied and so he could wait for two minutes longer, 'do you mean actually obstructive or do you mean she genuinely couldn't help?'

'I don't think Irene's obstructive,' she said after a moment's consideration. 'She said there used to be a clock in the study but she doesn't know where it's gone. She remembers seeing it when Lady F was still alive and she remembers the time Gil came to service all the clocks. He comes at the end of March and they have a joke about him putting the clocks forward, but I think he does do that because some of them are quite tricky and can be damaged if you just shove the hands about. Not that I know anything about clocks, so I don't know if that's true or not. But she says she doesn't know anything about him being forbidden to touch it.'

'Fascinating. I'll be really interested to know what else Gil has to say.' Because there was something else, surely, or he wouldn't have called.

'Mind and let me know.' Ashleigh hesitated. 'Do you want to drop by for a bite of supper when you're done? I'm not planning to be in the office much longer, because there isn't a huge amount we can do here right now. But I can rustle up a pasta or something.'

He was never sure, these days, where their on-off relationship sat on that tricky line between lovers and friends, and he didn't think she did either. 'I'm going to call in on my mum, as I'm so near. I'll probably pick up a bit of supper while I'm there.'

'Hmm.'

She knew as well as he did that when he went back to Wasby there was a chance he'd bump into Becca Reid, the ex-girlfriend they both knew he'd never get over. It was several years since Becca had ditched him, taking the other side in the row he'd had with Adam Fleetwood, and she still resolutely insisted on being his friend but no more. Ashleigh, still with her heart lost to a coercive ex-husband, understood the situation well enough. Thank God for that. 'I can pop by for a coffee later on, though.'

'Lisa's out,' she said, blurring that delicate line still further, 'and I expect we'll have a lot to talk about.'

'See you later.' He got out of the car, locked it, and went up to the front door, where a cardboard box labelled with the name of a notable wine merchant sat on the step, and leaned heavily on the old-fashioned doorbell. The jangling inside was loud enough to startle a flock of long-tailed tits from the feeder away at the side on the house, but it didn't generate a reply.

Jude frowned. He wasn't sure what he'd expected from Gil but he was pretty certain he'd be welcome. He tried the bell again and then, when he got no answer, tried the door. It was locked.

After a moment's thought, he followed the path around the side of the house. The back door stood open and a jacket hung on the back of a chair. There was an empty coffee mug on the table and the kettle, when he touched it, was stone cold.

'Gil?' Jude called, and got no answer.

He went through to the living room, then upstairs, looking in each room in turn but though the house retained every sign of normality and showed no trace of anything untoward, there was no sign of its occupant. Unsure whether that was reassuring or not, he went back out and stood in the courtyard. The pickup (he took a moment to run the numberplate through the app on his phone) was definitely Gil's.

He shook his head. He'd been thinking about the clockmaker as he'd been driving along, dredging his memory for everything he knew about him. His mother, when Jude had returned her clock those few years before, had expressed surprise that Jude had managed any conversation with him at all. *An odd man*, she'd called him, with a reputation for being eccentric. *He doesn't like people, he doesn't interact.*

Maybe Gil, who sounded like the kind of man who would turn out the lights on Hallowe'en even though there was no chance anyone would come guising, and hide from the meter reader if he didn't want to talk, had changed his mind after all, or else what he had to say was too difficult or too complicated and had led him to take fright. But how could it be, when all there was to talk about was a clock?

And a murder. If it hadn't been for Roger Duncan Jude might have let Gil be, accepted that the man just didn't want to talk to him, gone back to scratch his head and tried to carry on without that piece of the puzzle. There was a logical explanation. Gil was a craftsman who lived for his work. It was perfectly possible he'd become so absorbed in what he was doing that he had, ironically, forgotten the time.

He strolled around to the workshop, which huddled in a range of outbuildings behind a few young birch trees and a thin rhododendron that struggled in their shade which formed a screen to prevent him from seeing in though not, he thought, someone from seeing out.

'Gil?' he called again, and when there was no answer he put his hand to the door and opened it.

Inside, the cavernous workshop was still but for the shadows of birch and rhododendron dancing on the wall. 'Gil?' He opened a door at the back of the room that led to a storeroom full of spiders and dust, and then another which took him out into a small square of uneven paving which faded away through weed-filled gravel into a tangle of brambles. No joy there, no sign of disturbance or escape.

Back in the workshop, a shaft of sunlight slipped in through the dirty window and slid down like a finger, pointing to the bench by the window. On it lay Gil's phone, connected to a plug, unblinking and fully charged, and a dismembered wristwatch set out on the desk, its innards arranged with extreme precision around its empty casing, its face smiling upwards. For a moment Jude stared at it in perplexity.

It was possible, though surely unlikely, that Gil had regretted his decision to contact Jude and, overwhelmed by it, had taken himself off somewhere, but where? And why? He stared at the bench a moment longer, and then it dawned on him. There were no tools. When he'd visited Gil those years before he'd been struck by the man's precision, the way he'd sat at the bench and taken the clock apart for its initial check, how he'd had his open toolbox beside him and had taken each item out of it as he needed it and placed it back immediately, so there was never more than one item out of place. The toolbox had gone.

He shook his head. He wasn't so alarming that Gil would be afraid of him, so maybe the watchmaker had called intending to make some kind of confession and had changed his mind. Or maybe he really had just gone off to an emergency clock repair within walking distance, without a thought for the visitor he was obviously expecting.

Maybe. Gil was unquestionably eccentric, but that much? For a moment he stood there, then walked around the workshop, back into the garden, then again into the house. There were no signs of a struggle, nothing broken or out of place.

Gil was a grown adult not a child, and was in no way

vulnerable, so the idea of pursuing the matter further was ludicrous. He smiled, grimly, as he imagined Faye's face if he tried to trigger a missing person's inquiry and Gil turned out to have gone into Shap for fish and chips, or an uncharacteristic trip to the pub.

He'd call later, but if Gil chose not to answer, what more could he do?

When he got down to Wasby, still musing on Gil's strange behaviour, he found his mother at the gate deep in conversation with Becca. He pulled the car up with care, waiting to see whether his ex would stay to be civil or whether she'd turn and run at the first sight of him. He saw her often under just such circumstances and it could always go either way.

He sighed. Becca was a thorn in his flesh. For a while he thought he'd been able to let their relationship go but now he had to admit he never would, that he hadn't the strength of will to ignore her and that her presence brought him both pleasure and pain. Ashleigh, who had the life experience and understanding to cope with it, was sure Becca still cared for him, and he'd once thought so too, but his most recent approach had been so instantly and soundly rebuffed that his pride wouldn't allow him to ask her again. And so it went on, and would go on until one of them moved away so that they never crossed paths again and eventually drifted out of touch.

He got out of the car. 'Evening.' There was a smell of smoke, lingering on the air, a barbecue at one of the holiday cottages. He waited for Becca to comment on it, to go rushing off with some excuse about getting her washing in, but although she stepped back a little from the gate to let him past, she lingered.

'Are you passing with a purpose,' asked his mother, 'or just drifting to see who's about?' She gave him a meaningful look.

'I've been down to Shap to visit Gil Foley.' Out of the corner of his eye he saw movement and Becca's grey cat, Holmes, shot out from under her gate and across the road to rub around his legs.

'Is that right? They say Gil's getting odder and odder as he gets older.' Linda Satterthwaite nodded, wisely. 'Not that I know how anyone knows. He never speaks to anyone if it isn't about those clocks. And he's got worse. He had a fall a while back and it seems to have made him more eccentric than ever.'

'I didn't know about that.' Jude, who got on well with Holmes, bent down to make a fuss of the cat.

'He fell off a ladder trying to fix his own roof,' said Becca. 'I was sent out to call on him a couple of times. I got on with him okay, but then again I suppose I was a necessary contact. I think he just avoids people unless he needs to see them, and sometimes even then. He took against one of my colleagues and if he saw her coming he just wouldn't answer the door.'

Nodding, Jude straightened up. 'That makes sense.' Gil could easily have changed his mind and taken off somewhere.

'So maybe it's just you,' said Becca, waspishly.

'Are you wanting some tea, Jude?' asked Linda, in time to prevent him responding.

'If there's some going.'

'There's lasagne. And in return you can do me a favour and run Mikey into town afterwards, save me the trip,' said his mother. 'Fair's fair, I think.'

'That fits nicely. I'm going along to Ashleigh's later on.' He said it for Becca's benefit, to test if she still cared, and even though she was better at hiding her feelings from him than she used to be, he sensed that she stiffened. 'Work-related,' he clarified, though there was every chance the evening would end in pleasure.

'I'd better get on, then.' Becca snapped her fingers at Holmes, who ignored her. 'Holmes. If you want your tea come and get it now, or you'll have to fend for yourself. Bye, Linda. Bye, Jude.' And she turned and headed back to her cottage with Holmes at her heels.

TEN

'I don't know what you want,' said Gil to the man who had just untied his hands, and removed the blindfold, 'but whatever it is you won't get away with it.'

'We've got a job for you.' The man gave him a little shove across the room — barely a room, really, just a workshop in an outbuilding not unlike Gil's own, but with a shuttered window and nothing but a tiny square of glass right up at the top of the wall to let in the light. There was a workbench on the far side of it, against the wall, and a lamp stood there, switched on. In its spotlight stood the Capel Lodge clock.

Gil stood there for a moment, flexing his wrists and rubbing at them to buy himself some time. This was crazy. Abducted at gunpoint to fix a broken clock? Why? He bent down to rub his ankle, too, although that hadn't been bound. His mind, unused to close engagement with the actions of others, whirred. This was his own fault. He should have overcome his hatred of the telephone and told Jude Satterthwaite everything he knew straight off, or else he should have gone up to the police station and told them all about his apprehensions about the business up at Capel Lodge. They'd have laughed him out of the place, but they'd have known. But he hadn't done either of those things, and here he was in this godforsaken place and no-one knew where he'd gone.

'A job?' he said, feigning simplicity.

'Yes, you half-witted old soul. You're a clockmaker, aren't you? We've got a clock for you to fix.'

As slowly as he dared, Gil took a few steps towards it, though he knew it well. His father had made it, and he'd watched him do it. It had been a gift from Lady Frances's father to her mother, for their wedding anniversary, more than fifty years before. It wouldn't be hard to fix, or he didn't imagine it would. A couple of hours and he could go home.

But up at Capel Lodge a man had been murdered, shot dead, they said, and here behind Gil at that moment was a man with a gun. He hadn't been shy of showing his arrogant, brutal face, either. When Gil got back home he'd be able to tell the police everything about his abductor, give them a full description of his height and the narrow dark eyes, his age — somewhere in his thirties, perhaps — his clothing, his rough Manchester accent. Careless.

Careless, or ruthless? Gil reappraised his situation and it didn't look good. The path ruthlessness might take was increasingly obvious. Repairing the clock wasn't such a big job but to take it into a jeweller's shop risked identification, left a paper trail of email contact and names and payment, whereas Gil himself, a stubborn sole trader who lived in isolation and did things his own way, was a different prospect.

'You could just have brought it to the workshop,' he said.

'Sure we could. And you'd have recognised it and called the police.'

For no reason that he could fathom Gil sensed that this man was somehow involved in the death of Roger Duncan, might even have fired the shot that killed him. If he had no qualms about showing himself that might mean he had no fear of Gil identifying him. He might not know that Gil wasn't a man who couldn't be bullied into anything, still less silence, but even if he didn't he probably wouldn't take the chance. That was how these people worked. You got the job done and you disposed of the witness.

If that was the case — the worst case, but one that looked very possible — Gil could have only a couple of hours left to live, and when the clock was fixed he could expect nothing but a bullet to the head and his body tipped down a mine shaft somewhere up in the Pennines or sunk in depths of Ullswater where the currents would take him down and down into their icy grip and never let him go. And no-one would care.

Knowing something was required of him, he shuffled across the room towards the workbench, assessing his options. When he thought about life and death, which he did increasingly as his seventies slipped away, he did so with equanimity. You lived life in the present, brought nothing into it, took nothing out. He had no family to mourn him, no friends to raise a glass to his memory, and that had suited him. When the time came he was ready enough to shuffle out of his life, quietly and without either fuss or regrets.

But this wasn't the time. At the bottom of his soul he was a stubborn old man with a strong sense of justice and there was no way he was going to allow himself to be used and cast aside like the weakest, rusted link in an old chain.

Nobody, least of all this demanding, aggressive stranger, got to tell him what to do.

He approached the bench and looked at the clock, picked it up. It was heavy in his hands. His father had made the base of it from granite with gold fixings; he remembered watching him do it. It had been a trial, because Gil's father, like Gil himself, cared more for the internal workings than the external look and wasn't that good at handling stone, but he'd done it because Earl Capel had paid him handsomely for it. 'What's this?'

'It's a clock,' said the man, in contempt, 'you fool.'

Gil had a good aim — that was one thing that youthful flirtation with cricket had shown him — and if he managed to hurl the clock at his abductor and get in a lucky strike, who knew? He might get away. But in his head his father's hands fussed at the gold fixings, his father's tongue clicked against his teeth in patient exasperation, his father's brows shrivelled into a frown as if the clock disappointed him. Perhaps it was this very sudden shadow of his own death reminding him of his loss, but he couldn't bring himself to damage that clock.

'Okay. And—'

'It's a musical clock. It plays a tune on the hour. Or it used to.'

'I can fix it,' said Gil, confident of this at least, though he had no intention of trying. He put it down again, pulled back the chair that had been sitting waiting for him at the workbench, and tightened his grip on it until his knuckles were white. Then he raised the chair in a swift gesture, brandishing it in front of him, and rushed at the man.

He was stronger than he looked and his abductor had fallen into the trap, thinking that an elderly man who came quietly at the point of the gun had no fight in him, and no power. Brandishing the chair in front of him, Gil crashed the man to one side, scrambled over the flailing legs of both man and chair, and made the door.

For a second he had to pause to get his bearings. It was a bright summer evening, the sun declining to his left, but he had no idea where he was. In a courtyard not unlike his own, with outbuildings around a farmhouse. Thick woods crowned the brow of a hill to his right and sheep grazed in the narrow field in front of it. A glimpse of silver to his left told him there was a river and a rutted lane, thickly hedged, climbed away to his right. The lane tempted him, but if he went that way he would be easily caught so he headed for a gate, his only hope, aiming to cut across the fields and reach the woods.

Barely ten yards into his escape bid, as he struggled through the soft mud of the field, the crack of a gun came from behind him and a sharp pain ripped through his thigh. Fear and determination kept him running for a few yards, but no more. After that his left leg failed to work and he crumbled, terrified and frustrated, into the grass.

'He's going to need a doctor,' said a woman's voice above him, as whining and tedious as the man's. 'For Christ's sake, we can't leave him to bleed to death or die of an infection or something. We need him to fix the clock.'

Gil had been playing dead, but at this point it dawned on him that if he was that useful to them he might still have a chance. He dared to open his eyes a little, and saw a woman with red hair standing over him. She shuffled back as she saw him move and Gil, terrified that they might think he wasn't at death's door, let his eyelids droop again. He was in pain and there was no way he could stand. And he felt unbelievably weak, detached from his body, but his mind was sharp. There was a tightness to his leg, now, that suggested they must have cleaned up the wound and tried to bandage it, but any movement hurt.

'We can't involve anyone else. And even if we could, we can't go kidnapping doctors in the dead of night. Where do you think this is? Iraq?'

'We kidnapped him. If we want the clock fixed we have to keep him alive or get someone else to do it. It makes sense to get him looked after,' the woman insisted. 'Do you know any other clockmakers around here? I don't.'

'You can ask around.'

'I did ask, and everyone told me to go to this guy. If I ask again people are going to want to know why I didn't go to him and why I need a clockmaker so urgently anyway. Anyone else is a risk.'

'I don't want to have to go round murdering doctors to keep them quiet.'

Ask around. They weren't local. Weirder and weirder. What the hell was so important about the clock? And this talk of murder was even more unnerving when they said it out loud than it had been when it had just been a catastrophic fear in his head. More than ever, Gil wished he'd trusted himself to speak to Jude Satterthwaite. He didn't even know when that had been. Today? Yesterday? He'd been shot in the evening but the interlude of pain that had followed had been one whose duration he couldn't measure, and the room he was in was both curtained and shuttered so he had no idea whether it was day or night.

'He'll know,' said the man, after a moment. 'Maybe there's a retired doctor locally. A nurse, even. He'll know someone who won't tell if they want to keep him alive. Or won't tell until it's too late, at least.'

He seemed unconcerned by the idea of *too late*, so that

Gil sensed it applied to him rather than his captors. *Too late* meant he would be dead and they would have got away, but he still clung to a glimpse of hope. Perversely, he might now have days to live rather than those few hours. Somewhere there was someone he could name who they would bring to treat him, and somehow that person could be made to understand that they had to go to the authorities. If he was going to die it was much better to take a bullet being rescued than be slaughtered in cold blood.

Someone slapped his cheek, not too roughly. That must be a good sign. 'Hey. Wake up.'

He blinked his eyes open. It was the woman. He tried to get a good look at her face but the light was behind her. The man might not care about whether he saw him or not, but she did. Maybe that meant she was the weak link, the one who was prepared to let him live.

'Mm,' he said, trying to sound as if the pain had submerged him.

'You need to get that wound treated. Who can we get to come and look at you?'

'Hospital,' he mumbled, uncertainly.

'No hospital. We need someone who won't talk.'

'That'll limit it,' said the man, sarcastically. 'And we need someone who doesn't have a family to wonder where they've disappeared to at dead of night, too.'

'You must know some old retired doctor or nurse or someone,' the woman said in Gil's ear. 'Come on. Think. Someone you can trust with your life, eh?'

If only Jude Satterthwaite didn't have a high local profile Gil could have pretended he was a doctor, but Jude had been mentioned in the reports of the murder and for all Gil knew had appeared on the telly as well. He didn't dare risk it. It would have been dead handy from a medical point of view, too, because hadn't Jude once gone out with…?

'Nurse in Wasby,' he murmured, indistinctly.

'What?' said the woman sharply.

'Nurse.' It was a difficult balance, between making his meaning clear and sounding as if he was on the edge of consciousness. 'District nurse. Wasby.'

'You know a district nurse?'

'Where the hell is Wasby?' said the man.

'We'll find it. Don't worry. Right, Gil. A district nurse. What's her name?'

'Becca Reid.' He hoped desperately that he wasn't going to get her into any trouble but he thought she could handle it. She'd know what to do.

'Does she live on her own?'

He nodded and closed his eyes again as if he'd slipped back into unconsciousness and listened to the two of them debating above him in urgent tones about how they'd find her, and how they'd bring her to him without being seen, and how they'd make sure she stayed silent until whatever it was they wanted was safely complete and they'd made their escape.

Oh God, Gil said to himself, *oh God*. He didn't pray, didn't believe, but if he had he would have prayed he hadn't made a fatal mistake.

ELEVEN

'I've spoken to Wilf Hamley,' said Chris Marshall, with a broad theatrical grin, 'you know, the Capel family solicitor. About the will.'

Ashleigh had known he had something up his sleeve. The two of them had been sitting in front of the whiteboard in the incident room, under the plethora of pictures and questions. Someone (Jude, presumably) had been in earlier and written Gil Foley's name on the board with a question mark, but tucked away to one side as if even Jude couldn't bring himself to make the leap that a slightly eccentric recluse might just have behaved in a typical fashion after having (as he might see it) got himself into a difficult situation and just run for it.

Her gut instinct was that Jude was right, that was the problem. They'd talked about it the previous evening as they'd sat in her living room chewing over the endless possibilities for who might have killed Roger Duncan and reaching no conclusion. All the while she'd sensed that he was fighting his instincts, reluctant to push forward with an improbable connection between Gil's absence and Roger's murder. It was Jude's arrival in the incident room that had triggered Chris's comment, some news he'd clearly been waiting for a while to share.

Jude set a cardboard cup of coffee and his iPad on the table, pulled up a chair and sat down. 'I meant to ask you about that. I'm hoping for something big and meaty that will point us in the direction of the murderer. Am I out of luck?'

'If you'd asked me for something to further muddy the waters then I don't think you'd be disappointed. But no, I don't think this is going to answer any questions. Just pose more of them.' Chris sat back and stretched for a moment.

'Go on then.' All of them were used to Chris's fondness for a dramatic moment but this time, Ashleigh could see, Jude wasn't in the mood for it. She thought she knew why, too. No matter how much he tried to rationalise his concerns Gil Foley, vanished without trace after a murder at a funeral he hadn't even attended, was at the back of his mind.

Chris must have sensed his impatience, too, and adjusted his approach accordingly, becoming on the instant as dry and precise as any solicitor. 'Some background. Lady Frances inherited the bulk of the family estates on the death of her father, though the title went to a distant male cousin. She owns Castell Capel — a country house in north Wales — as well as Capel Lodge and a swanky flat in St John's Wood. There's also a significant swathe of investments. I don't have the exact number, but we're talking in the high seven figures. All of these go to Emma Capel.'

'I think I know Castell Capel,' said Ashleigh. Her parents had a holiday home not that far away from it, and she'd regularly passed the towering stone gateway with the name of the property carved into it. 'It's not open to the public, so I've never been inside. But I can imagine.' It had seemed forbidding and reclusive when she was a child and its dark foreboding echoed through the years and across the miles, reflected in that wall of death at Capel Lodge.

'It's not in great repair, apparently, but Emma can easily cash in some investments and fix it and still be a millionaire several times over.' Chris glanced down at his iPad. 'Lady F made several bequests to local charities, all of them considerably smaller than any of them had been led to believe — a couple of dozen charities, maybe, each getting a thousand quid. I'll forward you copies of the will so you can look at them and see if anything stands out that I've missed, but I don't think so.'

'What about the staff?' asked Ashleigh, remembering Emma Capel's bewilderment at having seemingly inherited people along with the goods and chattels, and Emma's comments about her distant cousin's offhand attitude to her employees.

'Not a bean to any of them. Not a penny. Except for Irene Jenkins and she was left—' Even recognising Jude's impatience, Chris couldn't resist a pause and a flourish, 'a book and a clock.'

Jude sat bolt upright at that. 'What? Which clock?'

'*To my companion, Miss Irene Jenkins, I leave a musical clock,*' read out Chris from his iPad, '*made on the instructions of my father as an anniversary gift for my mother and currently in the library at Capel Lodge.*'

'Well now,' said Jude, and his face was grim. The missing clock now seemed to lock the missing watchmaker well and truly into the mystery of Capel Lodge — but did it make him villain or victim, and how did it relate to Roger Duncan? 'And what about the book?'

Chris turned to his iPad again. '*Also, the first and oldest ledger from the estate records. She will know where to find it.*'

'You called her yesterday,' said Jude, turning to

Ashleigh, 'didn't you? Specifically about the clock? What exactly did she say?'

'That it wasn't there. I didn't ask about the will. I didn't know what was in it.'

'She must have known, though. And didn't mention it when we were specifically asking about that clock.'

'Must she?' Ashleigh thought of Irene, patient and submissive, moved by circumstance from being at the mercy of one employer to dependent upon the good will of another, asking and expecting nothing. 'I know you'd normally expect Lady Frances to have told her but she may never have thought about it. She wasn't brought up like that.' That time she'd spent in the study, first with Emma and then with Irene had given her a glimpse into a different way of life, an almost Victorian setup of assumed entitlement and abased acquiescence. 'She'd never have dreamed of asking, either.'

'I can't believe she didn't know. Lady Frances has been dead for weeks. The solicitor must have told her.'

'True, but old Hamley's probably been busy dealing with all those disappointed charities,' said Chris, cheerfully.

He was probably right. 'Shall I give her another call?' asked Ashleigh.

'That would be the quickest way to find out,' agreed Jude, still frowning. She could read the questions in his mind, the same ones that troubled her. How the hell were all these things connected? And where was Gil Foley? 'I'll wait. I was on my way to see Faye with an update, and if I'm going to go to her with questions it'll help if I can say we've at least tried to find the answer.'

'She might know the answer,' suggested Ashleigh, checking for the number of Capel Lodge.

'I'll be surprised.'

It wasn't like him to be so gloomy, but she knew he was

JO ALLEN

worried about Gil, thinking what might have happened if he'd gone straight down to Shap when he'd received the call.

'Miss Jenkins,' she said, when Irene answered in her usual composed manner, 'it's Ashleigh O'Halloran here, from the police. I'm calling to ask you a couple of questions about Lady Frances's will.'

'Her will?' said Irene, in what seemed like astonishment. 'I really…I mean, what has that to do with Mr Duncan?'

'It's a line of inquiry, Miss Jenkins, that's all.'

'You really are very thorough. There's not much I can tell you. I suppose you know what's in it?'

'We do, and I wanted to ask you about Lady Frances's bequest to you.'

There was a short pause. 'I'm not really sure I'd call it a bequest, Sergeant.'

'I wanted to clarify about the clock. Is it the clock I asked you about yesterday?'

Another pause. 'Yes, I suppose it is. I hadn't thought about it. I have so many other things to think about and so many other things to do, and Mr Hamley only told me about it a few days ago. And besides, it doesn't really feel right to go looking for things — taking things — before the will is signed off and probate granted.'

'And there's still no sign of it?'

'No, though I have looked.'

'And the book?'

'Oh dear. I have to confess. I'm baffled as to why she left me the book. I wondered if she thought there might be something in there that would interest me, but I have to be completely honest with you, Sergeant O'Halloran. The Capels have always had a very particular sense of humour, not one I've ever been really tuned in to. There have always been plenty of in-jokes, some of them going down the generations and a mystery to me. Lady Frances did like a puzzle. I expect there's something in the book she thinks would amuse me.'

'In a ledger from the estate?'

'It struck me as strange.'

Opposite her, Jude was flicking through his messages, but with only half his attention; the rest was focussed on the phone call. He mimed something, a complicated gesture of opening a book, pre-empting the question that Ashleigh was already primed to ask.

'Do you think we could have a look at this ledger, Miss Jenkins?' she asked.

'I'm sorry to say it's gone. I definitely saw it in there just after Lady Frances passed away. I was speaking to Carly in the library about the funeral and about Miss Capel's arrival and so on, and I noticed it was there then. Or rather, I didn't notice anything, but after you called yesterday I went to look and there is a gap there now. It's definitely that volume that's missing. The others are still there.'

'Thank you. And you've looked for it?'

'Only very cursorily. You'll understand we have other things to do. But now I know I will of course make sure we comb the place.'

'The clock, too?'

'Most definitely,' said Irene, with some force, and rang off.

Ashleigh laid her phone down and looked across at Chris and Jude. 'Looks like that will was pretty interesting after all.'

'Yes, Faye's going to love that,' said Jude, moodily. 'Two odd items left to the former companion, neither of them with any obvious significance and both of them missing? I can't for the life of me see how this is anything to do with Roger Duncan, but I'm one hundred per cent certain it's got something to do with Gil Foley, and I don't like that.'

'Maybe he stole the clock,' suggested Chris.

Jude, it was clear, hadn't thought of that. Nor had Ashleigh herself. The three of them contemplated the possibility and she she, like Chris found it plausible, but Jude was shaking his head. 'No. Nice idea, but that doesn't convince me. If we were turning up to speak to him I might buy it, but he called us.'

'Maybe he got cold feet over what he wanted to say.'

'Maybe,' said Jude, unconvinced, and went across to stand in front of the white board.

Ashleigh went and stood next to him. 'Is there anything we can do about Gil?'

'Nothing.'

She sensed his anxiety, his frustration. 'Perhaps if we—'

'I've thought about it. I've thought about everything. I'd love to search the place. I'd love to have people looking for him. But he's an adult and as far as we know he hasn't done anything wrong. We'll just have to wait for him to find his way home.'

TWELVE

'You're a fast mover,' Rose had said to Adam when he called her and suggested they should meet up, and she was right. It was barely forty-eight hours since Roger Duncan had been murdered and by any measure his suggestion that they meet for a date was entirely inappropriate but, even though he knew that and was secretly appalled by his own behaviour, he still went ahead. If he didn't, he might miss the opportunity and he'd never before felt something snap in his head and his heart — in a good way — the way it had happened in the moment he'd set eyes on Rose Duncan.

'I just thought you might need some support,' he'd said to her, 'someone to talk to,' and if the truth were told he hadn't been in the least surprised when she'd agreed because he was so sure she'd felt the same. And now here they were, sitting outside the pub on Langwathby village green, he with a diplomatic half pint and she with a pint, under the obviously disapproving eyes of the locals, though whether it was because of the pint or the date or a combination of both he neither knew nor cared.

He'd known from the minute he set eyes on her that she was the right girl for him. It wasn't just that she was beautiful, although he would hardly overlook that significant point in her favour, but he'd immediately sensed a steely composure about her, a devil-may-care attitude under that fitted black funeral outfit. She might have a job which at times required the most rigid adherence to public ideas of respectability; she might have to execute some wildly inappropriate suggestions from relatives as to how they wanted to say farewell to their loved ones; she might be working in a company so old that most of their records had yet to be digitised. None of these things undermined his sense that Rose was as hard as steel and probably as cold, that she was utterly composed and completely resolute.

He wasn't like that. Adam was hot-blooded and an occasional risk taker, a man who never forgot a slight and who too often allowed his fury to derail his common sense. That didn't mean they were incompatible; it meant she was the yin to his yang.

Now that he was approaching his forties and still single, and despite playing the field with the energy of a man unencumbered by responsibilities, he found he couldn't resist an ice maiden. He hadn't even known this woman for two days and he was already envisaging what it would be like to wake up next to her for the rest of their lives. There had been a hint of this weakness when he'd dated Becca Reid, whose chilliness towards him had reflected more how she felt about herself than about him, but even then the main attraction hadn't been Becca's looks (more muted than Rose, though good-looking enough, he supposed, and she had been passably enthusiastic in bed, at least for a while) but rather the fact that dating her had rubbed salt into the emotional wounds that Jude Satterthwaite had sustained when Becca had ditched him all those years before. Adam had moved on but he was confident the damage was done and Jude and Becca's relationship was irreparable. If he hadn't been, he might have been tempted to try again.

Not any more. Now Rose was the star in his sky, the leading light into harbour, and Adam, sitting gazing at her like a lovestruck teenager, was struck uncharacteristically dumb.

'It was nice of you to ask me out,' she said, after a while — a bland opening gambit but better than anything he could muster under the circumstances.

'I thought you might need some fresh company.' He pulled himself together, lifted his glass in a half-hearted salute. 'I know what it's like. People think they know you but then something happens, like a death.' Or a prison sentence. 'Then it changes you.'

'Yes, exactly. Being in the business of death, so to speak, people seem to think I can handle my own bereavement.' She looked demurely down at the stained top of the wooden table. 'But of course that isn't true.'

'Let's raise a glass to your dad, eh?' he said, emboldened. 'I'm sorry I never met him. I've heard people talking about him for the last two days, and all of it good.'

Rose lifted her own glass and whispered *to Dad*, then set it down again. 'He was such a lovely man. I'm going to miss him more than anything, but I have to carry on.'

'If there's anything else I can do—'

'It's very kind of you, but with the line of business I'm in, you can't afford to get overly concerned about death. And you did enough for me on Monday.'

'Yeah, I know what the police are like.' For a moment he had that dangerous feeling, trust in the strength of the alpha male. That had got him into trouble before. 'I know what it's like. I found a body once and, God, they don't spare you.'

'Of course they don't,' she said, amused. 'It's their job to find out who the criminal is and it could be any of us. We may know we're innocent, but they don't. Of course they'll be investigating both of us.'

'You don't know them like I do,' he said, darkly.

'Really?'

He hesitated for just a moment, ghosted by the brief thought that a woman who'd just lost her father might not want to hear about the shortcomings of the officers who were investigating it, but that thought was brief. With the encouragement of her smile he launched into the long and breathless tale of how Jude Satterthwaite had found his kid brother with drugs and hauled him down to the police station, and how that in its turn had led to Adam being dragged in and landing up with three years in jail.

'But that's good,' she said. 'Not about prison, of course. That seems really harsh for what you did.'

Her sympathy was gratifying. He had expected some kind of censure, but she had accepted him for what he was. Or, not quite. He hadn't told her about the aggravating factors in his case, how he'd assaulted a policewoman and broken her collarbone. 'You think it was good that they hammered me for just a bit of supply? It was recreational, that was all, and it's not as though the kid had to take it.'

'No, I don't mean that. I mean, it's good that you've got a team of officers who aren't going to let anyone get away with anything.'

He fought the urge to tell her everything — how Jude Satterthwaite lived rent-free in his head, how he was so consumed with rage (and, yes, jealousy) because his childhood friend had gone on to build a successful professional career for himself so that even those who professed to dislike him nevertheless respected him. Adam was his antithesis: for all his charm and the sympathy for his misfortunes he would always be a man with a violent record, never quite worthy of anyone's trust. 'They come down too hard on the wrong people.'

'You mean you? You should complain.'

'They don't listen.'

She nodded, sympathetically. 'But I have to trust them. I need them to find out who killed Dad. If they can't be trusted I'll have to do it myself.'

'That would be dangerous!'

She looked him in the eye. 'Yes, but not for me.'

Adam lifted his half pint, desperate to sink it and have another but knowing he'd have to make it last all evening, or move on to something soft. In his head Jude's actions against him, as he perceived them, were personal and vindictive and he was afraid that if he outlined them Rose would react in the same way as Becca Reid, who had fallen out with Jude over it, had eventually done. *It's in the past. Now all he's doing is his job. It isn't personal.* But it was, for him at least.

'They need to catch him,' he said, 'and soon.' He couldn't fault Jude on that, at least. The man had always taken on any problem like a terrier with a bone, worrying at it and shaking it and attacking it from all angles until he found a solution. Rather to his surprise, he found for once he didn't want to dwell on all the perceived wrongs he had suffered at the hands of Jude Satterthwaite. He just wanted to hear Rose Duncan talking and, though her pain and grief were less obvious than they surely must be, he wanted to help her. 'You'll miss your dad.'

'It'll be awful.' Her eyes filled with tears and he reached to his pocket for a hanky but there was nothing there, and in any case she had one of her own, as though she always carried something with her to offer to grieving relatives. 'So soon after my mum, too. And the worst of it is I can't imagine why anyone would want to kill him.'

'Maybe it was a random thing. A stranger.'

She gave him a sidelong look. 'The police were all over that. That blonde woman detective asked me all sorts of questions and if I had anything to hide, or if I'd seen something I didn't realise I'd seen, I swear she'd have got it out of me. She was very good.'

Ashleigh O'Halloran was good-looking, sexy and, as far as Adam knew, well and truly settled in Jude's bed. He'd always resented that his old foe had got lucky that way, too, but somehow that mattered less now that Adam himself was in the company of Rose Duncan. 'They say she is.'

'I liked the way you stood up for me to her but I thought she was okay. Just doing her job, you know.'

'I wonder who it was?' he said, daring to close his hand over her fingers and elated when she didn't move them away.

'I don't know. There can't be anyone who wanted to kill Dad. Everybody loved him, and it's not as if anyone would have trusted him with their secrets. I mean, he's an undertaker, not a solicitor or a financial adviser. He just did what people wanted when they were dead and tried to make it easier for the people who loved them.'

She twitched her hand away from his to dab at her eyes with the handkerchief and Adam was, for a moment, devastated, but he understood. He had always been a man in too much of a hurry but for him, and Rose, this was only the beginning.

THIRTEEN

Becca Reid was ready to turn in. It was nearly ten o'clock and the sun had finally set; outside in the garden the darkness deepened and the long shadows of the fell above and the small copse at the bottom of the garden reached out to consume her cottage.

'Holmes!' she called, softly, so as not to disturb the neighbours, 'come on in, you dirty stop-out!' but there wasn't a chance the cat would respond. There were too many things hiding in the shadows, too many creatures for him to hunt, mice and moths and even bats. These days he was starting to get a bit long in the tooth and rarely caught anything, but instinct still drove him and he remained unaware of his possible frailties.

Leaving the door open behind her, Becca made her way down the path and followed the sound of rustling in the bushes. In times gone by she would have left him to fend for himself, but it wasn't just the mice and the moths that were out there. There was a fox she regularly saw slinking about in the dusk or sometimes bold as brass in the daytime, and hedgehogs that would give him fleas, and she didn't fancy his chances if he got into a fight with a badger. Even Holmes might become prey, the hunter become the hunted.

That cat's your child substitute, her sister used to tease her, and time had turned was was once a joke into a hollow truth. Becca would have loved a child — preferably a houseful — but she'd failed to grasp the opportunity with the most likely man and was neither foolish nor desperate enough to shackle herself to someone who'd make her life miserable, just for the sake of being a mother. And she was a bit too old-fashioned to have a child for her own sake; though the world she inhabited was full of single parents with happy children there were many broken families too, and she needed to look no further than the Satterthwaites over the road to see how bitter a marital breakdown could be. You could never be sure about anything, but she reckoned a child got a fighting chance of making something in life with two parents who loved each other.

Still, she had Holmes, and it was certainly true that he occupied enough of her time to be company and make her feel needed but not enough of it to tie her down in any way. Sometimes, as she sat with the cat on her lap on a winter evening, she thought about that. If she had her time over again she might not have been so dogmatic in taking Adam Fleetwood's side against Jude. It had taken her a long time, and a short-lived and rocky relationship with Adam, to see through his charm and realise that underneath it there was a bitter, vindictive man with a very nasty side to him indeed.

But that was all done, lesson learned, and even if she wasn't too proud to go back and tell Jude exactly how sorry she was — it had been years since she'd ditched him — he was in a relationship with Ashleigh O'Halloran, who was surely the perfect match for him. The relationship might be on-off (she was kept reasonably up-to-date on its twists and turns by the insatiably curious and irredeemably indiscreet Mikey Satterthwaite) but she didn't think she was equipped to challenge it. What could she offer that Ashleigh couldn't?

'Holmes!' she called again, irritably, this time with success. A grey shadow bolted out from under a shrub and shot past her and back towards the house. With a sigh, she followed him up the path and into the dimly-lit kitchen.

A woman stood by the kitchen table. Startled, Becca had scarcely enough time to register both that she was there and that she was a complete stranger when the back door closed behind her and the key clicked in the lock.

She took a step away from both the woman and the door and turned, pressing her back again the kitchen unit. At her feet Holmes, too, stared, his spine arched, his tail fluffed out as if he sensed and shared her apprehension. She took another look at the woman — a heavily made-up face, brassy blonde hair, black clothing — and then turned to see what trouble lay to her left. No surprise, now. There was a man there, all in black. Unlike the woman he'd troubled to cover his face with a mask and he wore a black beanie on his head. He held her phone.

Becca clenched her hands against the unit and waited.

'Becca?' said the woman, and smiled.

She nodded. The windows were closed and the kitchen was at the back of the house. There was no point in screaming.

'Don't worry,' the woman said, reassuringly. 'We don't want to hurt you. We need you to do a little job for us, that's all.'

'A job?' said Becca, playing for time.

'Yes, nothing to worry about. A friend of ours has sustained an injury and we need to get him treated but we don't want to bother the people up at A&E. If you come along with us and treat him, it'll be fine. He gets better, the police don't find him, and you don't get hurt.'

'As long as you don't tell anyone,' growled the man in a voice he was surely trying to disguise.

Great. They were playing the good-guy bad-guy routine on her. Her heart thumped. Ignoring the man, who scared her more, she concentrated on the woman. 'What do you need me to—?'

'We want you to dress a wound.'

'Is it bad?'

'How would I know?' said the woman, and shrugged. 'I'm not a doctor. I just know it needs treated.'

Becca wasn't a doctor, either, but wound dressing was within her capabilities, which was just as well since it seemed that she would have no choice. 'I'll need to go to the car and get my bag.' Twilight or not, she might have a chance of attracting attention from a passer-by or a neighbour, if she only got the chance, and with luck they would scare this dangerous pair away.

'We've already got it,' said the woman, with a smile. 'No worries. All you have to do is come with us, do the job and then we'll drop you back here and you can forget it ever happened.'

The man stepped forward to join her, leaving the key in the lock. For a moment Becca saw the slimmest chance of escaping, but he realised before she could break for the door, retrieved the key and placed it in his left hand pocket. The other pocket bulged ominously and he laid a finger upon it, another warning. Either he had a weapon in there or wanted her to think he did. Whichever it was, it was serious.

'Look,' she said, in desperation, 'I don't think I can—'

'We're not offering you a choice,' said the woman. 'No arguing. Now.'

She said it with a smile and a laugh in her voice, a woman in complete control. Slowly, still keeping an eye open for an opportunity, Becca, moved away from the kitchen unit. The woman, carrying her bag, opened the door into the hallway and the man, dropping Becca's phone on the kitchen unit, slipped in behind her.

'Wait here,' he instructed as the woman cautiously eased open the front door and peered out into the gloom, and when Becca tested his intentions by shuffling forwards there was an immediate reaction — something shoved into the small of her back. 'I said wait!'

So she'd been right. It was a gun. That meant they were serious. Doing as she was told, she stole a glance beyond the woman. All she could see was the Satterthwaite's cottage on the other side of the road, and the curtains in the living room were closed. It was a pity Jude wasn't around. They wouldn't have dared come anywhere near the place if he had been, and if they knew who he was.

Reality asserted himself. If he had been there, what could he have done? The man was armed and she was beginning to suspect who their injured friend was. Surely it had to be someone who was involved in the murder of Roger Duncan — but how?

There was a car parked next to Becca's with blacked-out windows, and the woman opened the rear door on the passenger side and beckoned her forwards. Legs suddenly reduced to jelly as she realised that this was real, and that she was being taken away on and adventure from which she might not return, Becca walked as slowly as she could into the vehicle as the man her the front door behind them. The woman got in to the car beside her and produced a blindfold and, as she tied it around Becca's eyes, the engine revved into life and they were off.

It was as simple, as straightforward, and as irresistible as that.

FOURTEEN

Gil, thank God, had the common sense not to try anything. The minute he'd heard the door click shut and the key turn in the lock he opened his eyes and took a look around the place, and the first thing he saw was the winking red eye of a surveillance camera above the door.

That gave him pause for thought, and he took a moment longer to assess his situation. He was lying on some makeshift concoction of cushions and blankets, which suggested his captors hadn't expected him to stay long enough in this hell-hole to need a bed. His leg was roughly bandaged but the blood had seeped through the dressing onto the cushions and the shorts he'd been wearing on that hot sunny afternoon, whenever it had been. He didn't think he could move far anyway, because although his mind was still working he didn't trust himself to put too much weight on his leg, but if he'd thought he might have had a chance of getting out he might have tried. They weren't taking any chances, though. The snap of a key had been followed by the rasping sound of a heavy bolt being drawn, putting paid to any chance he might have had of using his tools to tackle the lock and making his escape before they came back. And if he got up and explored he would give himself away, because the camera might be connected to a phone and if he moved, sooner or later he'd have to admit he wasn't as badly hurt as he was pretending.

Then he'd have to fix the clock. And after that, what?

He turned over, away from that malicious blinking light, bitterly regretting having involved Becca Reid in all this. If any harm came to her he'd never forgive himself, but then again, if any harm came to Becca he didn't think he himself would be around long enough to feel any guilt. It was increasingly clear to him that his captors were responsible for Roger Duncan's murder and that it could only be because the undertaker had unwittingly seen something he shouldn't have. From what little he knew of Roger it was entirely characteristic that he would refuse to stay silent when confronted with a crime.

Maybe, he thought as he lay dozing, that was as far as they'd gone. Maybe they hadn't meant to kill him and it hadn't been a cold-blooded execution. Maybe that one death was enough, or too much, and they didn't want to kill again.

Or maybe they would kill as often as they had to in order to get away.

Frustrated, he lay there wondering how long they'd been away. In his period of unconsciousness he'd lost track of time; he was a man who lived by time, who was surrounded by clocks, not at all fazed by the symphony of ticking and the chorus of chimes that formed the constant soundtrack to his work. The silence of this rough place unnerved him. If he stayed much longer, the silence would send him mad.

After a while — maybe a long while, maybe not — the door opened. Gil flicked his eyes open and sensed darkness beyond it, though his view was impeded by the figures who came through it, the man, the woman and Becca Reid. They must have blindfolded Becca as they'd blindfolded him, because she was blinking and running a hand through her hair as she looked around her.

'My word!' she said, looking across at him. 'Gil! Oh dear!'

He allowed himself a tiny shrug. If he knew her then it was reasonable to expect that she knew him, so she wouldn't have got herself into any more trouble by admitting it. He moaned. 'What time is it?'

Becca looked doubtfully at the woman, who shook her head. Instead she crossed the room and stood looking down at him. 'My word,' she said again. 'Okay, Gil, let's have a look at you.' She looked at the woman. 'What happened?'

'Just treat the wound, and no chat.'

'Or else,' added the man.

Becca, who had her back to him, had the courage to roll her eyes, though she must be as terrified as he was. 'Can't you at least find somewhere more comfortable for him?'

'He won't be here that long.'

She dropped to her knees beside him and frowned down at the bloodied bandage. 'Does it hurt badly?'

He reached out and gripped her hand, squeezing it a couple of times, hoping she'd understand. How much could he say to her without risking her safety any more than he'd done already?

'Shouldn't have asked you to come,' he mumbled, as a test. The woman drew closer and listened. So that didn't mean he couldn't speak, only that he had to bury whatever he wanted to say so deeply that she wouldn't understand it and hope that Becca would work it out for herself. *They'll kill me if someone doesn't come and rescue me before I mend the clock.* How did you telegraph that through groans and mumbles, the briefest of touches? 'What time is it?' he said again.

'A watchmaker who doesn't know the time,' said the man, and laughed, a high, nervous, nasal laugh.

'You asked me that before and I can't tell you,' said Becca, disengaging her hand and reaching for her bag. 'I'm just going to cut the bandage away, okay?' She tugged and pulled and the cold blade of a pair of scissors touched his skin. 'Oh dear. This looks nasty. I can dress it for you but I think you need to rest for a couple of days at least. You look as if you've lost a lot of blood.'

Behind her the woman sighed in frustration.

'You're a good girl,' he said to her, watching through half-closed eyes.

'I do my best.' She wiped down the wound and he twitched as it stung.

'I know the lad you used to step out with.'

She nearly gave them both away at that point and he waited for her to say *Jude?* and for a flicker of recognition to appear on one or both of those hostile faces, but she didn't. Instead, a curious expression crossed her face and she shook her head.

'Oh, him,' she said, as if she was as acutely aware of the danger as he was. 'Do you know, I never see him these days.'

'He was a nice lad.'

'I'm sure he was nice enough but it just didn't work out.'

'He was easy to talk to.'

'Maybe,' said Becca, raising her voice, 'but I certainly won't be talking to him.'

'Or anyone else,' said the woman warningly.

'No. Or anyone else. Sorry, did that hurt you?' asked Becca, as he twitched again.

She hadn't, but he felt it was time to end that line of chat, so he pretended to drift off to sleep and then come to as she was bandaging the wound. 'You're a good lass, Becca.'

'I'm not, really. Just doing something anyone would do. Now, that's you cleaned up, but I don't think you should try and move any more than you have to. I can't dispense any prescription painkillers but I can leave you with some Ibuprofen. Have you had anything to eat?'

'Not hungry.'

'Oh, Gil. You'll really need to eat something if you're going to get better.' She squeezed his hand a final time and stood up, turning to her abductors, trying to take charge. 'He'll need rest and food. He can't take Ibuprofen on an empty stomach. I don't know what you want him for—'

'That's none of your business.'

'...but whatever it is, he isn't going to be any good for it for a day or so at least.' She picked her bag up and snapped it shut. 'That's all I can do for him. Can I go home now? I have to feed the cat.'

The woman almost laughed. She, of all of them, at least seemed able to find some humour in the situation. 'Yes, you're done here. We'll take you home. But don't forget — if you tell anyone what's happened this old man won't be getting any older.'

'I'll keep quiet.' Becca looked a bit shaken.

'Don't look like that. You won't get hurt. You'll be fine. In fact you can go away and tell anyone you want, but I know you won't. Because you're one of the good sort, aren't you, and you wouldn't want an old man's blood on your hands.'

'Did you shoot him?'

'What do you think?'

The man headed to the door. Becca followed and the woman followed close behind her.

'Okay,' said Becca as she headed through the door without a backward glance, 'I won't tell anyone.'

'Not even your cat,' said the woman, and was laughing as she closed the door and left Gil alone with his thoughts and his pain.

FIFTEEN

'Not even you,' said Becca, crossly, as she spooned cat food into Holmes's bowl. 'I daren't even tell you. Not that you'd have anything useful to offer if I did, you old sponger.'

She looked at him as he hunkered down by the bowl, tail stretched out behind him, unconcerned by anything but food, and turned her attention to the coffee machine, envying his simplicity. Today she reached for the rarely-used espresso pods, the ones she kept for emergencies, and this was most definitely an emergency.

She hadn't got back from the previous night's adventure until well into the small hours of the morning, and it wasn't until they'd pulled the car up outside the cottage and she was thinking that perhaps it hadn't been so bad after al, that the man had shown her his ruthless side and read her the full warning about what would happen to Gil Foley — and, despite what the woman had said, to Becca herself — if anyone found out.

And that was the problem. She took her coffee and sat down at the kitchen table, sipping the thick brew and massaging her aching temples. She'd barely slept, lying there going over and over everything that had happened, every word that had ben said. Becca was an honest woman — honest to a fault, she sometimes thought — and she didn't think that anyone that night had been telling the truth, but what they were trying to say had been beyond her. She'd sensed a hardness behind the woman that was at odds with her manner, and there was something about the man that made her think he was talking bigger than he acted. And of course there was Gil, who wasn't nearly as badly injured as he tried to make out and who had obviously been trying to communicate with her.

At some point in the night she'd decided she knew what he was trying to tell her. All that prattling about Jude, a man who was so dangerous to know that Becca had been forced into denying she even saw him these days and had thus got sucked into the lies and, in consequence, would struggle to try and remember what she'd said and what she ought to know.

Gil was braver than she was. He must have known the risks and that meant he thought whatever he wanted to say was worth the risk of trying to tell her, and now it was clear as day — insofar as anything was clear in her muddled brain — that he wanted her to tell Jude what had happened. Becca wasn't scared for herself, never really had been, except for that moment when she'd nearly blurted out her ex's name, but there was Gil to consider. If she walked into the police station that morning, or picked up the phone to Jude, she knew what would happen. She would be whisked off somewhere and placed under guard until the kidnappers were caught, which would be an ideal outcome for her but would mean leaving Gil to his fate.

She couldn't do it. She was a nurse, who saved lives

rather than tossing them away. She couldn't risk having him on her conscience.

She knew what Jude would have said if she'd ever confronted him with that particular dilemma. He'd have told her she had to tell the authorities, that giving in to the demands of kidnappers, even if those demands were for nothing more than silence, was the worst thing she could do.

She looked at her phone. The man had come into the kitchen as they brought her back and had been playing about with it, had told her he'd put something on it that recorded everything she said and everywhere she went, and while she wasn't particularly tech-minded she wasn't sure it was the truth, but the question remained the same. Did she dare risk it? If she called Jude and the kidnappers somehow knew, Gil would be spirited away at best and possibly murdered on the spot, and it would be her fault.

Poor Gil. He was an old man who seemed to care for nobody, but he was human and he shouldn't be regarded as expendable. She drained the coffee, praying that the bolt of caffeine would hit her veins sooner than usual, placed the cup in the sink, bent down to bid a swift farewell to Holmes, and headed out of the house.

Damn. Mikey Satterthwaite, looking the living image of his older brother, was loitering in his front garden with a cup of coffee, like a Mediterranean peasant keeping an eye on the village's comings and goings. She put her head down and ignored him.

'Morning, Becca,' he said — yes, exactly like Jude.

In a village like Wasby you might pretend not to see your neighbours but you couldn't ignore them without raising questions and that was something Becca couldn't afford to do. She put her bag in the boot of the car and turned to him with what she could muster in the way of a smile. It felt as fake as that on the face of the female kidnapper. 'Hi Mikey.'

'Are you okay?'

'Yes.' She slammed the boot. She liked Mikey, who was very similar to Jude in all the good ways but without lumbering her with any emotional baggage, and when she saw him she always stopped to chat. Not to do so now would seem suspicious. 'Sorry. I didn't see you there.'

He strayed from the front step to the wall, eyes on his coffee, hands clasped around the mug. 'Nice morning. Bit chilly.'

'It's a lovely morning, but I really do need to go. I have to get to work.' Though she had plenty of time and was leaving a full half an hour ahead of normal and Mikey would know that.

'Are you sure you're okay? You look a bit…' He tailed off and sipped his coffee.

'I'm very tired, that's all. You know how it is. It's these light nights. Holmes is always awake, chasing flies or whatever. I'm threatening to put him up for adoption. I don't suppose you want a cat, do you?'

Mikey grinned. 'That animal just about lives in our house, anyway, at least when Jude's around.'

It was Jude who had bought Becca Holmes as a present, and one of the things that annoyed her about both man and cat was the way they had a secret understanding which excluded her. 'It's obvious he isn't around now, then, because Holmes is being a complete pest and getting under my feet all the time.'

'Better than having Jude getting under your feet,' said Mikey, with an impertinent grin.

It was definitely better. 'I'm sure he has much better things to do than hang around here.' Desperate to get out of this inconsequential conversation, she edged towards the driver's side of her Fiat 500. 'I really have to go, Mikey. I have a busy day.'

'Yeah, me too.' He drained the coffee and placed the mug on top of the wall. 'Why don't I get Jude to give you a call?'

She felt herself going scarlet. Now Mikey would see it and think it was because she wanted to see Jude and she did, but not for those reasons. 'Oh God, no!' she said in confusion, before she could stop herself.

'Right. Okay. Sorry. I didn't mean to interfere.'

'No, I know you didn't. But honestly, Mikey. I don't want to speak to him but if I do I can call him myself, you know?'

'Yeah. Sorry.'

She got into the car and looked across at the cottage. Holmes was sitting on the living room windowsill as if he knew they'd been talking about him. Mikey stayed where he was, also staring at the cat. What could he possibly know? What could he have seen?

It felt like Fate nudging her in a different direction to the one she'd concluded was right, but she ignored it. As she turned the key in the ignition, she couldn't help watching for another car, for someone else watching her, couldn't help being afraid that the conversation had somehow been recorded, couldn't help thinking that deception wasn't nearly as simple as it was sometimes made out to be.

SIXTEEN

'Something occurred to me.' Ashleigh looked up as Jude shouldered his way through the door, obligatory cardboard cup of coffee in hand, on one of his occasional visits to the incident room.

'Is it to do with where Gil Foley has disappeared to?'

'He hasn't reappeared, then?' she asked, sidetracked.

'He isn't taking my calls if he has.'

'Maybe he's just seen your number and doesn't want to talk to you.'

'Maybe.' Though that wasn't really out of character, certainly not enough to raise the matter officially. 'I wish I'd got up a bit earlier and gone down to see if he's about.'

'He'd hardly thank you for disturbing him at seven o'clock or whatever time it was.'

'Fair point.' If the truth were told, Jude found himself worrying more about Gil than he was about Roger Duncan. The undertaker, after all, was dead and beyond help and all they could offer him and his family was justice, but Gil was different. Although they hadn't yet established any connection other than the missing clock — and God knew what that had to do with anything — he was, as far as he knew, alive. But *alive* didn't mean *not in danger*, or indeed *not a danger to others*, and Jude wouldn't be happy until he knew the clockmaker wouldn't come to — or cause — any harm.

He pulled up a chair and sat down. 'Never mind just now. Worrying about where the man's gone won't help. What was your thought?'

'Irene Jenkins called me this morning. Not for anything in particular, I think. Apparently Emma Capel wanted to know when we'd be out of the property.'

'I'm pretty sure Ms Capel could have asked us that herself.'

'I've already kept her updated. Irene phoned because she was a bit nervy, I think, and wanted some reassurance that we were still doing something. Anyway, I took the opportunity to talk to her a little more about the people who'd been in the library with all those weapons. That's what got me thinking. Roger Duncan was one of them.'

'Was he there on his own,' he asked, his attention caught, 'or with Rose?'

'On his own, I think. She couldn't remember Rose being there when I asked, and Rose isn't exactly someone you forget, is she?'

'Okay.' Jude switched the last of his attention from missing Gil to murdered Roger. 'And what's your revelation? That Roger took the gun for whatever reason, pulled it on someone and then they turned it on him?'

'I hadn't thought of that, though I suppose it's definitely a possibility, if we can come up with some kind of a motive and a suspect. Roger doesn't seem to have been that kind of man. But that isn't what I was thinking. I was thinking about the book.'

Jude considered it. God knew how anyone would make

sense of a dusty old ledger full of dry information, in spindly, faded writing, set down long before Frances or her father, or even her grandfather, had been born. 'And?'

'I wondered if he might have taken the book for whatever reason, and someone might have killed him for it.'

It made as little sense as anything else, but like everything else it was possible. 'As you say, Roger seems to have been as honest as the day.' Not that that precluded it. The most saintly of humans could be tempted. 'I'll think a little more seriously about that when someone comes up with a reason for him to steal it.'

'And who he stole it from, or tried to.'

'If it still exists.' Though what secret could the old estate records possibly hold that was worth stealing and killing for?

His phone rang and he glanced down at it. Mikey. What now? There had been a time when a call from his brother had always heralded some kind of disaster, the only personal calls he ever answered in work time. Mikey's wild days were over, now, and the difficult teenager had matured into a sensible young man, but although the calls came much more rarely in work hours these days, Jude couldn't rid himself of a residual fear that something was wrong.

He nodded down at it. 'I'd better get this. It's probably nothing, but you never know.' He picked up the phone, stood up, strayed over to the whiteboard. 'Mikey. How are things?'

'Dunno,' said Mikey, in a sepulchral tone.

'What's the matter?'

'Nothing, exactly, just something that feels a bit out of kilter. I bumped into Becca this morning and when I asked her if she wanted me to get you to call her she just about bit my head off.'

'I can understand that.' Jude frowned. There was never any point in hurrying Mikey along. He'd get there in his own time.

'I dunno. I thought she'd have jumped at the chance, like she always comes out of the cottage for some reason every time she hears your car. But no, there she is, denying all interest in you. Clear as day, a cry for help. I nearly said to her, *if you're being kidnapped blink twice.*'

'I'd have been more likely to think that if she'd wanted to speak to me,' Jude said, and laughed.

'Right. But you know what. something very funny happened last night, and I've been thinking it through and I've finally decided it's not my over-active imagination.'

Something very funny might have happened to Gil, too, but at least Mikey had seen Becca that morning. 'Go on.'

'I thought I heard her go out last night. Didn't pay much attention, because it's none of my business what she does. But she didn't come back until much later, which is really odd because I knew she was working today. I wasn't asleep so I got up and I had a quick peek out of the window.'

Jude strayed over to the other side of the incident room where it was quieter and stared down onto the courtyard. 'I'd probably have done the same thing myself.'

'Nosey as hell, you are, and I think I'm starting to go the same way. It wasn't her car. She came back in a strange car and the headlights were off. I couldn't see the make or model or plate. She got out of the back of the car and there were two other people, one of them in the back with her. One of them had her nurse's bag. They walked her into the house and they came back a minute later.'

'And so of course you hung around this morning to catch her and see what she had to say.'

'Like you just said. You'd have done the same.'

On balance, Jude thought he might not. The benefit of experience had taught him a degree of caution Mikey lacked. 'And so you asked her if she was all right and she just about ran off. Great work.'

'Yeah, okay. I get the point. But I wasn't sure and I didn't want to waste your time.'

'I'll give her a call. And Mikey."

'What?'

'This call never happened. And if you hear anything like this happening again, you don't do anything stupid like looking outside. You call me straight away. Okay?'

'*Watch the wall my darling while the gentlemen go by.* Is that right?' said Mikey, sounding much more cheerful now he'd passed his problem on to someone else.

'What?'

'It's a poem. *If you wake at midnight* and all that. *Them that asks no questions isn't told a lie.*'

'Stick by that advice,' said Jude, and ended the call.

He went back to the desk where Ashleigh was sitting, and sat down. 'Did you hear any of that?'

'Some of it.' She looked concerned. 'Do you think there's something—?'

'Mikey does get it right occasionally.' Jude dialled Becca's number. 'Damn. She declined the call.' She never did that. He put the phone down. 'Okay. I have a theory about this.' He glanced at the whiteboard, at Gil's name scrawled there. 'Just a theory.'

'I do, too. Gil's missing because someone needed him to mend the broken clock.'

'Exactly. And somehow he got hurt and Becca, for whatever reason, has been dragged in to help. But how that connects to Roger Duncan is anyone's guess.'

'At least if they needed a nurse we know Gil's still alive.'

DEATH IN GOOD TIME

He shook his head. First Roger, now Gil, now Becca, all involved. If someone had seen Mikey looking out then he, too, might get dragged into it. 'I need to speak to her.'

'Someone's obviously put the fear of God into her,' said Ashleigh, with sympathy.

'Yes, but surely she knows — she *knows* — you can't afford to keep quiet about these things. If she'd told me last night we could perhaps have done something and now she's not answering.'

The phone rang again. Mikey again, sounding more subdued this time. 'I meant to say something else. I've been reading up on the Capels. They have a really interesting family history. You should dig more deeply into it.'

'Is that really what you called for?'

There was a pause. 'No. I mean…I just wanted to ask. Becca's going to be okay, isn't she?'

'Yes,' said Jude without hesitation, 'she is.'

He ended the call and laid the phone down on the table, staring at it as though there was something else it could tell him. Of all people, it had to be Becca.

'Now,' he said, getting to his feet, 'I'm going to see Faye.'

SEVENTEEN

'Becca, love,' called Elaine from the reception desk just as Becca was heading for the door, 'could you do just one last thing for me before you go?'

'Will it take long?' Inwardly, Becca cursed. The day had been a struggle because of her lack of sleep, made worse by the enthusiasm of all her patients to discuss the murder up at Capel Lodge. Every one of them had formulated a fantastical theory to chew over with her, every one had heard something from someone who'd been there or who knew someone who had, and of course every one of them knew of Roger Duncan. 'I was hoping to get away sharp.'

'Not long. Maybe five minutes. There's a patient been waiting in room five now for quite a while.'

A patient meant scrubbing her hands and putting her uniform jacket back on and all the palaver that went with it. Becca sighed. 'Can't Jan—?'

'She's away to catch a train. Off down to London for the weekend, apparently.' Elaine shook her head, as if

London were a faraway place, riddled with danger and exoticism.

It might not hold as much danger as Cumbria, or at least not at that moment. 'Oh, I suppose so.'

'I knew you wouldn't let me down. Just pop your bag on the desk, sweetheart. I'll keep an eye on it.'

Truth be told, Becca was a little relieved to be rid of her bag. It had her phone in it and she'd been paranoid all day about saying something which might be picked up by her previous night's antagonists and misinterpreted sufficiently to put her — or Gil, or both of them — in even more trouble than they were in already. And although she was desperate to get home and get some sleep, she couldn't rule out the man and the woman coming back to fetch her to replace the dressing. At least in the minor injuries unit, out of which she worked, she was safe from that.

Room five was in the bowels of the building, a stuffy, windowless dungeon that generally only got pressed into use when there was an overload of patients, but she almost felt comforted heading there, as if it was a panic room she could wall herself up in. But it wasn't. She had a patient to see and in her exhaustion she hadn't even remembered to ask Elaine for their notes. Going back would be another few minutes of a day that couldn't end soon enough. She reached room five and pushed open the door.

Seated facing the door, Jude immediately leapt to his feet and moved across the room towards her.

For a moment she thought he was going to catch her up in a hug and when he stopped short she felt strangely bereft, because a hug was exactly what she needed and she had no-one to give her one. 'Oh!'

'I'm just checking you're all right,' he said motioning her to shut the door. 'Sit down and we can have a chat.'

'But I'm meant to be seeing a patient. Is it you? You aren't hurt are you?' Even she heard the anxiety in her voice, as if his welfare mattered more to her than that of any other patient.

'No, I'm here on official business.' He looked very grave.

Curse Mikey. She should have known he wouldn't be able to keep his mouth shut. 'I can't…I mean, I'm fine. You don't need to worry. Everything's okay.'

'But you didn't answer my call,' he said, and his eyelid twitched as though he were tempted to wink.

'No, because I was at work and anyway, it's not as if—' *Not as if we're together any more.* She wouldn't even have had that thought if she weren't so tired, so anxious. When his number had come up it was only the thought of Gil, lying in a corner looking like a shrivelled old man far older than his years, that had stopped her snatching up the phone and telling him everything.

'No, but it's serious. I need to talk to you about what happened last night.'

She drew in a deep breath. Gil was an old man, for God's sake, in his seventies, injured and utterly at the mercy of his captors. It was all right for her, but if she said anything, he would die.

'Last night?' she said, and managed a laugh. 'Is this about what Mikey saw? Bless him, but he has completely the wrong end of the stick. I was out with some friends, that was all. Not something I usually do on a work night, but that's all it was.'

'Okay, that's fine. I can tell you this is a police investigation and I'm very interested in the two people you were out with. Your friends. So I'm going to ask you who they were and when you've told me, you can go.'

There was a second chair in the room and Becca subsided into it. Jude resumed his seat, sitting back and trying, she thought, to seem more relaxed than he must feel. 'Right.'

'So who were they?'

Her breath shortened. Their conversations were too often stiff and restricted, but he never attempted to assert his authority over her. It felt uncomfortable being questioned by him like this, as though she'd done something wrong. 'I don't know—'

'Okay. So, not your friends after all, then.' He nodded, as if that was the answer he'd expected.

'Jude. I can't. Really. Don't ask me about it.'

'Fine. I won't.'

In the ensuing pause she looked at him, watching as he weighed up his response. His face was as neutral as always but she sensed a twitching of a smile on his lips which he either couldn't, or chose not to, control. They knew one another so well; he would know exactly how to get the story out of her and then someone else would die and it would be her fault. She steeled herself for his reaction.

'If you won't tell me,' he said after a moment, 'then why don't I tell you? This is to do with Gil Foley, isn't it?'

'I must be the easiest witness you've ever had to interview,' she said, crossly.

'It's not personal,' he said, as if that made her feel better. 'Doddsy would have approached it the same way, or Ashleigh, or any of us. We're not idiots.'

The cat was out of the bag and the weight of decision-making lifted. Becca could have cried with relief. Gil was Jude's problem, now. 'Did Mikey tell you?'

'That's between me and my conscience,' he said, 'and if your conscience is clear now because you didn't tell me, are you happy to share the rest?'

'I might as well,' she said, her emotions mixed. The situation was no more dangerous for Gil than it had been before, just a different sort of danger and one she need no longer take on responsibility for.

'Good.' He nodded, and then the professional mask slipped, just for a second. 'You are all right, aren't you?'

'It's not me I'm worried about. It's Gil. I don't know what happened — they wouldn't let me talk to him — but somehow he got shot. I don't know why.'

'Is he badly hurt?'

'I don't think so. It was a clean wound, as far as I can tell, and it didn't look deep. It's his thigh. Superficial, and there's no infection.' Gil's face loomed in her imagination. Eyes closed, skin ghastly white in the artificial light, like death itself, but he'd been able to talk. That was what that had been all about, that inconsequential rambling about *the lad you used to go out with*, the one who was *so easy to talk to*. 'With hindsight, I think he might have been faking. Not the wound, of course. That was real enough. But he was making out it's much worse than it is, and I went along with that.'

'Gil's a wily old bird,' he said, more cheerfully, 'and cussed with it, so that wouldn't surprise me. Tell me what happened, from the beginning.'

Encouraged, Becca ran through the story of her adventure the previous evening. 'They were serious, you know. They scared me.' There had been the blindfold, the threats, the warnings.

'I'm not surprised.'

There had been other things, too, things she hadn't dared think too much about because everything she knew was dangerous. Now she could give her memory free rein. 'I know I'm not the police, and I know you like facts—' she began, a little sheepishly.

'You know me so well. I do like facts but if I can't have

them I'll settle for any other information. Thoughts, ideas, guesses. Anything.'

'Wherever we went, they took me a very long way round.'

'Did you know how long? You didn't know what time it was,' he reminded her, because she'd told him how the kidnappers had been meticulous in making sure she hadn't known what time it was until she got home. Now she saw that for what it was, an attempt to confuse her, and with her mind clear she could pick over her experience with a fresh eye.

'No, but there was something. I know I was away for about three and a half hours, and I can't have been with Gil for more than fifteen minutes. But if I had to guess I'd say in reality I was only about half an hour from home.'

'Right?' he said, interested.

'Yes. We never went on the motorway. I would have known. So we must have been on country roads.'

'Okay.' She could see his mind working, whirring away, calculating how far she could have been driven in an hour and a half on country roads and, no doubt, finding the area covered daunting.

'Not too long before we arrived, there was a smell. A foul smell. I noticed it the other day when I was out seeing a patient. There was some leak from an industrial unit up outside Langwathby a couple of weeks ago, and they keep saying they've fixed it but it keeps recurring. I smelt it just before we got to wherever we were going and again a few minutes after we left.'

He reacted to that, almost in delight. 'That's a damn good spot. Well done. Maybe you should be in the police after all.'

She felt herself going pink, as if praise from him was something she wanted, as if she needed his approval.

'There might be other leaks. I don't know. I don't know what it was. It's just common sense.'

'You'd be surprised how few people have it. And you can bet your life I'll have someone checking out every industrial leakage in the county before I get home tonight. Anything else?'

'Only that the woman was wearing a wig. They did their best to stop me seeing them but of course I needed light to treat Gil. The man was wearing a mask but the woman wasn't, and I got half a look at her out of the corner of my eye. I didn't see her face properly, and she was really heavily made up, but she was blonde. So even at the time I reckoned that they were covering their bases and didn't mind if I did get a look. Because maybe he was recognisable, or known to the police or something, and she wasn't. And then I wondered if I was meant to see her and get the wrong idea of what she looked like.'

'And you're sure it's a wig?'

'I've seen a lot of them in my time, with cancer patients. I didn't think about it at first, because I was too scared.' With Jude it was easy to be honest, at least about that. 'But I've seen a lot of wigs in my time. And when I think about it, she reminded me of someone. She reminded me of Rose Duncan. Same height, the blonde wig and no local accent.' Though that could be many people.

He was nodding again. 'But you don't think it was Rose?'

'I think that might be what they wanted me to think.' She picked at a fingernail, self-consciously. 'I was at school with her, did you know that?'

'I don't think I did. Though I could have worked it out.' He had gone to the same school, but three years ahead, and at that stage the two of them had never paid one another any real attention.

'Yes. We were friends for a few years, but she was so much cleverer than me and moved up to the top set in all our classes, and then we did different subjects and drifted apart. I always wanted to be a nurse so I did the science subjects and she was really creative and arty.'

'You didn't keep in touch?'

'I haven't seen her for years, so maybe I wouldn't recognise her voice, but she was much more well-spoken than the rest of us, almost posh. I was really surprised when I realised she'd joined the family business. I never saw her as an undertaker. She always wanted to be an art historian.'

'People change their plans,' he said, and nodded. 'Brilliant. Thanks, Becca. That was very helpful.'

She shook her head at him, suddenly infuriated. 'Are you like this with everybody? I'm not an idiot, and you're just being bland. I've told you everything I know, and God knows what it'll cost Gil, and all you can do is fob me off with platitudes. What's going to happen now? What are you going to do for Gil? And what do these people want.'

'Okay,' he said, 'fair point. Right. I haven't had time to think through what you've told me but I'm pretty certain it has something to do with Roger Duncan, though God knows what, and I think Gil is probably still in significant danger.'

And me, she thought, though her pride wouldn't let her say it. *Am I in danger?* 'I think they'll come back.'

'Yes,' he said, calm as a parent reassuring a child about a recurring nightmare, 'I expect they will, but you'll be fine. It looks as if they need Gil to be well, for whatever reason, and so they'll probably want you to have a look at him.'

'I'll go,' she said, cursing herself even as she said it. She wasn't brave in the way that Jude or his colleagues were brave, knowingly and readily confronting danger whenever it was required, far more often than anyone could have expected of them. She was just a nurse who plodded along doing her job, changing dressings, washing wounds, checking blood pressures, day in and day out and for that she was called, along with all her colleagues, *an angel*. When she came across the dying it was expected, and it was rare that she came across the type of violence that others saw, but Gil had touched something in her. It was his faith in her, her trust that she would help him, and that meant she couldn't do anything that might harm him. Initially that had meant keeping silence but now that the Satterthwaite brothers between them had thwarted that plan, the only alternative she could see was to play along, play the game, do her best to keep things normal and at least not expose the old man to any further risk until the police had come up with some sort of plan. 'Of course I'll go.'

He was shaking his head. 'No question of that, I'm afraid.'

'I'm responsible for Gil and he needs medical help.'

'No, Becca. You can't. I won't allow it.'

'How dare you—'

'Not at a personal level. At a professional one. I can't let you. This is a serious matter. Gil's life is at risk already, and yours will be too, if you go back. I spoke to my boss before we came out and everything's arranged. There's someone waiting outside who'll take you somewhere safe until this is all over.'

She stared at him. It had been serious before but this made her feel more scared rather than reassured. 'But my job—'

'All sorted. I've spoken to your boss.'

'And my clothes. I don't have my clothes.'

'My mum can go in and pack a bag for you. We'll take your phone and check to see if there's a tracker on it, though I'm willing to bet that was a bluff and if it is we'll get it back to you. If not, we'll get you another one.'

He'd thought it all through. Almost all of it. 'But Holmes—'

'Mikey can feed him. He can make himself useful for once.'

'This is all so sudden,' she said, and felt in her pocket for a handkerchief, fighting tears of fear and relief and God knew what else.

'Yes, I know. But we know what we're doing, I promise. We'll be doing our damnedest to make sure Gil is safe.' His phone rang, and he glanced down at it. 'I'll need to take this.'

He stepped outside and a moment later the door opened again. She jumped, but it was only Elaine, with a cup of hot chocolate from the vending machine. 'I brought you this, just to see you through to whenever you get something else.' She winked. 'Patient okay?'

'Yes,' said Becca, rather crossly, 'he was fine.'

'Good looking lad, too,' said Elaine, as if she hadn't been working with Becca long enough to be fully conversant with the whole sorry Satterthwaite saga, and winked.

'Handsome is as handsome does,' said Becca, accepting the cup and resigning herself to being swept away on a tide of other people's making.

EIGHTEEN

Jude was wasting the evening waiting by the phone and pretending to work when the doorbell went. He went into the dim hallway with a degree of apprehension because he wasn't expecting anyone, then went back into the living room and took a quick peek through the window. It was his father.

Awkward. The two men had been supposed to meet for a drink that evening and Jude, as he so often did, had cancelled in the name of work. His father must have seen the light on and decided to take him to task. He opened the door.

'Not at work after all, then?' said David Satterthwaite, and sighed a huge, amateur-theatrical sigh.

'I didn't say I'd be at work. I said I'd be working.' Not that he was doing much of that, just sitting with his laptop open waiting to hear something from Faye, but with no result so far.

'Sounds like an excuse to me.'

David, who was always alert to a potential slight, had been in the pub. 'No,' said Jude, good-temperedly, 'not at all. I had some stuff I needed to do. Really must do, in fact.'

He looked over David's shoulder. Adam, whose campaign of low-level harassment extended to renting the flat directly opposite and making himself constantly visible, had come out of the building and was loitering in the small square of slabs and scruffy perennials that passed for his front garden and watching them with interest, a cigarette dangling between his fingers.

After all, David was the lesser of the two evils. If, as he surely would, he made a scene on the doorstep Adam would be over at once, pretending to be civic-minded and no doubt seeing aggression on Jude's part where none existed. 'I'm waiting for an important phone call so I couldn't come out. But I can spare you half an hour. We can have a coffee and then I'll run you home.'

'We were supposed to be out for a drink, lad. I was hoping for something a bit stronger than a coffee.'

Jude led him into the kitchen, where they would be away from Adam's disquieting stare and where the chairs were less comfortable and so more likely to persuade his father to curtail his stay. There was a stock of non-alcoholic beers in the fridge and one remaining full-strength, which he offered to his father. 'Have a seat. I am sorry about tonight. I was hoping we could make another time, when I'm not so busy.'

His father, who was on the whole a happy drunk, grinned at him. Relations between the two men had been strained ever since David had upped and left his wife when she had been diagnosed with cancer and had shown no regrets in so doing, but at least there was a relationship of a sort. Neither Mikey nor their mother had spoken to him since. For Jude, who unequivocally took his mother's side in the matter, their meetings were always a matter of duty, something he grimly set his mind to as he would to a long run on a wet winter night, undertaken for his own good rather than for his pleasure. Nevertheless he was reluctant to cancel, and at least half an hour would set his conscience at rest for a week or so.

'This'll do.' David wrenched the ring off the can and poured it into the glass Jude offered him. He was sixty now, and as clumsily insensitive as ever to the nuances of Jude's attitude towards him, reverting to a false theatricality after a couple of pints and quick to take recourse in his own injured feelings at Mikey's continuing silence. 'Anyway, there was a reason I wanted to talk to you tonight, in your own interests. And it would have been a shame if you'd missed out on it, because it might actually help you with your work.' He left a dangling contempt on the final word.

'Is that right?'

'Yes. It's this Capel funeral. Of course you'll know the background — I bet you have a hundred underlings doing that for you — but they might just be a bit narrow, you know? Keeping it to the here and now.'

'Very possible.' There was nothing suspicious about Frances Capel's death, but Jude was happy to let David ramble. It kept them off more difficult subjects for a decent interval, until he could ease him out of the door. 'And you're the local history buff, after all. Let's hear it.'

'They're the talk of the town these days, aren't they?' said David, lifting his glass and making Jude wait. 'The Capels, I mean. I thought you'd be wanting all the gossip.'

'You know me. I'm interested in everything.' Jude stretched his legs out and took a long swig of his joyless beverage, listening for his phone and wondering what was happening — in Wasby, where Faye had arranged for armed police to be waiting in Becca's cottage, or somewhere not too far from Langwathby. He would hear about it in good time from Faye, who was in the office overseeing the search for Gil.

'And I'm the man to go to. Not that I want to give you the wrong idea. Wouldn't want you looking at your old dad as a suspect in a murder, eh?'

Irritated, Jude fell into the trap. 'I'm glad you're here, actually. Mikey mentioned something about the Capel family history being relevant.'

On the instant, David's eyes narrowed. He could never grasp how his younger son could be so unforgiving, could rebuff any — admittedly half-hearted — attempts to rebuild, and in Jude's opinion he never would until he could accept some sort of responsibility for the whole mess. But that was what happened in families. They got themselves tied in knots of right and wrong and historic mistakes, perceived or actual, that too often echoed through the years and the generations. Maybe that was what had happened with the Capels. 'And he said to ask me, eh?'

'He didn't mention you.'

David puffed himself up for a second in injured vanity. 'We did a couple of visits there with the local history society a few years back. But aye, I know a bit about the Capels. Not from those visits, because the old girl was never there when we went and all we got to do was see round the Lodge, but there was a lad I taught who was doing a local history project a while ago. An interesting story, but damned if I can see a connection with your dead vicar.'

'Undertaker.' Jude's phone pinged and he manoeuvred it out and snatched a quick glance, but it was his mother, assuring him that she'd managed to retrieve anything she thought Becca would need and handed it over to a police officer for delivery, and that Holmes was under Mikey's tender care.

He thrust the phone away. It would have been too difficult to respond to that just then. It was relatively early, nine o'clock and still light. If Gil Foley's kidnappers came back to Wasby, if they were caught or — God forbid — not, then it would be much later on. The planning might be taking place back at the police headquarters, and armed officers might be waiting, but no action was expected until it could take place under the cloak of darkness. 'Go on. You know me. I love a good story.' And his father, for all his faults, never forgot a detail.

'Once upon a time,' David began, and paused for effect.

Jude, used to him, took a long drink of his zero-alcohol beer and waited. It was passable, at least.

'Decades ago, a couple of generations at least. Back in the War, it was, when Frances Capel would have been a toddler without even a title to her name. Her father was in the army, and when the War broke out her grandfather, the seventh Earl, was determined to do his bit for the war effort but he was too old to fight. The family had moved out of London to Capel Castle, up in Snowdonia, and he moved the family into the servants' quarters and offered the castle to the National Gallery.'

'Why would they want it?' Jude asked, knowing some interaction was expected of him.

'For their works of art. They knew London would be bombed and they wanted to get all these precious things out of the way. So they commandeered a load of places that they considered suitable for any of their movable treasures — things from art galleries, libraries, museums, some of the most iconic items you can imagine. And they shipped these things out all over the country, in cellars, in caves, in mine workings and in private homes. It's quite the story.'

'And the Capels got paintings?' Jude asked, thinking of the missing clock, the missing ledger. 'Not *objets d'art*? Not books? Not clocks?'

'Definitely paintings. They had a gallery of their own, you see.'

'That doesn't surprise me. Her grandfather seems to have had an eye for a bargain.'

'He was a bit of a magpie, and his father before him. They both collected everything, from neolithic arrow heads to vintage cars.'

And weapons, of course, but how many? 'Clocks?'

'What's this obsession about clocks? Yes, I'm sure they will have collected clocks, but only in passing, as it were. But these pictures were the thing. They had their own gallery so they were able to store the pieces in suitable conditions, and they had plenty of space. A lot of the items had had to be sold to cover death duties, you see, and Earl Capel himself wasn't that struck on pictures. He was much more interested in the occult and sacred mysteries, as he used to call them. Ley lines and so on.'

'And what's a ley line, for those of us who only know about practicalities?' said Jude, and grinned.

'Oh, some new age claptrap, but a lot of folk are interested in them. They're lines channelling the earth's energy or something, and they're supposed to connect churches and places of spiritual interest.'

'Stone circles and the like?'

'For sure. Capel Lodge is built on a ley line, the same one that goes through Long Meg stone circle and a load of other churches in the area. Not that I believe in that kind of stuff. Too many coincidences and all that, and it's a bit too much of a stretch of the imagination for me to believe they're all linked. But the old Earl was convinced.' He drank, deeply, already halfway through his beer.

'Right. And back in Wales…?' Jude snatched a glance at the clock, wondering how soon he could move him on.

'Of course. You want that story. Back in Wales the National Gallery shipped a load of paintings out to Capel Castle. Not their Old Masters, nothing world famous, and it was just as well. Late one summer night, a farmer on his way back from a lock-in at the local pub saw a light in the sky. Capel Castle was on fire.'

'Arson?' asked Jude.

'I knew you'd say that. You have a suspicious mind. But yes, they reckon so, though it was never proved and no-one found a motive. Earl Capel rushed into the gallery and retrieved some of the paintings but he couldn't save them all. The gallery was consumed and one wing of Capel Castle itself badly damaged. A number of minor works were lost.'

'And perhaps someone—'

'You're not solving a crime here,' said David, wrestling the conversation back to the story. 'No-one proved arson, though the gallery officials tried to blame the Earl. Covering their own negligence, I bet, because he left the more valuable paintings and retrieved only the items he was particularly interested in. Ran past a line of Rosettis, I'm told, and a very fine Millais, and a few others. Hedleys, Redgraves, Tissots and so on.' He looked at Jude as if he expected the names to mean something to him.

'So what did he save?'

'A series of sketches by Burne-Jones, ideas for a series of paintings based on the tarot deck.'

'Right.' At last, Jude found something in his father's story that made sense to him, though he still couldn't see how it might link to the death of Roger Duncan. Ashleigh had a passing interest in the tarot, something he'd always thought a little too esoteric for a police officer, and he even had a deck himself that she'd given him, though his interest in it was limited to curiosity, and when he came to think of it he realised she hadn't mentioned it for months. At that moment, he knew, she would be working in the office, waiting to see if the kidnappers came back for Becca and, if they did, what they would do, where they might be.

'So he left the valuables and took the ones he liked,' prompted Jude.

'Exactly. He went back in for the last one, a painting of The Emperor from the deck, the only one in the set that Burne-Jones ever completed, but he couldn't reach it. He was overcome by smoke and had to be rescued by his valet. He was never the same afterwards. Couldn't bear being held responsible for the losses, apparently, and the suspicious circumstances surrounding the fire just made it worse. Then his son — Lady Frances's father, who became the eighth Earl — was badly injured in the last days of the war. The seventh Earl lingered on for twenty years or so. His son became a virtual recluse, and retired up here, to Capel Lodge, where he lived out the rest of his life sitting in his rooms and sending his representatives out to buy up stuff for him to sit and gloat over. He died back in the 1990s, I think. And Lady Frances has been ruling the roost ever since.'

'And look how it turned out.' For a moment Jude entertained the image of the damaged eighth Earl sitting in a darkened room like a dragon with a golden hoard, unable to use it and able to gain satisfaction only from possessing it. 'Lady Frances didn't care much for it, it seems, and was starting to get rid of it.'

'I heard she'd given some pieces away.'

'Any guns?'

'God, Jude, I don't think I'd want to live with your brain. Guns, clocks, books. No, I never heard anything about what it might be, only that it was odds and ends.'

'Anything to report?' he asked, when he'd driven David the couple of miles or so back to his house and headed home to put in a call to Faye. It was ten o'clock, around the time that Becca had been abducted the previous evening, and he knew he was pre-empting matters, but he couldn't bring himself to wait for her call.

'Nothing yet.' She, he could tell, was as tense as he was. 'We've got Becca Reid safely tucked up in a B&B in Keswick, so she'll be fine, and the whole of your village crawling with plain clothes officers. Let's just hope they're discreet. These country villages are the worst places. Someone always notices.'

It was just as well Mikey had had his eyes open the previous night. 'Any luck in finding where Gil might be?'

'Not yet, and not through want of trying. But the same applies. I've sent up a helicopter and a couple of drones, but we can't buzz the whole countryside with them, much as I'd like to. We'd just alert them. But we're working on it, and rest assured. I'll let you know the minute something happens.'

He made himself a coffee and wished he had the courage to phone Becca to reassure her, make sure she was all right. But he couldn't, and she probably wouldn't want to speak to him if he did, and all he could do was the same as Faye and Doddsy and Ashleigh and the rest of them were doing and wait to see what happened when the kidnappers turned up at Becca's cottage again.

NINETEEN

'Not a thing,' said Faye, her eyes dull from yet another long night, when Jude called into her office the next morning. 'Nada. Not a car that didn't have reason to be there, not a dog walker who didn't come in and out of their own front door under the eye of our surveillance team. You seem to have been brought up in the dullest village in the county. It's no wonder you grew up to be so interested in other people's business.'

He would have chuckled at that if it wasn't for the fact that Gil's whereabouts were still unknown. 'And a few bored special ops lads, eh?'

'I'm sure we'd all rather they'd have had a very exciting night and brought us Gil Foley, alive and well, along with a couple of suspects for questioning, but here we have it. We're no further forward than yesterday.'

'Do you think they got wind of something?'

'More likely they didn't need to come back.'

Her face was grave. She would be thinking the same as he was, that it might be good news or it might be bad.

'For better or worse,' she said, as if to be sure he shared

her concerns. 'Trust me on this, Jude. It's my absolute priority. And I can promise you Becca Reid is fine, too.'

His relationship — or rather, the lack of it — with Becca was widely known, but he was never sure that Faye, who lacked emotional intelligence, would have understood how much it mattered to him even now the two of them were no longer together. She had shown herself ruthless in ending inconvenient relationships; he was anything but. 'I'll get on, then.'

'Any developments on the Duncan murder?' she asked, with a restless look down at her laptop in response to a notification, only to roll her eyes at it and look away.

'No, but I'm working on it. Someone must have seen something.' He paused and turned towards the door. 'I'm going to head up to Long Meg. It's not that far from Capel Lodge.'

She raised an eyebrow, always notoriously wary of senior officers getting their hands dirty and going out into the world and made even more tetchy by the tension of the situation. 'What is it this time? Some clue only you can find, growing wild in a hedgerow by moonlight?'

'Not that. I want to speak to Geri Foster.' That, at least, was a more robust reason than his real one, to have a sniff around Capel Lodge without seeming too obvious.

'Can't Ashleigh do that? It's what we pay her for. I expect you to be a manager.'

'Geri's tough as old boots,' he said, 'and one of those women who see other women as a challenge. I get on with her better than most. I've a reasonable chance of getting something out of her. And I can call in on Capel Lodge and have a chat to Irene. See if she remembers anything else, or has found anything out.'

'About the clock?'

'The clock, and the book. It was left to her, remember.

She might have racked her brains and come up with some reason why or some idea what's happened to it.'

'I'm sure Miss Jenkins is perfectly capable of using the phone,' she said, but she stood aside as if to approve his decision. 'But for God's sake try not to go anywhere near that bloody sewage leak or whatever it is.'

Despite her strictures, he had no option. Capel Lodge and Long Meg were both within an easy few minutes' drive of the micro industrial estate whose unfortunate incident might have set them on the trail. He drove with extra care as he took a route that took him through Langwathby but avoided the place itself, noting the occasional police officer making discreet observations of outlying properties, seeing the low pass of a drone over a collection of abandoned farm buildings on the edge of the village. Ten minutes from there on country roads might take them to the local villages of Lazonby or Temple Sowerby or Melmerby, to any one of a hundred isolated properties that lay somewhere between them.

Conscious of the need for discretion, he resisted the temptation to drive around and see what he could find, though he paid careful attention to everything along the route he took. At least he had reason to be up at Capel Lodge and at Long Meg, and he thought it most unlikely that Gil would be being held anywhere near there. With so many police, uniformed and otherwise, in the area, the risk of discovery was too great.

He stopped the car in the field next to Long Meg, close to the New Age travellers' camp where Geri had said he would find her. It was a place he knew well, its occupants a strange mix of the affluent, stepping out from the rat-race for a few weeks to settle in the affluence of their camper vans or luxury tents, and the longer-term adherents to a more austere way of life. Only a few years before there had been a reasonable collection of what Chris dismissively referred to as flat-earthers, genuine hippies who lived as close to nature and as removed from modernity as possible. These days their number had dwindled to just Geri Foster's parents, Storm and Raven, lingering on in a ragged canvas tent in the corner of the field, literally and metaphorically overlooked by their neighbours.

Geri was waiting for him, hands in pockets and clad in sensible wellies even though the ground was dry. As he pulled his car up in a lay-by just beyond the gate and got out, she walked swiftly across from the corner where Storm and Raven lived and leaned on the field gate. 'Chief Inspector. Hello again. What am I supposed to have done this time?'

He suppressed a smile. Her fierce formality was, he suspected, intended to intimidate him, but it failed. He was too used to that from Faye. 'Just a catch up. I know you spend a lot of time around here these days because of your mum. I wanted to ask if perhaps you've seen anything.'

She raised an eyebrow, exactly as Faye did. 'Is that it? Don't you have people in uniforms you can send up to ask about it?'

'I was in the area anyway.'

'I suppose that makes sense.' Her expression sobered slightly. 'No nearer to catching whoever did that poor man in, then? What a terrible business. It does look as if they might have put one over on you for once.'

Geri's attitude towards the police varied from the ambivalent to the downright aggressive; she was a woman who lived within convention but loved outside it and always rooted for the underdog. Jude suspected she would be quite happy to see the villains get away. 'It's early days.'

'It's five days. I always thought if you didn't catch them quickly they got away. But you'll tell me that justice works

DEATH IN GOOD TIME

slowly and you always get your man, so we'll have to agree to differ.'

'You have a pretty good view from up here,' he said, turning to look one way towards the slate roof of Capel Lodge, a few hundred yards away as the crow flew and rather longer via that twisted web of country lanes, and the other towards the chapel nestling against the woods.

'We do, and I've already been asked about it. Several times.'

'I'm just satisfying my curiosity.'

'Are you sure you didn't just come to get out of the office?'

He did laugh at that. 'I like it up here, that's true. And, by the way, I learned something about it yesterday. It's on a ley line.'

Geri had been brought up in tune with the Earth, a tree-hugger who knew the stars and the natural world, as well as a hundred strange theories about their provenance and their influence. 'I didn't know you believed in all that stuff and nonsense.'

'I don't. It was an observation.'

'If you listen to Mum, everywhere's on a ley line around here, or so it seems. There's even one that goes through your police headquarters, right the way up through the town and up here. If I believed in them I'd say that was why you're always drawn up here but I dare say you loiter in plenty of other places without any spiritual heritage at all. But my parents believe in it, and they like to live on them.' She turned back to the tent. 'Sometimes I think that's why my mum is still alive. All that positive energy.'

'I wondered how she was.' Raven, who shunned modern medicine, had been dying for a long time, with an undiagnosed illness he suspected was breast cancer.

'She should have been dead months ago.' Geri sighed. 'I don't know why. I Googled it and read a lot of articles I didn't understand about metastasis of cancer cells or something. Apparently sometimes the cancer just grows very slowly and I can only imagine that if her lifestyle is a healthy one after all then that's what keeps her going. Not that I wouldn't have liked her to get treatment and live a bit longer. She's only sixty.'

'Is she in pain?' he asked.

'Yes, quite a lot, but she seems very happy in herself. She just thinks nature isn't ready for her. But it won't be long now. In the meantime she just sits there reading her tarot cards and always pulling out the positive ones. I swear to God she cheats, but who am I to say anything? If she wants to kid herself everything's fine, it's up to her.'

'You think it matters that she cheats with the cards?' he asked, sensing the opening.

'Of course not. The tarot is even more nonsensical than the ley lines. Now you sound as though you're interested. I never thought you'd be the type to go soft in the head over fortune telling.'

Tarot, Ashleigh would always say when he teased her about her unusual hobby, wasn't about fortune telling. 'I'm interested because apparently Lady Frances's late grandfather was very enthusiastic about that sort of thing.'

'My word,' she said, in mock-admiration. 'You are thorough. Investigating some old man who's been dead for decades?'

'I have that kind of mind. It goes down a rabbit hole. I discovered last night that he saved a set of sketches for a tarot deck from a fire, although the only painting from the deck was lost. Which is a shame, because it would have been immensely valuable.'

'Oh right. I see. And when you say lost...?'

'Destroyed, apparently.'

'Which one was it?'

'The Emperor.'

'Well,' she said, cautiously, 'that follows. Because from what I've heard the old Earl had a guid conceit of himself, as the Scots say, and I'm quite sure he would have fancied himself as the Emperor. It's a very positive card. It represents masculinity, positivity, leadership and authority.' She shot him a sidelong look. 'Rather like yourself.'

Her habit of alternating insults and compliments amused him. 'I wonder why he didn't try and save it until it was too late?'

'We can hardly ask him,' she said with a shrug. 'Since you're here, you might as well come and say goodbye to my mum. She always liked you. And I'll see if I can rustle up what passes in this godforsaken place for a cup of tea.'

TWENTY

'I'm so sorry,' said Irene as she answered the big front door of Capel Lodge and found Wilf Hamley, Lady Frances's solicitor, standing on the doorstep, neat and buttoned up even in the summer, in full tweed suit and cricket club tie, 'Miss Capel isn't here at the moment. She's gone down to London to deal with some business.' It was with the ex-husband, who'd suddenly realised a St John's Wood flat was now at play in their marital blame-game, but Wilf didn't need to know that. He fancied himself as a big noise locally and Lady Frances had rather liked him, but he was better suited to dealing with land disputes and simple wills rather than more complicated matters like high-roller divorces, and anyway Emma's own solicitors were already joining battle on her behalf.

'It was yourself I was after, Irene, if you have a minute.'

Wilf was a tall man and looked down upon her, not just literally but also, she thought, metaphorically. Some people asserted their seniority and presumed superiority by keeping to a cruel formality, as Lady Frances had done; Wilf preferred to patronise. Irene, who had spent all her life in service and had grown so comfortable in it that she'd struggle to adapt when she was at last in charge of her own destiny, was much happier with the former. For a moment she thought about calling him out on his familiarity, but decided against it. What was the point? He wouldn't choose to hear it and if he did he would choose not to listen.

'I'm very busy, Mr Hamley,' she said, and looked at her watch to make the point.

'It's important.'

'You'd better come in.'

As she led the way through the echoing hall to the library, Carly popped her head out from a door further along. 'I thought I heard the door…oh, Mr Hamley. Irene, shall I get you some tea?'

'No, thank you Carly. Mr Hamley won't be staying long.' She could guess why he was there. It would be about the will and so she supposed she needed to talk to him, but she was sure he was making more of it than was necessary, to give himself a chance to look around, to be in on the gossip. Tea would only give him an excuse to linger.

'Shocking about poor Roger,' he said as she closed the study door behind them and ushered him to the threadbare tapestry chair she normally occupied. Lady Frances's — now Emma's — rather grander and more comfortable seat she took herself, noting his raised eyebrow at her presumption. As if it was his business!

'I'm sure the police are closing in on the killer,' she said, inwardly outraged.

'They've asked everybody enough questions,' he said cheerfully, 'that's for sure.'

Solicitors were like undertakers, thriving off other people's misfortunes, and no doubt Wilf would be hoping to pick up a bit more business out of the murder. She'd had the impression that he and Roger had been close, which made his untroubled demeanour over his friend's murder particularly unsettling. 'Can I ask you to get to the point, Mr Hamley? As I said, I'm rather busy. Miss Capel has asked me to oversee an inventory of the property as a matter of urgency.'

'With a view to a sale?' he asked, perking up.

'I'm afraid you'll have to discuss that with Miss Capel herself.'

'Of course. Of course.' He fussed a little over his cuffs, coughed, took a nervous look at the door. 'I wanted to talk to you about the bequest left to you in Lady Frances's will.'

She stared back at him, hoping she'd managed to copy the stony expression Lady Frances had perfected for those of whom she disapproved. 'The antique clock and the book which never came to me?'

'I'm not familiar with either item,' he said, turning his wedding ring over on his finger like a liar, 'but I believe the clock might have considerable value.'

'I think it most unlikely. Lady Frances's attachment to it was purely sentimental.'

'Then why did she leave it to you?'

'Presumably for the same reason she left me a specific book from the library.' Irene allowed herself to glower at the telling gap at the end of a shelf where the ledger had been. 'As I had no idea that that Lady Frances had made this bequest, I'm afraid I can't tell you what that reason was.'

'You aren't helping me, Irene,' he said, baring white teeth in a fake smile. 'It will be very difficult to settle the will until we have those items accounted for.'

'Why?'

'The law requires that every estate must be carefully accounted for in every detail before probate can be settled.'

This was unbelievable. Wills made decades before they were needed must surely bequeath items of property which no longer existed, jewellery that had long been lost or stolen, sums of money too large to be covered by the value of the estate. What happened then? Did estates atrophy, wasting away to nothing, or did the beneficiaries fight themselves into an exhausted bankruptcy over them? Irene had no significant formal education but she'd learned a huge amount both from Lady Frances and from her grandfather, the seventh Earl, and a lot of it was raw cunning rather than book learning. Wilf Hamley was up to something and whatever he wanted, she needed to handle him with care.

'Then I'm afraid you and Miss Capel's solicitor will have to find another way round it,' she said and sighed with what she hoped was convincing regret.

He sat forward a little in his chair. 'I have reason to believe, Irene, that you know exactly where the clock and the book are.'

'Are you accusing me of stealing them?' she asked, and dared laugh. 'How can I? They're my property.'

'Not until probate is settled. If you let me have them we can move on. You would, of course, get them back as soon as matters are settled.' He smiled again, but the threat in his tone was implicit and, as if to enforce it, he cast a glance across at the empty wall where the weapons had been. Thank goodness the police had taken them away. She really wasn't sure she would have trusted Wilf Hamley if they'd still been there.

'I'm sorry to disappoint you, Mr Hamley.' She folded her hands on her lap in a submissive gesture, like a bullied wife, as she used to do when Lady Frances was in one of her more quarrelsome moods. 'I don't have them. I don't know where they are. I would never have taken them without Miss Capel's express permission and if I had then I would give them to you. But I don't.'

'But R—' he began and stopped himself.

'That's all I can say. I'm sorry to disappoint you, but I don't have them. You've had a wasted journey and I, as I said before, am very busy.'

'With the inventory,' he said, with meaning.

'That's correct.' She stood up and opened the door. The radio was on down the corridor, and Carly was busy dusting the tops of the picture frames in the hallway.

'Miss Capel will be very upset if probate can't be settled,' said Wilf, keeping a wary eye on the housekeeper.

Oh, you liar. 'It would be a terrible shame for her, Mr Hamley. If there's one good thing about my bequests,' (she said it with slight emphasis) 'disappearing, it's that no-one needs to worry about me because I expected nothing and will receive nothing.' And so, he would know his threat about the delay would be irrelevant to her, even if it was true.

He switched tack immediately, lowering his voice. 'I must warn you, if it were to come out that you did steal them—'

'I did not.'

'Even if it were thought that you had stolen them…if the police were to question you on the matter… if you were convicted?'

'I won't be convicted.'

'Even the accusation would be bad for you. Miss Capel has no time for servants, they tell me. She even inquired about how easy it might be to make you all redundant.

DEATH IN GOOD TIME

Lady Frances didn't make any other provision for you in her will. If Miss Capel has cause to dismiss you without notice or compensation, how would you manage?'

'I'm seventy years old, Mr Hamley. I have family in Wales who will be glad to look after me. I'll be just fine.' She preceded him through the door and into the hall. 'Please don't threaten me again.'

'I'm sure I never threatened you Irene. All I wanted was to speed up the process of probate for everyone's benefit.'

With relief she put two hands to the big wooden front door and forced it open. 'I really think you should leave.'

'Good morning, Irene,' he said with a genial smile, and even managed a wave as he left.

Before he'd reached his car she'd turned her attention back to that old door, gripping arthritic fingers on the handle. It opened more easily than it closed and in her nervousness she struggled with it.

'I've got it, Irene.' Carly was beside her in a moment, taking the door handle and wrenching it shut. 'There you go. Nothing to worry about. Good job he's gone, eh?'

Naturally Carly would have been listening at the door. 'Yes.'

'Are you okay?' said Carly as the two of them stood in the hall, listening while his car started up and crunched down the drive. 'Come down to the kitchen and 'll get the kettle on. I've been keeping the police sweet with cake, but I've got a secret stash of chocolate digestives we can raid.'

Irene was overcome with warmth, so much so that she forgot her momentary resentment at Carly's appropriation of her business. It was to be expected that everyone in this rural prison traded in gossip; it kept them sane, and Lady Frances had set them a fine and malicious example. 'I'll do that, thank you. But if you give me five minutes I'd better give Miss Capel a quick call and let her know what he said about probate.'

Leaving Carly to head to the kitchen, she made her way back into the library. She'd never expected that of Wilf Hamley. What a liar he was, him that had always been so deferential to Lady Frances and unfailingly polite to Irene herself, and now here he was, out for what he could get and all but threatening violence. She thought of Roger Duncan on the day of the funeral, her last sight of him fussing round Emma as she got out of the car, his gracious acceptance when he'd been invited to join them at the wake. That had been the last she'd seen of him, unless you counted the white tent in the vegetable garden and the tail lights of the hearse disappearing down the drive.

She'd never given much thought to who'd killed him. That was a job for the police, in whom she had been brought up to trust absolutely, both in terms of their probity and their wisdom, but now Wilf Hamley had turned up, bold as brass and demanding the clock and the book she didn't have. She almost laughed, but it wasn't funny. Most of what she'd said to him had been true and most of what he'd said to her was so obviously untrue, but there was one facet on which he had been honest and she had lied.

Emma Capel certainly wanted to get rid of her, not because of any personal shortcomings but because of the subservience she represented, and if that happened she was in trouble. She had no family in Wales, or none who would want to take on the burden of an older woman who would be able to do increasingly less as time went on, and Wilf would guess that she was relying on Emma to at least see her right in terms of letting her go — with a small pension, perhaps, or a cottage where she could live out her days in quiet comfort. The clock, even if she got it back, wasn't worth anything, probably no more than a few hundred pounds, but Emma's good will was her pension.

Wilf had left her with no choice. She picked up the telephone receiver and dialled Ashleigh O'Halloran's number.

TWENTY-ONE

Jude left the car by a locked gate not far from the abandoned Long Meg mine, just outside Little Salkeld. He was five minutes early, and occupied his time by inspecting the ruins from a safe distance. They would be an ideal hideout for a kidnapper if they weren't so obviously unused — fenced off, dangerous and with KEEP OUT signs on all sides. The place would be full of bats, no doubt, and the birds were zipping in and out with food for their young, while the surrounding trees rippled with life. Sometimes you saw squirrels down here. And often you bumped into someone you knew.

He turned and looked along the path that led to the riverside walk, past Lacey's Caves and the broken sandstone banks of the Eden, and saw an elderly woman striding along towards him, swinging a rolled-up golf umbrella in a businesslike manner. He waited.

She slowed as she reached him, looked sideways and then back along the path.

'Irene?' he said amused. There was no doubt in his

mind because not only did she fit the descriptions and the photographs of her that had appeared in the background files for the Duncan murder, but she had also asked to meet someone in exactly that spot. 'It's okay. There's no-one about. We haven't met, but I'm DCI Jude Satterthwaite.'

'Oh!' she said, and went a little pink. 'I didn't think… when I called and asked to see someone I was expecting Sergeant O'Halloran.'

'Yes, I'm sorry if that caught you out. She called me when she got your message because I was up in the area already, so it made more sense for me to speak to you. I take it you're all right?'

She went even pinker. 'Yes. I have no doubt you think this is all terribly extraordinary.'

'Just a little unusual.' Irene, in the call that had come through to Ashleigh, had been adamant about not meeting at the house and preferably not being seen to have a deliberate meeting at all. He came across plenty of people who over-estimated their importance as witnesses, but Ashleigh hadn't thought Irene fitted that mould. 'What can I help you with?'

'Oh dear. I don't want you to think I'm foolish but I'm afraid I just had a rather unpleasant experience with Wilf Hamley. Lady Frances's solicitor.'

He nodded. 'I know of him.' They'd met, he was sure, at some do he couldn't remember and hadn't been able to avoid — another funeral, possibly. As he thought about it Wilf swam into his memory as entirely true to type — a bluff, slightly pompous, country solicitor who wore tweed and smelled of cigars. He couldn't have been too much older than Jude himself but he looked and acted like a man well past retirement age.

'It's the clock,' burst out Irene, suddenly and obviously

furious. 'My clock, the one Lady Frances left me, the one that's disappeared. And the book. Mr Hamley came round to the Lodge this morning and accused me of stealing them. Quite aggressive, he was. He said if I didn't come up with it, probate couldn't be granted, and I'm sure that's nonsense.'

'It definitely is,' said Jude, fascinated by this turn of events.

'I'm so glad to hear that! When I told him I didn't have it he said the police would have to be involved and then Miss Capel would cast me out — as if I was some Victorian lady's maid of doubtful character! And *of course* I know Miss Capel would never do any such thing, even though she thinks she doesn't need a companion, but I'm afraid he unnerved me and I'm worried about what he might do next.'

Irene Jenkins wasn't what he'd expected. By all accounts she had been efficient, timid and submissive throughout her service to Frances Capel, but here she was arranging clandestine meetings with the police and holding forth in her own defence. 'He's a brave man to threaten you,' he said gravely.

'Did I do the right thing? One never wants to waste police time on trivialities but they always say you should go straight to the police if someone tries to blackmail you.'

'Quite right.' If only Becca had followed the same, simple reasoning. He frowned at the thought. 'What did he say?'

She ran him through the interview in a surprising amount of detail. 'I don't know why he behaved like that. I don't have either the book or the clock, but if I did they would belong to me and there would be no reason why I wouldn't produce them, at least to show him. And yet there was something about him — he is such a sly, knowing man — that made me wonder if he knows where either the book, or the clock, might be. And I think he wanted to know if I knew so he could get hold of the other.'

'If he knew, why would he ask you?'

'Perhaps they're somewhere he can't get them, or if he doesn't know perhaps he thought I'd tell him without asking questions. He's such a clever man, so very careful not to be explicit in his threats. But you know how it is. They are thick as thieves, these country people. These solicitors and doctors and vicars and undertakers, carving up the births and lives and death between them. Less so nowadays, of course, but in some places their little secret societies still survive and their sole aim is to help one another to a profit.'

The passion of her speech surprised him. 'You don't think they just regard themselves as part of a community?'

'I don't see that the two need be exclusive. I grant you no vicar ever got rich, so perhaps I was a little unkind to Reverend Bowen. But solicitors and undertakers have always been businesses and even the doctors nowadays work out of practices they part-own and have more concern for profit than for patients.' She slashed savagely at a clump of Queen Anne's lace with the umbrella, and a bumble bee rose from the quivering blooms in startled alarm, hung in the air for a couple of seconds and then lumbered off on its ungainly way.

'Did you have any concerns about Mr Hamley before this?'

'No, none at all. But it made me think, Chief Inspector. I never had any concerns about Mr Duncan either, from the little I saw of him, but the two of them worked together very closely. The network out here is strong.'

He thought she might be overstating it, but what she

had to say intrigued him. 'You say you had no concerns about Mr Duncan before this. Do you have any now?'

She pursed her pale lips. 'I think so.'

'Why?'

'It was something the solicitor said.' She poked with the stick again, more gently this time, and her face creased into a frown that told Jude that Irene Jenkins, for all her submissiveness to her employer, wasn't prepared to be bullied by someone to whom she owed nothing.

'Go on.'

'He said *but R—* and then stopped himself. I don't know who R was but I can guess. As I said, thick as thieves, him and the undertaker.' She sighed.

At least the doctor and the vicar had now escaped from Irene's sweeping generalisation. 'Thank you, Miss Jenkins. That's very helpful.'

She gave him a grateful look. 'No, thank *you*, Chief Inspector. For listening. And for treating an old woman like myself politely and with respect.'

'I like to think I'd always do both of those things.' He smiled at her. It was a running joke in the office that he was popular with elderly ladies of a certain class. 'And of course you must feel free to contact us at any time.'

'I'm not afraid of him, of course,' she said, after a moment. 'He's a coward. You can always tell. Lady Frances might have taken to violence as a last resort, perhaps, to protect herself and her home, and I suspect Miss Capel would, too. They're both true Capel women with steel in their souls. Wilf Hamley never would. His threats are based on the assumption that I'm weak and can be bullied, but he's wrong.'

'Nevertheless, I want you to know you can always call for help if you think you need it.'

'Thank you, but I shall be fine.' Irene took a look down

the path in the direction of a barking dog. 'So nice to bump into you and chat,' she said loudly, for the dog walker's benefit,' but I have to get back. Miss Capel will be looking for me.'

Amused, Jude stuck his hands in his pockets and sauntered a little way in the other direction, until she was out of sight. Everyone said Lady Frances had been something of a conspiracist but Irene, it seemed, was more than capable of trying to hide her tracks if she wanted to and that immediately raised his interest.

'Burma!' called a woman's voice from around the bend in the path along which Irene had just passed. 'Heel, boy! No, heel. Oh, damn. Let me just clean that up and we'll get you on the lead.'

His heart sank. He recognised the voice, he recognised the dog's name and the last thing he wanted was another verbal duel with Geri Foster for the sake of her ego and her entertainment. If he headed back towards the car she would see him when she rounded the bend and if he headed the other way to would be impossible not to engage with her, even if he pretended to be in a hurry. He took a split-second decision and stepped over the low wire fence that separated the path from the woods. If he was quick he could be out of sight over the steep drop down to the river before Geri had finished cleaning up the dog's mess.

He knew the area well. The path he'd just left ran along the side of the steep riverbank but there was another below it, closed to the public after a particularly wet winter a couple of years earlier and never repaired. He trusted himself to follow it along to the viaduct that carried the railway over the Eden, and then he could pick up a lane up through the woods to the car.

He made it out of the woods and slithered through the lush bracken and the swarms of flies with the devil-may-care feeling of a schoolboy playing truant. Musing on Irene, he reached the riverside path, overgrown since its closure but still discernible. The summer had been dry and the river was low, rocks showing like ribs in its bed. Around him the woods hummed with low-level sound — the buzz of hard-working bees, the rustle of wind in the trees on the hill, the chatter and chirp of birds, the busy sound of the river braiding its way around the rocks. Above the water a dragonfly shimmered in iridescent green. Over the opposite bank, to the south, a helicopter made a pass across the hamlets around Great Salkeld.

His plan came to nothing about three hundred yards along the path. Much further back there had been a *Footpath Closed* sign but here someone had decided to take public safety to an extreme and it was blocked with barbed wire. The wire was untarnished and so must have been put up relatively recently. That meant another landslip. He would have to go back; frustrating, because it was only twenty yards or so before he made the lane that would take him up to the car.

For the sake of a few moments, he might risk it. The worst that would happen was that the path gave way and he slithered down to the dry river margin, but it didn't look unsafe, so any danger must be further on. With care, he negotiated the barbed wire and rounded the corner to the lane.

There was more barbed wire here. Curious. He snatched a cautious look up the slope. It was as he remembered, a tumbledown cottage with cramped outbuildings sheltered under a thicket of tangled trees and forbidding rhododendrons, an old cottage that had once belonged, he seemed to remember, to the Capel Estate and seemed to have functioned as a gamekeeper's cottage. At the bottom of the lane what looked like a former boathouse was in a state of disrepair.

But the place was still in use. He stopped, acutely aware of his own visibility, and backed away, back along the path, over the wire and up into the shelter of another belt of scrubby vegetation that drew on the water from the river to keep it growing. From there he called Faye.

'I've had a breakthrough,' he said, when she picked up.

'Have you, indeed?' She sounded even more waspish than usual. The strain must be telling.

'Yes. I think I know where Gil Foley is.'

'I should have guessed. There's a whole team of us been working on that since yesterday and no nearer to finding out, and here you are going for a walk in the woods when you should be at your desk and coming up with inspiration. You'd better be right, because I don't want to be sending the tactical ops and the firearms people in and then finding you've rumbled a couple of lost hikers.'

'I'm down by the Eden, just below Cave Wood. There are some old buildings down here that used to be part of the Capel estate.' He gave her the exact coordinates. 'I met Irene Jenkins on the path and she told me about how Lady Frances's solicitor had tried to threaten her into handing over the missing book and the clock, and I took a wander round to give her time to get clear and then guess what? I saw Ashleigh's car.'

'That's truly remarkable,' said Faye, acidly, 'since Ashleigh is in my office right now and her car is park in the car park. I can see it.'

'Yes, and from the riverside path I could see it, too. A white Ford Focus, correct numberplate. I ran it through the app to make sure I'd got it right. The numberplate must be cloned. It had me fooled for a moment but Ash's car has a big scrape above the wheel arch and this one doesn't.'

'That's just a bit clumsy of them, no?'

'I don't think so. They have to assume we've realised Gil's missing, even if they don't know exactly how much we know and when we found out — and certainly if they know, somehow, that he'd called me before he disappeared. They'll guess that we'll be keeping a lookout and they don't want to attract any attention. And they're right. If a random copper sees that car somewhere where it looks a bit unusual, they'll run a numberplate check just like I did. They'll see a white Ford Focus registered to a serving detective currently working on a case in the area, and they won't give it a second thought.' It was risky, but it was smart. It might also be the kind of gesture someone made when they were arrogant enough to be sure they'd get away with it.

'All right.' Faye was starting to sound businesslike. He could almost imagine her allocating time and resources even as she was speaking. 'I'm not going to insult your intelligence by asking if you had the sense to be discreet, but I am going to ask if you think they saw you, and if you had the chance to check the place out.'

'I'm extremely discreet. I beat a hasty retreat over a barbed wire fence and now I'm jammed into a hedge that was the first hiding place I could find. I'll be asking you to authorise the dry-cleaning bill for my suit.' He waited for a laugh but she wasn't in the mood for a joke. 'I'm sure no-one saw me and if they did they almost certainly won't have recognised me. As soon as I saw the car I backed away, just played the part of a walker who came across the barbed wire and turned back.' He hadn't even stopped to take any photographs, though he'd allowed himself a few seconds to commit the details to memory. 'The lane comes down the hill from just outside Great Salkeld. There's a cottage that looks empty and a barn which looks in relatively good nick. The barn has a security box on the outside. And an alarm.'

'On an old barn?'

'I know. Odd, eh? And shuttered windows. With bars.'

'Right,' she said, briskly. 'You've convinced me. Get back to the office. I can't risk you being seen. As far as I'm concerned it's out of your hands, now.'

TWENTY-TWO

'I've moved everything up as quickly as I can,' Faye said, as Jude came into her office and took the seat she indicated, 'and it's gone over to Firearms Command. That's all we can do, other than listen in.'

'Is there anyone down on site?'

'I've managed to get an undercover officer repainting the road sign in Little Salkeld, so at least they can't slip out unseen. We have to wait while Firearms get their act together.' She rolled her eyes.

It was easy to get frustrated and Faye, who was a control freak, succumbed to this particular emotion more quickly than most. She would be aware of the constraints. It took time to put together a plan that didn't risk Gil's life. It took time to assemble the components of it, to scope out the building without risk, to seal off all the exits and formulate an approach that brought an optimal outcome. 'How long do we reckon that'll take?'

She shrugged. 'It's not my baby, now. I've asked to be in touch with them throughout. That's all I can do.'

'Do you mind if I listen in?'

'Be my guest,' she said, and looked at her watch. It was just after one o'clock. 'I expect we've a couple of hours to wait, at least, if they decide not to wait until under cover of darkness.'

It was a bright day and darkness was a long time away. It was, Jude thought, unlikely that they had the time to wait that long. 'Right.'

'You know as well as I do,' she repeated, 'that there's nothing we can do but wait. I'll call you as soon as there's something happening.'

'Right,' said the man, snapping the light on so suddenly that Gil knew his game was up and he couldn't play sick any longer. 'Get up. It's a bad leg, not a brain injury. I don't care how much pain you're in. I don't care how weak you think you are. I don't care how long it takes. You're going to fix that clock and you aren't going to stop until it's done.'

As slowly as he could, Gil eased himself to a sitting position, blinking in the light. He'd known this moment would come. All he could do was spin it out for as long as he could and pray that Becca Reid had had the sense to realise she was his only chance and tell someone. And then, of course, to hope that they got to him in time.

If she'd told Jude Satterthwaite, he thought he might still have a chance. He liked the man. Jude struck him as thoughtful, sensible and thorough, and he seemed to have reached a senior rank in the police very quickly, which had to say something about him. Even the people who disliked him because of what had happened to Adam Fleetwood (which surely meant, by extension, that they had things in their own lives to hide and must now know there would be no hiding place for them if he ever found out) spoke very highly of him in a professional sense.

No, if Becca had spoken and the police were on the case, all he needed was time, and he could at least buy some of that for himself. Just not much, and maybe not enough.

The worst of it was that he knew exactly what was wrong with the clock. He'd known when he'd looked at it that day in Capel Lodge when Lady Frances had expressly forbidden him to touch it and her companion had looked at them both in compete shock. There was nothing wrong with it. It was old and it needed a thorough clean, and on a good day he could have had it done in half an hour, maybe even less.

Thank God, this wasn't a good day. He looked at the man's boots like a dog expecting to be kicked. 'My leg hurts. I can't get up.'

The man reached down, grabbed him by both wrists and hauled him roughly upwards. Wobbling on his dodgy leg and weak from loss of blood and lack of food, Gil leaned on the rough stone wall to hold himself up.

'Here.' The man thrust a walking stick at him. 'You'll manage. Now get on with it.'

Gil's brief thought of using the stick as a weapon ended when he took a step and his leg almost gave way under him; the potential means of escape became a necessary prop. He yelped with pain, more loudly than was necessary, and managed somehow to hobble across to the table that stood directly beneath the bare light bulb. His tool case was set to one side and the clock, with its monolithic granite base and its gold hands jammed at ten to two like a clown's grin, was centre stage.

He lowered himself into the chair that was set ready for him and the man removed the stick from his grasp. It was a carver chair, an old and rather attractive one, and it held him and his dodgy leg as if he were in a cage. Even that hobble across the room had made him feel light-headed. 'I need something to eat.'

'Aye.' The man produced a petrol station sandwich, ripping the packet open and handing it to him, placing a bottle of mineral water down beside it.

Gil ate as slowly as he dared, keeping an ear open for any sound outside, but the place was in silence and there was no sign of the woman. She might be keeping watch somewhere, perhaps, or — and he shuddered at this — making arrangements for the disposal of his body. The sandwich was dry and tasteless, and even though he chewed every mouthful thoroughly, to his captor's obvious frustration, he finished it far sooner than he liked. Still he fussed, rubbing the crumbs off his lap and onto the floor, taking a long drink of water until time ran out and, setting the bottle down, he took a sidelong look at his captor and turned to his task. Unscrewing the base with difficulty — no need to pretend, here, as the screws were long untouched and he had lost his touch over the past couple of days and fumbled at them before he finally undid them — he lifted it off, removed the glass front and exposed the internal mechanism. He replaced the screwdriver with extreme care and exchanged it for one of a different size, then gradually disassembled the clock, piece by piece, laying all the components out in their place, gears, levers, screws. His father had been chaotic in his work but had always seemed able to find whatever he wanted without a thought, so there must have been order in his mind, too, though today Gil's obsessive neatness had an additional benefit: it bought him time. With all the pieces laid out, he began cleaning, item by item, each one laid back down on the table in its place.

'Hurry up.'

He raised a hand, kept his eyes fixed on his work, carried on at his own measured pace. Once he'd taken pleasure in designing clocks for himself as his father had done, but latterly he took found more fulfilment in restoring someone else's superior work to its best possible condition, listening for the chime of a clock as it might have sounded a hundred, two hundred years before. Over the years he'd developed from a creditable creator into a flawless repairer and this clock, which looked increasingly likely to cost him his life as he was certain it had cost Roger Duncan his, would be the best job he'd ever done, the cleanest, sweetest piece of work.

Eventually, as the man stood watching and whistling under his breath as if to hide his impatience, Gil oiled and wiped the last screw for the last time and began the process of reassembly. It took him far less time than he'd hoped; once he tried a deliberate fumble, dropping a screw on the floor in the hope that it might make his task impossible to complete until another part could be found, but the man pounced on it and placed it beside him without a word.

Finally it was finished. He took one last gamble, the most time it could buy him, and set the clock at one minute past the hour, then sat back. 'That's it.'

'Make it chime.'

Gil puffed out his cheeks in one long sigh. 'Ah.'

'Put the bloody thing forward. Or take it apart again and I'll do it.'

'Putting it forward will damage the mechanism.' It was a lie he knew he'd get away with. If the man knew the first thing about clocks he'd have fixed it himself.

'I can wait for an hour,' the man said more softly, now, as if he was nervous. And well he might be. He must be expecting to find some clue or other, or maybe the clock itself was the answer, in some peculiar way Gil didn't understand.

The man pulled up a chair and sat down, staring at the clock intently.

'Right,' he said. 'We'll wait.'

'Can you give me an update?' said Faye, into the radio, to the firearms commander who was parked up somewhere near Little Salkeld. Her face was grave. She knew as well as Jude did that if they were right, and if Gil Foley was incarcerated in that barn on the banks of the Eden, his life was in grave danger.

'We're just getting everything in place.'

The radio crackled. Jude leaned in to hear it better.

'What resources do you have down there?'

'One unit of armed officers just arrived,' said that crackling voice. 'We're waiting to deploy others on the riverside path.'

'Have you any idea what's going on?'

'I've a lad down the lane with listening equipment. He can't get any closer, but he's picking up voices. Male, two. Can't hear what's being said.'

'How long will this take?' muttered Faye to herself, but they both knew there was nothing that could be done to speed up the process.

The ticking, seeming so much louder in this bare space than it had done in the affluent surroundings of Lady Frances's study, offered Gil no comfort and the clock's gold hands nudged around too quickly, a jolt every minute. On the half hour it gave a jaunty chirp which made the man jump, but if he was expecting anything he didn't get it. 'It plays on the hour, right?'

'On the hour.'

They resumed the silence. The ticking filled the room, on and on, relentlessly. The hands jumped minute by minute, closer to the moment of truth.

At one minute to the hour, the man got up and stood with his hand resting on his jacket pocket. Gil sat back, understanding. The man had a gun and if the clock didn't deliver — maybe even if it did — Gil would die. He sat back, wondering if anyone would miss him and knowing the answer. Only when their clocks needed mending. Only when they remembered. *Oh no, old Gil died, didn't he? Who's going to sort the grandfather clock?* But that would be all. And if it wasn't for — he hoped — Jude Satterthwaite, no-one would even have known he was missing.

With a shuffle of its mechanism audible only to Gil's trained ear, the clock moved to strike. He placed his hands on the edge of the table, gripping it. And then the chime. One. Two. Three. Four. And another shuffle and the clock began to play *Oh My Darling Clementine*.

Gil dared to look at the man's face and wished he hadn't. It was dark and drawn tight with fury and frustration.

'That's it?' said the man.

'Yes.'

'You haven't done anything smart? You haven't stopped it doing something it should? You haven't stopped it playing a message?'

'It's a clock,' said Gil, wearily. It was too late to change his fate now; there was no need for politeness. His father's clock had run down on him. 'A musical clock. It plays a tune. That's all it does. And tells the time. Obviously.'

DEATH IN GOOD TIME

'You bastard!' The man shouted. 'You utter bastard!' He his hand twitched in convulsive fury to his pocket and he fired at the clock. It exploded into destruction. A chip of something — stone, rock, gold, who knew? — stung Gil's cheek and he drew his hand up with a yell of protest and pain. It was too late. He'd done everything he could and Becca Reid had let him down.

The reverberations of the shot died away, though they lingered on in the disrupted rhythm of Gil's pounding heart. He lowered his hand.

The man swung his arm and the wreckage of the clock, the beautiful clock that had caused his father so much grief in its making, crashed to the floor. Glass, steel, wood, gold and granite, already mangled beyond any hope of repair, hit the ground together in a cascade of constituent parts.

'No!' said Gil, as the man raised the gun again and this time pointed it at his head. 'No!' And he met the man's gaze as he prepared to die.

'Shots fired!' came the shout from the other end of the radio.

'Shit!' said Faye, powerless.

'We're going in!'

She pushed the radio away from her, and looked at Jude, as the drama of Gil's life played out a dozen miles away.

'Armed police! Armed police!'

Something crashed at the door so that it shook on its

old hinges. Distracted, the man turned and Gil, sensing his last opportunity, dived off the chair and rolled under the table. Above him a second shot whistled through the air and crashed into the wall and seconds later the door burst open and a shaft of June sunlight speared across the floor.

He crammed his arms over his head and cowered, knees crunching on the remains of the clock, yelping with the pain from his leg. Boots, four, five pairs of them, thrashed across the floor across the pool of light and out towards what must be a back exit. 'Stop! Police! Armed police!'

'I'm here,' Gil called out, or intended to, but his voice came out in a whimper. 'I'm Gil Foley. They kidnapped me. Help. Help!'

More boots came in. Two pairs of them, a woman's and a man's, stopped and one of them bent down to help him up.

'Gil, eh?' said one of them, cheerfully. 'We've been looking for you. Are you all right, my man?'

Safe. He smiled at last. He should have known Becca would come up trumps.

'Can you get up?' said the other. 'There's an ambulance out there. We'll get you to hospital and they can look you over. But you look in pretty good nick to me.'

Gil struggled up to his knees and shuffled backwards, painfully, until he was away from the table. The woman police officer took another step forward, another step on the broken, beautiful works of the clock.

'Stop,' Gil said to her. 'Stop. Just for a second.' And he reached out and felt among the wreckage until he came up with what he wanted — the slender golden minute hand. He held it out.

'Here,' he said. 'You might want to give this to Jude Satterthwaite.'

TWENTY-THREE

'I thought I'd call with an update,' said Jude, sounding businesslike but, Becca thought, with a certain lightness to his tone.

'Good news?' she asked, with a surge of hope in her heart, because good news meant she could get out of the repressive situation in which she found herself, stuck in a B&B in Keswick with a discreet armed police presence and nothing but the telly, her phone, her Kindle and the view from her window for company.

'Some of it's definitely good and some is not exactly bad.'

A car door slammed, a car engine started. 'About Gil?'

'Yes. The good news is we got to him in time. The bad news is that we had to send people in to get him before we had the property secured, and so whoever was holding him got away.'

'I'm so glad about Gil.' And it was true. She'd had him on her conscience, had lain awake at night worrying about him, not sure whether it was her speech or her silence that had placed him in more danger. The only comfort she could take from it was that she trusted Jude, absolutely, to do whatever was best. 'But if they got away, that means I have to stay here, doesn't it?' There wasn't even any football to watch on the television. She was bored of *Bargain Hunt* and *Cash in the Attic* and at thirty-five she thought she'd left it a bit late to get involved with the ins and outs of cricket. Apart from that her options for entertainment were limited.

'Yes, I'm afraid so. If I'm honest I think they'll have more important things to do than think about you, but you know me.'

He said that often to her, and it was true. She did know him, so well that she laughed. 'You always were a bit cautious, and you're getting worse as you get older.'

'I don't think you've any reason to be alarmed,' he said, 'and I'll be very surprised if we don't run this precious pair of kidnappers to earth very quickly, because they left their car, and even if we don't find them soon they'll have more important things to think about than you, I would imagine.'

Jude would have plenty of other things to do, too. She should let him get on, but it was rare these days that he phoned her and she was bored and lonely without any work to do or even Holmes getting under her feet, so she made no attempt to be public-spirited and hustle him on. 'Is Holmes doing okay, do you know?'

'He brought my mother a most unwelcome present, but apart from that he's doing fine.'

Holmes was as fond of a prisoner as Jude must be, and in his case a live mouse — or worse — trapped under the kitchen dresser was something to be proud of. She stifled a smile. 'And Gil's all right, you say?'

'Yes. He's up in the hospital in Carlisle getting looked over, but he's fine. He'll need a square meal, but that's about it. I wasn't expecting to speak to him until tomorrow but he's very keen to talk and wants to get back to his normal routine as soon as possible. I suspect because all the time he's with people, whether they're police or NHS staff, he feels uncomfortable and on display.'

'That sounds like him.' Becca strayed to the window and looked out at the blue of Derwentwater and the flashes of white as sailing dinghies tacked to and fro.

'Very much so. Ashleigh and I are on our way up to Carlisle to speak to him. He's full of good cheer, apparently, and as she's driving and I had a few minutes it seemed a good opportunity to keep you in the loop.'

'I realise, now,' she said, watching a mother pushing a baby in a pushchair along the street immediately below her window and feeling a sudden, painful pang of longing. 'You were right. All the time when he was talking to me he was trying to tell me to tell you about it.'

'It might have saved us a moment if you had.'

'I was so afraid he'd die.'

'Well, he didn't and he'll be fine.'

You could never tell with Jude. Sometimes when he sounded clipped and dismissive it was because he was annoyed, and sometimes it was because he cared. It wasn't beyond the bounds of possibility that in this case, it was both, and she wasn't sure how she felt about that, especially not with him heading off up to Carlisle with Ashleigh and, no doubt, heading back down again later in the evening, going off duty together. Jealousy wasn't an attractive look, nor was it a pleasant feeling. 'I don't need you to take time out of your busy day to make sure I'm all right.'

'I'm a bit of a spare part at this point in this investigation. Faye's in charge of it, not me. I'm just a humble foot soldier.'

She thought she heard Ashleigh laughing in the background as if this were some in-joke. 'I really appreciate it.'

'Hopefully it won't be too long before you're back home again.'

There was so much she wanted to say to him and didn't know how to say it. She wanted to apologise and at the same time to explain herself. She wanted him to understand that she couldn't risk being the one who was responsible for Gil being further injured, or killed. Below, the baby had thrown a toy out of the buggy and the mother had stopped to pick it up, hand it back, make a fuss over the child, tickling its feet until it laughed.

Back in the old days she and Jude had talked about children and now the prospect was receding as fast as the afternoon sun. She was almost nearer forty than thirty, now, and realistic about her missed opportunities, but she wondered how he felt about it. Regrets? Or had he got to the stage now where he shrugged it off, or did he still see a future for himself and Ashleigh and a clutch of knife-sharp mini detectives?

She didn't think she'd ever know.

TWENTY-FOUR

Being a victim of crime had its advantages; they'd put Gil in a room of his own, with a police officer stationed outside to keep any curious passers-by at bay. This suited him down to the ground. With no-one other than the police interested in visiting, he was reconsidering his declared intention to get out of the place as soon as possible. He might be better off in hospital, because as soon as he got home he would be besieged by people who'd once come to him for a clock repair and considered this a valid reason to come in and mind his business, flooding him with goodwill and overwhelming him with home-made casseroles for which he'd be expected to pay with an account of his adventures. At least here the staff only came in when they had a reason to and were too harassed to spend any more time with him than was necessary, and at least the police, when they came (he hoped it would be Jude Satterthwaite, whose sardonicism he appreciated) would be precise and to the point.

He was in luck with that, too. When he heard voices

outside his door and recognised one of them, the door opened and the familiar figure of the chief inspector appeared in the doorway accompanied by an attractive blonde woman. Some people, it seemed, had all the luck.

'Good to see you, Gil.' Jude closed the door behind him. 'This is my colleague, Ashleigh O'Halloran.' He took a seat at a respectful distance and left a second, near to Gil, to the blonde. 'Strictly speaking she's the expert interviewer but I thought I'd tag along and see how you are.'

Gil was amused. Jude was a nosey old sod. It would be typical of him to want to hear the story first. 'Afternoon,' he said to the sergeant, rather gruffly.

'Afternoon, Mr Foley.' She smiled at him. 'I know Jude wants a quick catch up and then I'm afraid I'm going to bore you by going over everything in minute detail, probably several times. Needs must, I'm afraid.'

'That was a bit of an ordeal those lads put you through,' said Jude, as Ashleigh O'Halloran got out a notepad and pen.

'I'm a tough old bugger,' Gil said. 'Hard to kill.' Though there had been that moment, after the clock had smashed on the floor and he'd been staring down the barrel of the gun, that he thought they'd succeed. 'Did you get them?'

'Not yet. That's partly why my colleague will be giving you the third degree, so we get every piece of information we can. We're on the trail. Your friend with the gun escaped on foot, so it's unlikely he'll have got far.'

'Got the dogs on him, have you?' asked Gil, with relish at the thought of the hunter becoming the hunted.

'Dogs, drones, helicopters, the lot. No expense spared.'

'Your lads were great,' said Gil, thinking of that wash of relief when he'd heard the shouting and realised it heralded the arrival of the cavalry.

'From what I've heard. The officer in charge is beating himself up a bit about having let them go, but you were always our priority. We may have had to come in before we had the place secure, but we'll get them. Are you happy to talk right now?'

'Aye. I talk through the hole in my head not the one in my leg.' He grinned.

'Good. Let's have a quick run through what happened.'

Gil retold the story of his kidnapping, of Becca's visit, of the rescue. Out of the corner of his eye he saw the sergeant jotting things down, and there seemed to be a bewildering number of question marks. 'She's a smart lass, that young woman. I knew she'd tell you.'

Jude managed a wry smile. 'She doesn't tell me much these days.'

'All go wrong, did it?' asked Gil, relieved at an opportunity to talk about anyone other than himself.

'You could say that.'

'But she did the right thing. Tell her thank you, from me. When I'm back out of here I'll thank her properly.' He'd write her a letter and send her flowers, probably, because turning up to thank her in person would test his social awkwardness to the maximum.

'I'll do that.'

A nurse tapped on the door. 'Sorry. I was just in to check your blood pressure, Gil. I'll come back later.'

'I think all of our blood pressure has been up this afternoon,' said Jude when she'd gone, and laughed. He seemed almost relieved to have been interrupted. 'And so, let's talk about the clock, shall we?'

At last Gil was on safe ground. 'Aye. I can talk about clocks until the end of time.' He chuckled at his own witticism. 'Did they give you the minute hand?'

'They did, and very interesting it was, too, though I'm not sure I've made any sense of it yet. Did you?'

Gil considered. He hadn't had time to pay too much attention to the faint writing he'd spotted scratched on the minute hand, and the last thing he'd wanted was to draw his captor's attention to it, either. 'It said Capel. Is that right?'

'As far as I can make out. And considering Capel is the name of the person who owns it and so seems a fairly reasonable thing to be written on it, I'm interested as to why you thought it was worth salvaging. Although to be honest, while I have no idea of the significance of that clock, I'd like to know anything at all about it and you seem to be the only person who knows.'

'Bloody good job for you that I survived, then.' said Gil, and laughed.

Jude Satterthwaite acknowledged that with exactly the right balance of humour and seriousness. 'You know all about the clock, though.'

'I do. My father made it. I watched him. And I can tell you, there was nothing written on the minute hand when it was made. It was the bit of it he let me do.' That had been the part a young Gil couldn't possibly make a mess of but yet allowed him to play a role in what was, after all, a significant commission. 'If it had been a clockmaker who took the hand off, scratched on it and then put it back, or even anyone who had any knowledge of precision work, I might never have noticed. But I'd say it was an amateur.'

'An amateur like me?'

The detective had long, thin fingers that looked as if, under different circumstances, they might have found a creative outlook. 'No. A complete amateur.'

'It's not a difficult job?'

'No, because you don't have to get into the workings of

the clock. You have to open the glass cover — someone had forced it, it's always been stiff — and then you unscrew the nut that holds the hands on, take them off, do whatever you want to do and then put it all back again. But if you know clocks, you can tell that someone had tampered with it, and so of course I had a look to see what it might be.' That might have been why it had stopped so suddenly, rather than gradually running down, if whoever had tinkered with it had been less than fastidious and introduced grit or dust into its delicate mechanism.

'That's very interesting. And now, I wonder what else is so special about it? Irene Jenkins told us about its provenance and how your father came to be commissioned to make it, but that didn't enlighten me very much.'

Gil considered. 'It's got no real value, other than the craftsmanship and its uniqueness. Old Lady Frances was proud of it, though. Last time I was up there at the Lodge to do the clocks I had tea and cake in the library with her.' That had been an ordeal, and he'd survived it by answering her questions and listening to her talking about herself. 'The new housekeeper had made cake and brought it in, and Lady Frances had said something about the clock playing tricks on her. She said it didn't play the tune she expected it to, and her father always said it was like a code, but when I offered to look at it, she wouldn't let me.'

'When you fixed it, it played a tune. Was it what you expected?'

'Yes. It played *Clementine*, which is the tune it always did, the one her mother wanted. But the lad who kidnapped me was expecting something else. I don't know what he thought he'd hear.' Some message, maybe, about God-knew-what. But he hadn't heard it. Gil shook his head. It didn't seem to make any sense to Jude Satterthwaite and it certainly made no sense to him, but, thank God, it wasn't his problem.

'Did you know it was left to Irene Jenkins in Lady Frances's will?'

'No, I'd heard at one point she wanted the clock buried with her.' That was what he'd meant to tell Jude when he called him. It had seemed a triviality but now he knew it was important.

'How bizarre. Where did you hear that?'

'I used to play cricket with the undertaker years ago.' Poor Roger. Gil thought of him again, a decent man, someone who knew when to speak and when to be quiet. For almost the first time in his life he wished he'd made more of an effort to speak to people, to socialise. He might have been spared his own ordeal if someone had been keeping half an eye open for him, though popularity hadn't done anything to help Roger. 'He was never what you'd call indiscreet, but sometimes he'd say something, have a bit of a laugh about Lady F's oddities.' Roger would have known Gil would never bother to tell. 'Though apparently she changed her mind. I bumped into him one day, at the station in Penrith and he told me about it. In the end she wanted to be buried with a book.'

'A book?' said Jude, and for the first time he sounded genuinely startled.

'That's what he said.'

'Well, that is interesting. I don't suppose he said what kind of book?'

Gil shook his head. Thinking of Roger made him suddenly aware of his own brush with death, of his own pain. He felt suddenly very tired.

'That's okay,' said Jude. 'I'll find out.'

'You could ask Rose.'

'I'll do that. Good shout. Thanks for your help, Gil.

And if you'll excuse me I'll leave you to Sergeant O'Halloran's tender mercies and go and make a few calls, see how we're getting on with rounding up these attackers of yours. Not that I think they're much risk to anyone.'

'The clock didn't give them what they wanted, did it?'

'Doesn't look like it,' said the detective, and made his exit.

TWENTY-FIVE

The clock hadn't given the kidnappers what they wanted but the book, if they found it, might.

'I have so many questions,' said Jude, setting down his cup of coffee on the table in the incident room where the team were assembled waiting for him, 'and Gil's just raised a few more. I don't quite know where to start. But I think I'll start with the practical one, which is for you, Doddsy. Where are we with actually finding these people?'

He looked across the table at where Doddsy, looking frustrated, was stroking his chin and frowning. It had fallen to him to meet with Faye for a briefing while Jude had been occupied with the press office, going over the carefully-worded statement that had to go out following the obvious activity at Little Salkeld and taking a few questions over the phone from a journalist who could be trusted not to be too sensationalist in her reporting.

'Not much further forward, apparently. Our man got away on foot and the dogs lost the trail at the river. Faye's incandescent.'

It couldn't be helped. If they'd waited to seal off all

possible escape routes, they might have trapped at least one of the kidnappers but Gil would almost certainly have been dead. Jude knew how Faye's mind worked and how much, like all of them, she hated letting a criminal get away, but when she calmed down she'd see there had been no alternative.

He cast his mind back to the topography of the area. Beyond the buildings the track joined the path at the water's edge. It was June and there had been a prolonged dry period so that the mighty River Eden, looping around in one of its more friendly moods, was fordable if you were desperate enough or a good swimmer, and if the kidnapper had somehow managed to make it past the police cordon upstream he could have risked crossing the river on either the weir or the viaduct.

'If he's got across the river he can't have got far,' he said.

'He had an accomplice, though,' Ashleigh reminded him. 'Gil said the woman wasn't at the property the final time, but she could have been nearby. He might have managed to get to her and they made off together.'

'They'd need another car.'

'Maybe we'd better look for a Mercedes with your numberplate,' said Doddsy. 'There'll be stuff in the Ford Focus that'll help us, I'm sure. They weren't expecting to be raided and they'd left stuff in it, I'm told.'

'Good.' Jude would rest a lot more easily when the two of them were safely behind bars, and he was sure Gil would, too. And Becca.

He took a sip of his coffee. It was evening but they wouldn't be going home until they'd brainstormed their way through the puzzle, and they could be there long into the night. 'Right. Let's go through some of these things I don't understand.'

'I don't understand any of this.' Chris Marshall shook his head. 'I like a puzzle myself, but this is a weird one, isn't it? Lost art and books and clocks and God knows what else are fair enough, but if you'd told me we'd be looking at this kind of thing a few months ago I'd have expected it to be centred on Lady Frances, not the undertaker. It's generally the people who write the wills who get bumped off, not the ones who follow the instructions. I even went and looked at the death certificate, but there's no suggestion she died of anything other than natural causes. And there was nothing in the will about the funeral arrangements. That was all done verbally.'

'She knew she was dying,' Ashleigh reminded him, 'and from what I understand everyone else knew, too. But yes. I take your point.'

Any one of the procession of well-wishers who had come to pay their last respects might have lifted a gun from the wall of death. Any one of them could later have taken advantage of her funeral to murder Roger Duncan in the walled garden. Frances Capel's death might still prove to be the catalyst for the murder.

But why? He shook his head and moved the discussion on.

'Ash and I are just back from seeing Gil Foley,' he said, 'and had a very interesting chat that left me with more questions than answers. He's a tough customer and I think he has to take a lot of the credit for his own survival. Fair assessment, Ash?'

She nodded. 'Definitely. He gave a remarkably thorough and detailed account of what happened, too, under the circumstances. He's highly resourceful, too. He did find something on the clock after all, and he managed not to say anything.'

The gold minute hand was already in an evidence bag

and on its way to the lab on the off-chance that, amid the chaos and Gil's careful deconstruction and reconstruction, some shred of forensic evidence might have survived to identify the person who had tampered with it, but Jude had photographs, printed off in a hurry and enlarged to a strange, pixellated graininess. He opened the folder he had with him and laid them on the table. 'Here. Gil reckoned he could read the word *Capel*, which makes sense up to a point, but he swears it wasn't on the hand of the clock when it was made. I've had a good look at it, and I think there's something else, too.' In the chaos and the artificial light, Gil must have missed it, scratched faintly into the soft metal with something as small and sharp as a pin. 'I can barely read it but I think I see what it says. I might be mistaken, but I'd value your thoughts. See what you think.'

The three of them, Ashleigh, Chris and Doddsy, took the images and stared at them for a while.

'It's a tough one,' said Chris staring down at the image in front of him, 'because that second one is so faint. But if I have to give you an answer, I'd say that says *castle*.'

'Agreed.' Ashleigh dropped the photo on the table.

'That's what I thought, too. Any ideas?' And, when they shook their heads, Jude moved on. 'Next up. According to Gil, Roger told him Lady Frances had wanted to be buried with the clock but had changed her mind and asked for a book instead, though of course it's possible she changed her mind again and asked for something totally different instead.'

'Eccentric old bird, wasn't she?' said Chris, cheerfully.

'I'll say.' Frances Capel's peculiarities had more than muddied the waters for them.

'We should probably talk to Rose about it,' said Ashleigh. 'There's a chance she'd know, even if there's nothing written down.'

'Yes, we should, and after what Irene Jenkins said we need to speak to the solicitor, Wilf Hamley, too. But I'd like to proceed very carefully with Rose, for a couple of reasons.'

'She's the main beneficiary of her father's death,' said Doddsy, 'but we covered that. When he was killed she was clearly in view of someone else.'

'Yes, but she may have had the opportunity to take the gun and she might easily have passed it on to someone else to do the deed for her. And there's something else. When Wilf threatened Irene and insisted he thought she had the book — though it's worth saying she thinks he knows where it is — she said he said *but R—* and went no further. She assumed he was talking about Roger but he might not have been. He might have been talking about Rose.'

Ashleigh shook her head. 'Okay. But why would Rose have been involved in kidnapping Gil?'

'It was something Becca said.' Jude rubbed his chin, thoughtfully. Becca was smart, and saw things others missed 'She said the female who abducted her was wearing a blonde wig, and she noted a similarity to Rose, which might or might not be because of the wig.'

'Did Gil notice any similarity?' asked Doddsy.

Ashleigh shook her head. 'No. He just described her as blonde. I asked if he knew Rose but he never met her. He only knew Roger through the cricket, and that was years back.'

Under pressure, both Gil and Becca would have had other things on their mind than a careful observation of things they weren't supposed to see. 'And having said that, who's to say it wasn't a double bluff?' Jude scratched his head.

'You mean, Rose putting on a wig that was obviously

fake to make it look like she was trying to look like Rose?' Chris shook his head. 'Bloody hell. I'm confused.'

Which was, of course, what the kidnappers would have wanted. 'They've shown they're not afraid to take chances. Cloning Ashleigh's car numberplate was brave. They also aren't afraid to bluff.' There had been no tracking device on Becca's phone.

'Capel Castle, or Castell Capel to give it its proper name,' said Ashleigh, thoughtfully. 'Sorry. I'm jumping back a bit in the conversation. But that writing on the clock hands makes me think. I wonder if that's the answer. Could there be a connection with the story about the art collection?'

'What do you mean?' asked Chris. 'I can't see how that can have any relevance to whatever happened to the undertaker.'

'I can't say I can, but as everything seems to have something to do with one or other of Lady Frances's possessions, I think it's worth a look.' Ashleigh looked across at Jude. 'I'm happy to look into that if you don't need me to do anything else.'

'Excellent. Thank you.' He tapped his finger on the table. 'You're right, Chris. It's pretty much ancient history. But one thing we do know about Lady F is that she liked a puzzle. She also, as a lot of charities learned to their frustration, had a habit of raising expectations and not delivering. That makes me wonder if that's happened to Irene. Lady F left a series of clues, a puzzle to solve, and maybe someone found out and got the wrong end of the stick, thinking whatever was left to her was going to be worth the search.'

'I didn't get the impression that Irene had any expectations at all, other than perhaps some small memento or other, and maybe a place to live out her life.' said Ashleigh.

'I thought the same, but maybe someone else didn't.'

'And killed Roger and kidnapped Gil?' said Doddsy, with a sigh.

'It's worth looking at, at least. And let's think about these things. Who might have killed Roger? We were short on suspects, weren't we? But now I think we have more. I think we have the kidnappers, because they're clearly violent and desperate to get whatever they think has been left to Irene. We have Wilf Hamley, who knew Roger well and worked with him at a professional level, and who may well have worked with him on matters other than their mainstream business — and who's prepared to threaten Irene, even though she thinks he's unlikely to do anything more. Wilf, like Roger, would have a reasonable expectation of knowing Lady Frances's wishes.'

'If she's as mischievous as it sounds, maybe she was leading them up the garden path, too.' Ashleigh fidgeted with her watch, irritably. 'I don't think I'd have liked her. I don't mind a bit of fun, but God, if you take it too far you end up making things pretty damned difficult for us.'

And dangerous for others. 'Yes. So maybe Roger and Wilf were in it together. We know from Irene that Wilf was in the library on a number of occasions. He was at the funeral and he may well have had the opportunity to slip out. If he was chatting to Roger no-one would raise an eyebrow. So perhaps he decided Roger was double-crossing him, or trying to cut him out in some way. I'd like to look at him in much more detail than we have done already.'

'I'll take that on.' This was right up Chris's alley.

'Right. And then there's Rose. I haven't really considered her, but perhaps we should. She didn't want to be an undertaker, according to Becca. It may be that she felt trapped in the business and that killing her father was the only way out, or it may be that she needs the money. The business is in reasonably good nick but there's not a great deal of cash, so she certainly wouldn't have been able to take anything from it without a sale, which her father is most unlikely to have agreed to. It's possible she killed him for that, and this business of kidnapping Gil is entirely separate.' Though he doubted it. 'Or it could be that she was involved with the kidnappers for whatever money she thought she could get out of it.'

'Becca noticed the resemblance,' noted Ashleigh. 'Perhaps she was meant to. Perhaps they were fitting Rose up. But we need to consider the possibility.'

'Yes,' said Doddsy with a sigh. 'And if she was at Capel Lodge she would have had the chance to take one of the guns. And the clock. And the book.'

Chris whistled. 'We should definitely look closer.' It was clear he hadn't considered her a serious suspect.

'There was no obvious motive. And the last person we need to look at is Irene.'

Doddsy sat back and looked at him. 'What, a frail old lady who's spent her whole life running round after her boss? You might have persuaded me to take that seriously if she'd cracked and put poison in Lady Frances's soup after years of misery. But the undertaker? And a gun?'

'I know,' Jude said. 'She doesn't look the type. But whatever she's owed by Lady F, or thinks she is, it's important enough for Wilf Hamley to threaten her about it. Of the people involved in this, she's the only one who's had completely free access to everything at Capel Lodge. Not just the guns. Not just the clock. Not just the books. And while I struggle to see her turning a gun on a man much stronger than she is, it's certainly not impossible.'

TWENTY-SIX

'I'll go and see Rose tomorrow,' said Jude, as he and Ashleigh crossed the car park to where their cars were parked, side by side. Chris, who usually ran in to work, had accepted a lift home from Doddsy; the two of them were already in the car and heading towards the exit, red tail lights glowing as the June day finally faded into its brief period of darkness. There was little more they could do that night, only come in early next morning and start again, hoping that somehow the kidnappers were picked up in the meantime. And think. He'd lie awake wrestling with the problem for much of the night.

'Do you want me to come with you?'

Ashleigh could easily do the job and it was probably a more efficient use of her time than his, but he was keen to meet Rose Duncan, especially given that Adam Fleetwood seemed so suddenly taken with her. 'I don't think so. I'll see. I think you could be more usefully employed here.'

'I hope so. I was thinking just now.'

'Right?'

'I'm still on about the pictures.'

'The ones that were in the fire?' Like Chris, he'd been dismissive of so loose a connection, but he respected Ashleigh's opinion and so it was worth a second thought.

'Yes. I was reading up on them. That story you said your dad told you feels relevant. The background to it is interesting. I only had an hour or so to try and find things out and what I did come up with is fascinating.'

'Is that right?'

'Yes. The Earl — the seventh Earl, I think he was — was widely praised for his bravery in the immediate aftermath of the fire but after the war, when the paintings were returned, the tone wasn't quite so uncritical. There were allegations of arson and there seem to have been accusations levelled at him, but it wasn't immediately obvious what they were. That caught my attention so I kept looking.'

'Because of all those things at the Lodge,' he said, understanding. 'The collections.'

'Yes, and there's an extraordinary amount of stuff at the castle as well. I found an old newspaper buried away online, from the late 1940s, in which it was suggested that he started the fire deliberately, or had the fire started deliberately to cover his own negligence. He'd been left in charge while the custodian who was there was taken ill. The fire took place mysteriously on the night that the new man was due to arrive and take over. I wondered if he'd made some mistake that caused serious damage to the paintings, and started the fire to cover up.'

'That's a mighty leap to make.'

'It's often the cover-up that does the damage rather than the crime. The Earl seems to have been a very proud man. It was extremely unusual for someone who wasn't a professional curator to be left in charge of anything and it would have been a huge responsibility. All it would take would be a leak in the roof he hadn't spotted, or knew about but hadn't got round to having fixed.'

Jude toyed with the idea and found it pleasing but irrelevant. And there was another problem. 'Even if we could link it to Roger Duncan, we could never prove any arson or negligence.'

'No. But I kept looking at the pictures he did save and the one he tried to save but failed. The one he nearly died for.'

Jude had done a quick dive into the internet himself after he'd spoken to his father, and had found the sketches for the Burne-Jones tarot deck. They had been curiously hypnotic, like a dream from which it was impossible to wake, done in pencil with a touch of coloured crayon that hinted about how vibrant and exotic they might be when they had been completed. There was no visual record of the completed picture, which appeared not to have been fully documented before the fire. 'The Emperor.'

'Yes. And you know what the tarot are like. They take hold of people.'

'I know what they're like for some people.' But he did know, and he wasn't sure it was healthy. Even a dyed-in-the-wool sceptic like himself occasionally dug out the deck Ashleigh had brought him back from a holiday in Sri Lanka, fanned out the cards and looked at them with curiosity. He always told himself it was because each card contained a small grey cat, yawning, sleeping or hunting, exactly as cats in all centuries and all countries had always done, and exactly as Holmes still did in the sleepy gardens and hedgerows of Wasby. You didn't have to believe to be fascinated.

'I think it's a fair bet that the Earl was completely

obsessed by them. You only have to look around the library, even in the hall. There are images everywhere, and they certainly weren't chosen for their quality. Some of them look pretty cheap and nasty and others look a bit more expensive and old. A couple of them are prints, not originals, and there's a print of Dalí's *The Empress*. There are loads of books on the occult, and a few symbols I recognised carved into the ends of the shelves. I bet he had a fantastic collection of different decks, and a lot of odds and ends that were related to it. And that made me think.'

Jude allowed himself a wry smile at the thought that a tarot deck as cheap as his own was unlikely to feature in the Capel collection. 'About?'

'I'm astonished, under the circumstances, that he didn't go for *The Emperor* first, rather than the sketches. From what I've seen of the others, it would have been very special. The Emperor is a very positive card.'

'That's what Geri Foster said.'

'Geri reads the cards? That's astonishing,' she said, and laughed.

'I don't think she does, but Raven does. You might almost say she lives by them.' And, it seemed probable, would die by them. 'Geri's spending a lot of time with her just now. I imagine she knows all about it, even if she doesn't have a lot of time for them.'

'A bit like yourself, eh? But yes. The Emperor is a good strong card.'

Jude thought back to the sketch. 'A painting by Burne-Jones would be worth a lot of money, wouldn't it?'

'It wasn't a big one, maybe the size of a laptop screen. But yes. I don't imagine money would have been the motivation for the Earl. He might have convinced himself that it had come to Castell Capel through the hand of fate and he was meant to be its custodian. He seems to have been that sort of man. And of course it wasn't for sale. I noticed in some of the newspaper reports that a lot of the other paintings were damaged, some beyond repair, but only one was destroyed. The Burne-Jones *Emperor*.'

It was an appealing theory. Maybe it was true, and maybe there had been some elaborate plot. 'He'd have needed help.'

'His manservant went in with him and rescued him. I'm willing to bet that the two of them staged that great act of courage on his part to distract from the damage and had replaced the ruined painting beforehand, probably with some old canvas from his own attic. Or, of course, he might just have wanted it for himself.'

'What value would it have now, I wonder?'

'It's hard to say. A full-size Burne-Jones would go for millions, I think, and this isn't huge, but its provenance will be of interest and it seems to have been a remarkable work.'

Jude knew nothing about art, but he did know about human nature and its raging optimism. If someone wanted it for its monetary value they would have high hopes for it, and a price in the high tens of thousands might make it worth killing for. 'Isn't there a risk it would be too hot to handle?'

'Not if it's sold to a private collector, no questions asked. I suppose whoever had it might try and pretend they found it in an attic somewhere and try and get compensation from the National Gallery, but they wouldn't get it. The painting doesn't belong to the Gallery. It belongs to the nation.'

'Interesting.' He flicked the key fob at his car and the Mercedes's lock clicked open. Another time, even a few months before, he'd have invited her back with him and they could have discussed the case over a bite to eat and then gone to bed, but there was a degree of reticence about her these days which he didn't want to think about too much. 'You never mention the tarot any more,' he said, to change the subject.

'No. I've rather given up on them.'

'Oh?'

'Yes.' She turned towards her own car, the Ford Focus with the scraped wheel arch. 'I won't say I had a revelation, but I let myself make a very bad judgement on the back of them, and I haven't picked them up since then. Months. Maybe longer. I'm not saying I'll never go back, but you can get too confident, let them tell you what you want to hear. Sometimes you need to learn a bit of humility. And anyway, I tore one of them up so the whole deck is useless.'

He guessed the decision she was talking about. She had ended their relationship and he had gone back cap in hand to Becca and been rebuffed. Since then everything between them had changed and a relationship that might have had a fighting chance of permanence had deteriorated into friends-with-benefits, a sense that both of them were looking over their shoulder at lost loves.

'Do you still see Scott?' he asked, emboldened by this sign that she, too, was thinking about how things stood between them.

'You'll disapprove.'

'It's nothing to do with me.' But he did disapprove, because Scott Kirby, Ashleigh's ex-husband, was a coercive philanderer whose inexplicable charm always led her to forgive him even as she swore that relationship, too, was dead. He'd seen it often, people who kept giving a partner yet another final chance and ended by paying a high price in emotional or physical pain. To a degree he was guilty of it himself, unable to let go of something that hadn't worked out.

'Well, I am, but only occasionally. Because we were friends all our lives and you never give that up, do you?'

You never did. 'I'll see you tomorrow.'

'Bright and early,' she said, and then turned back. 'Oh. Something just occurred to me. About the hand on the clock. That writing on it.'

Capel Castle, a mournful sound, like the cry of a strange bird. 'Yes?'

'That second word. It didn't make sense. Their home in Wales wasn't Capel Castle it was Castell Capel. I wonder if it said something else. I wonder if it said *Capel Capel*.'

Which would be even stranger. It didn't matter that the time was ticking on towards midnight. He fished out his phone, opened it up and enlarged one of those grainy photos of the scratches on the metal. 'I think you might be right. But what does that mean?'

'I don't know for sure, but *capel* is Welsh for chapel. If Lady Frances really was sending Irene on a treasure hunt and the clock was the first clue, then I wonder if that's going to lead us to the second clue and that would be the book. In the chapel. And buried with her.'

If it was a treasure hunt it wasn't just Irene who would be following the trail. It was them and it was the kidnappers. 'No. Even Lady Frances would draw the line at having Irene open her coffin to get whatever she wanted her to have. What a waste of time and effort that would be.'

'It needn't be in the coffin, though. It could be somewhere else in the chapel.'

He nodded. 'I'll check with Rose first thing. And then we can go up and have a look.'

'I'll see you tomorrow then.'

She got into her car and he got into his, and checked the clock. It was too late to phone Becca. He sighed and followed Ashleigh's car out of the car park and down into the town until their ways diverged and they went their separate ways.

TWENTY-SEVEN

When Rose Duncan's phone went off at eight the next morning it was Adam who cursed.

'Can't you leave it?' he said, rolling over and laying a proprietary arm across her body.

'It might be a customer.'

'Let them ring the office. No-one's going to grudge you not being in on a Saturday after your dad's died, and even if they do, you're the boss now.'

'It might be important.' She rolled over, away from him and reached out for the phone, leaving Adam to stare at the smooth beauty of her back, the curve of her shoulders and the glimpse the duvet allowed him of her backside, with a shiver that was part lust — he recognised that — and part, to his astonishment, something much deeper, much more difficult to define. 'Hello, Rose Duncan.'

'Sorry to bother you so early, Ms Duncan. It's Jude Satterthwaite here.'

Adam's frustration at the interruption to his plans was deepened beyond measure when he recognised Jude as the source of it, but it didn't take him long to rationalise it into smugness. His old foe was up and working on a Saturday morning and Adam himself was lying in bed after a night of making love to a beautiful woman, and with every intention of carrying on once the call was over. He exerted a slight downward pressure on her body and she rolled over in response, pressing the phone to her ear.

'Chief Inspector,' said Rose, with the shadow of a giggle as she pushed Adam's head away. 'How can I help you?'

'I know it's an unconscionable time—'

'I know you put in all the hours in the public service,' she said, smoothly. 'It's quite all right. I was wide awake.' She reached out her hand and brushed her fingers teasingly against Adam's thigh.

'I wanted to ask couple of questions about Lady Frances's funeral.'

The conversation sounded as if it might be interesting and Rose, who was willing, would be all the more tasty for waiting a few minutes. Adam settled his head against her bare shoulder and divided his attention between listening to Jude Satterthwaite talking business and the beat of Rose's heart promising him intimate, unbridled, undisputed pleasure.

'Yes.' Rose stroked Adam's head, as if he were a pet dog. 'Of course.'

'I wondered if your father had mentioned anything to you about Lady Frances's instructions about her interment.'

She pushed a lock of damp hair away from her face. 'Lady Frances was…eccentric. She regularly changed her instructions, I know that much. The hymns, the coffin, who was to be allowed to read, what they were allowed to read. Everything.'

'I didn't mean the funeral itself. I mean the actual interment.'

'Oh. Yes. As far as I know the plan was always to have her buried in the chapel. I think most of the family are buried in Wales, where the main house is, but a few of the more distant members of the family are in the chapel. Lady Frances wanted to die and be buried here because she was so fond of the place. For some reason she never liked Wales.'

'What's the procedure for burial in the crypt?' Jude asked, with that ferret-like interest which had always irritated Adam, even when the two of them were friends, and had led them down too many long lanes and into deep hedges and had caused them to miss many a boat and bus and — more woundingly — many a pint.

'It's pretty straightforward. You have to have permission from the vicar in charge, which is obviously a formality because in this case the chapel belongs to the Capels so there is no vicar, only the local man in the village. The chapel is kept locked and the key is available from the house.'

'Is the crypt locked?'

'As far as I know, but I'm sure the key would be available to anyone along with the chapel key. The week before the funeral my father went to ensure the crypt would be open. It contains a series of large stone coffins — I suppose you'd call them sarcophaguses, really — and we had to make sure that there was one available and that it could be opened. Dad had checked before Lady Frances's death but he and I went down to the chapel to confirm, on the Friday before the funeral.'

'Very Gothic,' whispered Adam, daringly, in her ear, half-hoping Jude would hear.

'Very Gothic, in fact,' echoed Rose.

'It certainly sounds it. And when was the coffin taken into the crypt?'

'Immediately after the service had ended and the mourners had left. I was keeping an eye on things above ground, as it were. My father supervised that particular part of the proceedings.'

'And he was there all on his own?'

She ran her hand through her tangled hair restlessly, as though she were thinking of her father. 'I really couldn't say, but I imagine he would have been the last to leave.'

'And were you aware of any instructions Lady Frances left about anything that should be buried with her?'

'She was buried wearing her mother's wedding ring and her father's medals..'

'Were there any other special instructions?'

'Nothing that I'm aware of.' Rose turned over again, even closer to Adam. He fought the temptation to take the phone from her, cut off the call, and leave Jude to his joyless, office-based existence. 'There was some talk about her being buried with a clock, but that was one of the things she changed her mind on. I think she discussed the arrangements with Wilf Hamley, as well as my father.'

'Okay, that's fine. We've traced the clock. Thank you very much for your help, Miss Duncan. I'll stop bothering you now and leave you to get on with whatever it was you were doing.'

'Goodbye.' Rose ended the call and burst out laughing.

'Do you think he knew?' asked Adam, gathering her in towards him.

'No, of course he didn't. Why would he know what you and I are up to, and why would he care?'

Jude Satterthwaite was a sly old bastard with an instinct for all sorts of things he shouldn't have any thoughts about, and after all these years he still knew Adam too well, but even if he guessed it didn't matter. There was a charged satisfaction in letting Jude know he was having a good time, and what mattered was what he and Rose were about to do and enjoy doing. 'Come here. We've got unfinished business.'

'Don't take this the wrong way,' she said, holding him off though in a way that suggested something more important than any lack of desire, 'but that business can wait.'

'Was it something I said? Or something he said?' Adam took the phone away and tossed it somewhere towards the bottom of the bed.

'Neither, but that call reminded me I have something else I need to do today and I'm going to need your help.'

'Anything,' said Adam, even as he cursed Jude Satterthwaite.

'I'm going to have to go and see Wilf Hamley and I want you to come with me. For safety.'

'For safety?' He laughed out loud. 'Wilf Hamley? Isn't he the solicitor that was wittering on about land titles and common access and all that stuff at the wake?' No-one would have dared talk about that subject at Capel Lodge while Lady Frances had been alive, but Wilf had struck him as the kind of man who found it easy to be brave when there was no danger.

'Yes. I want to talk to him about something and I want to do it before the police get a chance.'

How could he refuse? How could he even question? It was like being a fly, trapped in a web. If it had been pure lust that had brought him to Rose's bed it would never have held him; he would have laughed and refused, carried on having his way with her the way he knew she wanted him to, then packed up his clothes and headed off to watch from a safe distance while she took on her own challenges and Jude tried to keep up with her. Even now he sensed he was in control and if he refused her she would just sigh and then surrender herself to his kiss.

The thought of the sigh was too much for him. With or without the physical compensations he would do whatever Rose Duncan wanted him to. 'Whatever,' he said and then, in case that sounded churlish, he recast it. 'Anything. Anything you want me to do. For you.' Even if it cost him.

'I knew you would. You are such a hero Adam. I almost think I love you.'

As she drew his face towards hers and slid her finger tantalisingly down his back, he succumbed. It wasn't the first time he'd been sucked into something he sensed was too big for him, laced with potential danger, but today he did it not for the excitement and the adrenaline, not even for the pleasure of putting Jude Satterthwaite's nose out of joint in some way he didn't understand. Today, for the first time ever, Adam was doing something for love.

Even on a Saturday morning in June, Wilf Hamley presented himself with stiff formality. When Rose and Adam, hand-in-hand (she didn't seem to care whether the locals disapproved of such a new relationship just days after her father's death and he was more than happy to maintain a touch as long as he could, and preferably for ever) strolled up the street to his large villa at the top of the hill in Lazonby, he was in the front garden. It was a warm morning, though with a stiff breeze, and he was dressed in thick tweed trousers and a pink cashmere pullover, standing over a rose bush with a pair of secateurs in his hand and a bright metal pail on the grass at his side.

'Good morning, Rose,' he said, without straightening up.

Snip-snip. A dead flower dropped into the bucket. Adam had the impression that he'd been expecting them to walk on by but Rose was having none of that. Still clinging on to his hand, she pushed open the gate and strode across the neat grass, towing him behind her. 'Hello, Wilf. Can I have a word?'

'Yes, of course.' He looked faintly startled, as if any departure from the preordained script of his life was hedged with alarms. The look he gave Adam was one of intense disapproval. 'I'm sorry, I don't know who—'

'This is Adam Fleetwood. I think you met at the funeral.'

'Good morning,' said Wilf to Adam, rather more severely than he had done to Rose.

'Now, Wilf. I don't think I'll even be five minutes.' She let go of Adam at last, but only to place both hands defiantly on her hips. 'I've just had the police on the phone.'

'I think we all have.' He snipped busily away at the bush, detached a luscious orange blossom on the edge of perfection and held it out to her. 'There you go my dear. A rose for a Rose.'

She didn't take it. 'I'm sorry, Wilf. I don't think that's appropriate, in the context.'

'No offence was intended,' he said, and took a sidelong look at Adam, who had the creeping sense that Wilf, unlike himself, had guessed what was about to happen and was attempting a distraction.

But even in the past few days Adam had learned that his love was not a woman to be easily deterred. 'The police wanted to know about the interment.'

'That's your line of business, not mine.' Left looking foolish with the rose in his hand, Wilf made a play of tucking it through the cashmere jumper, caught at it and pulled a thread. The fabric was too weak for the flower and it sagged, ridiculously. The colours clashed.

'Normally, yes, but I know you and my father had several meetings about what Lady Frances wanted done. He told me she'd requested it remain confidential.'

'You know yourself, my dear, that client confidentiality is paramount.'

'It's extremely unusual for me not to know everything that goes on in the business and I did wonder why I was excluded in this case, but I respected her wishes and didn't ask.'

'A very professional approach,' he said dryly.

'I regret it now.' Rose was tall and Wilf was still playing about with the rose bushes; when she pulled herself up, she dominated him. 'I had a call from the police asking me if I knew anything and I had to tell them I didn't.'

'The truth, then,' he said, 'according to what you just said.'

'It was, and I wish it wasn't. So I came here to warn you.'

'Warn me?' he said, with a dangerous glint in his eye. This time he straightened up and they were evenly matched for height, but he was so much stronger. Adam took a step forward and placed an arm around Rose's shoulder. It was unusual for him to place his aggressive nature in the service of the good guys, and he liked the buzz it gave him.

'Yes, Wilf.' Rose didn't flinch. 'I told them you spoke to him. I told them the little I know.'

'Good of you to be so kind, eh?' he said with a dry solicitor's laugh. 'And now you seem to have jumped to the wrong conclusion about a perfectly reasonable request from a dying old lady on the basis of my professional discretion, what do you expect me to do? Flee the country?

Pay you? Because if you're even thinking of the latter I would remind you that both blackmail and slander are criminal offences.'

'I'm not warning you for your own good,' she said evenly. 'At least, not like that. I'm coming to tell you that if this turns out to have anything to do with my father's death, and if you are in any way responsible, then I'll kill you.'

'Very sweet,' he said, and laughed again, then looked at Adam and the smile faded.

'That's all,' Rose said, and turned with Adam at her side, down the path, through the gate, onto the broad pavement and down to the main street, where she paused.

'Let's go to my place,' he said. 'Or back to yours. Carry on where we left off.'

'Oh, Adam.' She leaned in towards him for a quick, intense embrace. 'Yes, let's do that. I'm sorry. I shouldn't have involved you.'

He knew why she'd done it. The look he'd had from Wilf Hamley told him that his notoriety had got as far as Lazonby that Wilf knew he was a violent man who, in the past, had never allowed his rational self to control his rage, and so the solicitor had restrained himself. Adam was different now, a changed man in the space of a week, and yet his heart warmed at the thought that even his presence, even his bad reputation, had been of some use to poor, bereaved Rose.

'If he had anything to do with what happened to your dad,' he said, 'he deserves everything he gets.'

'I meant it, you know. Dad was all I had. I will kill him. You'll understand. You feel like that about your detective friend. When somebody wrongs you they live in your head and your heart, like you're haunted. I don't want to be like that with Wilf. If he's done anything, I'll make him pay for it.'

He squeezed her hand. 'Why would he hurt your dad? Didn't they get on?' It wasn't impossible, that friends and colleagues fell out to such an extent that one of them would have been glad to see the other dead. Rose was right. You had only to look at how the relationship between himself and Jude had deteriorated so badly.

'Yes, they got on fine. But Wilf… Well. Dad had heard some things about him. And if the police start looking at what he's been up to, it'll get very, very interesting.'

TWENTY-EIGHT

'I've had a very interesting research session,' said Chris when Jude pulled up the car at the side of Capel Lodge and called in response to the message he'd left, 'so interesting, in fact, it was almost worth coming in on a Saturday for.'

'Let's have it, then.'

'It's the solicitor. Wilf Hamley.'

'He's on my list for today.' After some thought, Jude had put a visit to Wilf Hamley on the back burner, at least until later in the day. His phone call with Rose had persuaded him that the chapel should be his priority and so he'd decided to call in on Capel Lodge unannounced and collect the key. That had the added advantage of giving him the opportunity for a quick look around the place himself; Irene's ultra-cautiousness had prevented him from doing so the previous day. Although the whiteboard in the incident room was plastered with a collage of photographs of the building and its grounds, there was nothing like first-hand experience. He knew the area around Little Salkeld and the Eden like the back of his hand, but he'd never had cause to set foot over the cattle grid at the lodge's impressive stone gates. 'I'm meeting Ash up at the chapel, and then we're going down to call on him later. Do I take it you've got a few questions for him?'

'I'll say. You might start by asking about the state of his business.'

'It's struggling?' Jude thought about Wilf Hamley, interested in whatever object of value he thought Irene had or would fall heir to, lying and bullying in order to get it. What else might he be capable of? It would be interesting to know if he knew the story about the Burne-Jones *Emperor*.

'It looks like it. Soliciting's gone a bit cut-throat. The small country practice has had its day, I think. They get bought over by chains and rebranded and all that sort of thing. In fact, there's an offer in on the practice.'

Would that necessarily be a bad thing for someone like Wilf? He'd no longer be his own boss but he would, equally, be absolved of a lot of the responsibility of running the business. 'What age is he?'

'Forty-four. I managed to rouse a woman called Sarah Garland, who's one of the partners of the firm that wants to buy him out and she says it's a very fair offer, something that he could easily retire on, even at a relatively early age, if that's what he wants to do, or continue to work for the company as either full-time or part time.'

'What was his response?'

'He accepted the offer in principle. That happened several months ago, but he's been dragging his feet over it, to the point at which the prospective buyers are becoming frustrated and pushing him, but he won't budge. He always has a reason. Paperwork not quite ready, accountant on maternity leave, that kind of thing. Sarah reckons that's a big red flag.'

'In terms of buying the business? Is it insolvent?'

'No, just about washing its face, though nothing like enough for him to retire on him as it stands. She says there's no obvious benefit to him financially for delaying the buyout, and her instinct is starting to kick in. She suspects fraud.'

'Right.' Jude looked north across the grounds and the river in the general direction of Lazonby, as if he could see Wilf Hamley there. What would he be doing? Putting on a normal front and pretending everything was okay, to his wife and his neighbours? Panicking, planning? 'I think I see the picture. I've come across it before.' A one-man business, a rich old lady giving the family solicitor power of attorney and trusting him to make financial decisions for her. A struggling business, a 'loan' that was meant to be paid back as soon as funds allowed, but never was. Difficult times, a few more thousand pounds borrowed with no questions asked, and so it went on, until the sum of money involved was so big it was unrepayable from current or potential funds, and so there was nothing left but more drastic action. 'I suppose Lady Frances kept control of her own money right up to the very end?'

'You can bet your life she did, but not everybody does. I've seen it, too. Fraud doesn't have to be on a big scale to ruin you as a solicitor and if he gets done for it he'll never work again.'

If that were the case, Wilf Hamley would have to find the money from somewhere to repay a client and buy himself enough time to bury the transactions in the accounts, hoping neither the new owners nor the account holder would notice. 'Have the purchasing solicitors raised that with him?'

'Sarah said *not yet*. I rather got the impression they're very keen to get their hands on the business and don't want to rock the boat. I expect when the matter is concluded they'll go over his accounts very thoroughly and if they're right and there's something incriminating, it'll end up in my or Ash's inbox.'

For a moment Jude almost felt sorry for Wilf Hamley, desperately struggling to make up the shortfall without realising how neatly the prospective purchasers of his business were luring him into a trap. Then he remembered Irene's account of his visit, and Roger Duncan lying dead in the kitchen garden. Had Wilf, the undertaker's friend and associate, killed him in his desperation to get to whatever prize Frances Capel had hidden, and so save his financial hide?

That was certainly plausible. It was less convincing that he'd kidnapped Gil to get hold of the clock, but not impossible he could be working with whoever had done it. 'That's good stuff. I'll look forward to having a chat with him.'

Chris rang off and Jude got out of the car and walked round the building. The gate into the walled garden was open and he strayed towards it to take a look, but there was no sign of the brutal murder which had taken place there just a few days earlier. Roger had died a few yards away, on the path by the border, but someone had washed it down or spread a thick layer of fresh gravel there so that there were no signs of violence and the place looked what it was meant to be — a haven of tranquillity, humming with bees mining the huge yellow trumpets of courgette flowers and shimmering with dragonflies around an ornamental pond. He stared into the garden for a moment and then walked round to the forbidding, grey front of the house and rang the bell.

It jangled in the depths of the building, and it was a few moments before Irene answered it. 'Good morning,

Chief Inspector. I'm afraid Miss Capel isn't here just now.'

Jude wasn't surprised. In Emma Capel's place he'd have kept as far away from this insanely outdated house and its burden of history as possible, and he suspected she would have disappeared on a permanent basis much sooner if she hadn't felt some sense of responsibility to the man who'd been murdered in her garden.

'It wasn't Ms Capel I was after. I understand there's a key to the private chapel kept at the house, and I wondered if there was any chance I could go down there and have a look.'

'Yes, of course. Come in and have a seat in the library while I go and look for it.'

This was exactly the kind of invitation he'd been hoping for. He followed her through but didn't take a seat, wandering round and taking a quick look at the books and paintings. Ashleigh had been right. The contents of the shelves, more or less organised, held a proliferation of books on the spiritual and the paranormal — witchcraft, ley lines, henges and stone circles, folk tales. There was an entire shelf on tarot cards, their history and meaning and guides to reading them, and when he nudged open a drawer fitted into one of the shelves he saw half a dozen decks of different designs.

When Irene came shuffling back in with a key that must have been six inches long and two hundred years old, and a second half its size but equally black with age, he was standing in front of the picture that Ashleigh had talked about. It was a print of a woman sitting on a rock against a background of a blue sea, her dress falling away from one shoulder, holding an orb in one hand and a sceptre in the other.

'Is this a Dalí?' he asked, turning.

'Yes. A print, of course. I'm not sure Lady Frances was terribly fond of it, but it was the last gift her late grandfather bought for her and so it has a sentimental value. I find it strangely attractive.'

'That's ringing a bell. Wasn't there a Dalí destroyed in Castell Capel during the war? I'm sure my dad mentioned it. He's a bit of a local history buff.'

She looked slightly put out. 'Oh dear. I didn't realise that story was so widely known. We don't like to talk about it, but I don't suppose there's any harm now the poor man's dead and doesn't have to bear the shame. Though that wasn't a Dalí but a Burne-Jones, and very different from that.'

'I know nothing about art, but I think even I'd recognise the difference between the two.'

'Yes. It's very obvious. This is quite plain, I think, and rather painfully clever, whereas the Burne-Jones — it was the Emperor, not the Empress — was much more accessible, so rich and exotic. You can't imagine the colours. The reds, the blues, the greens. They were breathtaking, quite jewel-like.'

Jude thought of the sketches he'd researched on the internet. 'Surely you can't have seen it?' She was nowhere near old enough.

'Oh no, of course not. Only a reproduction. In real life it would have been so much more vivid, I expect. Such a tragedy it was destroyed.'

'There's no chance it can have survived?'

She gave him a curious, blank look. When he'd seen her the day before she'd been alive, interesting. That, he understood, was because she had been prepared for him, acting a part, whereas today he'd caught her unawares and she had to tread more carefully. 'No, none. If it had done it would have been returned to its true owners. The seventh

Earl really was the most upright and honourable man.' She held the keys out to to him. 'The chapel key. And the smaller one is for the crypt.'

He took them, feeling the weight of time and history in his hands and accepting her desire to move the conversation on. There were plenty of other things he could learn from her without making her any more uncomfortable. 'Do you get many people wanting to visit?'

'Very few. Maybe a dozen in a year. The chapel has limited archaeological and historical interest, despite its age. And of course, a lot of the time the Lodge is empty except for the gardeners and Carly, so there's no-one to supply the key.'

'There's just one?'

'Yes. It's not exactly easy to lose.'

A key like that wouldn't be easily copied, either; it would be a specialist job and anyone wanting a second key cut ran the risk of being easily traced.

'Nobody's been down there recently?' he asked.

'We closed the church completely to visitors after Lady Frances's death, as a mark of respect, so no. I don't recall anyone asking for the key for some time, as a visitor, at least.' She was too polite and too aware of her position, he suspected, to usher him out, but he got the message and headed towards the door.

'May I ask you something, Miss Jenkins?' he said, as their feet echoed in the stone-flagged hallway.

'Of course.'

She reached for the door and he, noting her arthritic knuckles, opened it for himself. 'I hope you don't think it's personal, but I did wonder. You gave a lot of years to Lady Frances—'

'I was with her from sixteen and I will be seventy-three in September,' she said, with a degree of pride.

'Lady Frances was a wealthy woman.' Not exceptionally so, but certainly enough to be ranked one of the wealthier in the county when all her assets were taken into account. 'After all those years, didn't you have any expectations from her, in terms of a bequest?'

She didn't meet his eye. 'I would show myself up very poorly if I admitted that. Lady Frances remembered me in her will and I'm grateful.'

For a useless book that couldn't be found and a clock shot to pieces by a violent man. 'I think you're entitled to feel a little hard done by.'

'Perhaps a little,' she admitted. 'Lady Frances always said she would make sure I was properly rewarded for everything I'd done for her, but in my heart of hearts I suspected something like this might happen. Not that she intended it to. I don't believe that. I told your sergeant how fond she always was of treasure hunts and complicated riddles and surprises and so on, the more complicated the better. But latterly she was showing some signs of...of lack of competence. I don't mean to sound disloyal, you understand.'

'There's nothing disloyal about the truth, Miss Jenkins.'

'I know but one doesn't like to speak ill of the dead. I'm quite sure Lady Frances did intend to leave me something, and I'm quite sure the clues she left were part of her game. But I'm equally sure that either she never finished laying the trail, or that someone else got there first.'

And, as he returned to his car, Jude knew exactly who she was thinking of.

TWENTY-NINE

Ashleigh was already parked near the chapel when Jude arrived, leaning on the bonnet of her car and checking her phone. The chapel lay at the end of a lane that cut through woods on the eastern side of the Long Meg Stone circle and ended at a locked gate. Her car was parked in the slight widening of the lane that passed for a car park and bore the wide tread marks of tyres that must have belonged to the hearse. He parked his car beside hers.

'How are you getting on?' he asked as he got out.

'I'm doing fine. You?' Like him, she'd made a concession to the fact that it was Saturday and was casually dressed in jeans and tee shirt — ideal for the two of them to look around without seeming to be too obviously officious, or attracting unwelcome attention from passers-by.

'I think I've made a very significant breakthrough.'

'Right?' She pocketed the phone and came over to stand next to him at the wall, looking over into the churchyard.

'Yes. I went to the Lodge to get the key from Irene and she's made the most monumental slip.'

'I love it when you give someone the rope to hang themselves,' she said. 'Not literally, obviously.'

'I know what you mean. And I don't think Irene necessarily implicated herself in murder, either, but she certainly said enough to make me think she's been dabbling her fingers in some kind of fraud.'

'Art fraud?' she said, her mind moving the same way as his. She turned and looked intently in the direction of Capel Lodge as if she could see it and gain some inspiration.

'Yes. Tell me about the Burne-Jones *Emperor*. You researched it. What was it like?'

'I told you. There are no pictures of it. Either it hadn't been catalogued or any reproductions have been lost. There are no images of it anywhere, other than the sketches that were saved from the fire. They're in the archive at the National Gallery, but not on public display. If you want to see them you have to make an appointment or make do with what's on the internet.'

'I don't know that Irene would be too *au fait* with complex Google searches, though I may be wrong. She strikes me as very traditional and does everything by the book. And yet when I was speaking to her she explained to me the difference between that print of the Empress they have on the wall and the Burne-Jones *Emperor*.'

'Maybe she has seen the sketches,' said Ashleigh doubtfully.

'Maybe she has, but she was talking to me about the colours. *The reds. The blues. The greens.* There are barely any colours on the sketch, is that right?'

'Yes, that's correct,' she said interested. 'That is a slip, then, and a real one. Unless she's somehow conflating a memory of what someone might have told her. Could the be possible?'

'I don't think so. She said they never talked about the painting while the old Earl was alive and I got the impression Lady Frances was fairly tight-lipped about it, too. Do you know, up until just now I was sure we were on the wrong track.' He, too, looked back towards Capel Lodge. Maybe he should have pushed Irene further. 'I'd just about convinced myself no-one knows anything and that meant there was nothing to know, that Lady F had just sent everybody off on a wild goose chase.' Just as Irene had said.

'And,' said Ashleigh, laying her hand on the wall and frowning at the broken gravestones of lost generations, 'that's what she told you and that's what you're meant to think. That it's all about a book that's vanished and a clock that didn't work.'

He frowned. 'It doesn't make sense, does it? If that's right, why did she tell me about Wilf Hamley threatening her?'

'I know. She could just have left us wondering and now she's implicated herself.'

He cast his mind back to the conversation he and Irene had shared beside the river. The ensuing adventure and Gil's rescue had meant he hadn't given it nearly as much attention as he now saw that it warranted, but when he stopped to think about it he recalled how obvious Irene's righteous anger had been. 'He scared her and her instinct kicked in. She did what she was always brought up to do. Call the police.' Poor Irene. If she was up to no good, if she had the Burne-Jones painting stashed somewhere, or even if she didn't but was afraid someone else had, then she'd given herself away. No wonder she'd been so keen to add that resigned postscript to their conversation. *Either she never finished laying the trail, or that someone else got there first.*

'Do you think we'll find the *Emperor* in the chapel?' asked Ashleigh.

That would be an unexpected bonus. 'I think we'll find something.' Unless it had been a wild goose chase all along and Lady Frances really was enjoying a laugh at their expense, either up in heaven or down in hell. He couldn't imagine which tarot character she would associate herself with — the Hierophant, probably, knowing all the answers, pulling all the strings from the other side. 'Let's go and see.'

'Let me just check the car's locked.' She turned back to her car, paused, peered back the way they had come, along the lane towards Long Meg, not too many yards away. 'Oh, wait. What's that? Just at the end of the lane, by the stones? I'm sure that wasn't there when we—'

Jude began to run. He didn't know why, because what Ashleigh was pointing at looked like nothing more than a bundle of old mud-coloured rags, a half-stuffed scarecrow picked apart by the birds and abandoned contemptuously in a field, but it only took him a second to realise that it hadn't been there when he'd driven past. Whatever it was, it shouldn't be there. Something was badly wrong.

'Mum!' called Geri Foster's voice from the edge of the New Agers' field as he reached the spot and looked down to see Raven, crumpled and peace at his feet. 'Where are you?' And then Raven's husband, Storm, his voice rumbling above the rippling, knee-high grass that filled the field. 'Raven! Raven!'

Three crows rose from the trees and made a pass above them, sinister and interested. Recognising the tangle of worn clothing in which Raven's still figure was swathed, Jude dropped to his knees, reached for her thin wrist and felt for a pulse.

'Sweet Jesus!' said Ashleigh, arriving at his side a

second later. 'It's Raven, isn't it? What's happened? Is it too late?'

He nodded and laid Raven's hand down by her side while Ashleigh called above his head to Geri and Storm. The dry ground thundered under their feet as they raced towards the stone circle through the meadow of poppies and meadowsweet. A butterfly, bright as a jewel, settled briefly on the rough cloth of Raven's scarf and fluttered away again.

Jude got up to meet them. 'I'm sorry, Storm—'

Storm slowed. 'What?' he said almost in disbelief, and looked down. 'No! My Raven!'

He was a big man, so much more so by comparison with the wife who had faded away in front of him to barely more than a skeleton, but even he seemed suddenly shrunken and diminished as he sank down in the grass, took the love of his life in his arms and gently cradled her. His broad shoulders quivered with silent sobs. Geri, made of sterner stuff, kept her expression cynical but her hard expression couldn't conceal the pain and her eyes brimmed with tears.

'Come on, Dad,' she said, gently for her, because she was habitually offhand.' It's not like we didn't know it was coming.' She turned to the two detectives. 'It had to be you who found her, didn't it? It had to be bloody you.'

Jude stepped back, hands held up in a gesture of submission and regret. There was nothing he could say. 'I'm so sorry.'

'She wasn't even old,' Geri said, despairingly. 'She was barely sixty! She was my mum and I'll never have another one! It's not fair!'

'I'll call an ambulance,' said Ashleigh, straying a few steps away, 'and get a uniformed officer along. You just spend a bit of time—'

Geri focussed her fury even more sharply on Jude. 'The police. So now no doubt you're going to tell me it's a suspicious death and take us all in for questioning. A police matter. Don't touch the body. Well, if my dad wants to hold his wife he bloody well will and you won't stop him!'

He shook his head, feeling the loss of good-hearted Raven more keenly than expected. Geri wasn't an idiot. She knew there would be protocols. 'None of that. We need a police officer to record the death and handle the paperwork. It's routine.'

'I never want to hear that word again.'

'Indigo,' said Storm, from the ground, using the name he and Raven had bestowed on their daughter and which she had been quick to reject alongside everything else they had offered her. 'Indigo, moppet. That's not fair. She was ready to go. It was her time, a good time. The right time.'

'But why here?' Geri sank down beside him, and arm across his broad shoulder. 'Why not at the camp with us? Why did she leave us?'

Jude withdrew to where Ashleigh was closing down the call to the emergency services.

'They're sending a uniformed officer over, of course,' she said, under her voice. 'I know we could deal with it, but I thought under the circumstances it's better if it's someone Geri doesn't know. It's Tyrone Garner who's coming along. I don't think Geri knows him.'

So much the better. Tyrone, who was Doddsy's partner, was an exemplary young officer and would be more than capable of dialling down the temperature of grief and anger that strangely surrounded a peaceful passing. Jude would never claim to have been close to Raven and she'd always been suspicious of him, but she'd been a simple, decent soul and the world would be poorer without her.

'Should we go?' Ashleigh asked, looking troubled. 'I really hate to intrude.'

'No. Let's wait until Tyrone gets here, at least. I still want to look in the church, but I don't want to leave them on their own if there's anything we can do.' Raven's death changed nothing. Roger Duncan's murderer was still free, a valuable painting still the treasure for which potential killers were hunting. Lives, he was almost certain, were still at stake. 'We have time.'

They withdrew to the shadow of the trees and stood side by side, while Geri and Storm knelt by Raven's body. Storm was sobbing loudly and Geri looked down on her mother with an expression that implied she was fighting emotions Jude knew she'd regard as weakness. Geri prided herself on her pragmatism and hard-headedness, but he wished she'd allow herself a moment of emotion at the death of the mother with whom her relationship had been rocky.

After ten minutes or so a police car drew up. Tyrone Garner, his face already composed into an expression of sympathy and concern, got out and came across to them.

'Everything okay, here?' He flicked a look at Jude and his expression flicked with concern. 'Boss, is something—?'

'It's routine,' Jude reassured him. 'We were passing on our way somewhere else. Raven has been ill for some time.'

Geri was on her feet in an instant. 'I can deal with this. Don't think I don't appreciate the two of you standing over us like a pair of avenging angels. I do. But there's nothing to avenge and I can handle this myself. Constable, let me explain what happened.'

'We'll speak to you about it shortly,' said Jude to Tyrone and, on receiving a nod of acknowledgement, turned his attention to Storm, who was still cradling Raven in the summer sunlight. The butterfly had come back and was fluttering around his head, now, but he didn't wave it away. 'Storm. We have another appointment, but just let us know if there's anything we can do for you.'

Storm shook his head. The first flood of his tears had stilled now, though they would surely return later, as regular as the tide, ebbing and flowing, sometimes higher, sometimes not. 'You were always good to her. Both of you. She didn't trust the police but she liked you.' He swallowed. 'If someone official had to be here I'm glad it was you.'

In truth, the two of them had done nothing except call for assistance. 'I'm so sorry she's gone.'

'It was a shock,' said Storm, laying Raven's grey head down on the grass and taking her tiny hand in his big one, 'but this is how she always wanted to go. It was the right time. She knew that. I knew when I went to the tent and she wasn't there that it would be too late, but this was right. This is a ley line, did you know that?'

'I did.'

'It runs from Capel Lodge through the camp and the stones to the chapel. It makes sense to me that she wants to be here at the stones, not in the camp. She always felt the energy of the Earth. She knew it was time to come here and be consumed by it.'

Mikey's girlfriend, who had a thing about death and an obsession with the Long Meg stone circle, talked a lot about the energy of the Earth and portals to the underworld. With her Jude always had a slight concern that her morbidity was inappropriate to the point of being a danger, but for Raven the belief had been a harmless one, and so what if it had given her comfort at her natural end? 'We'll leave you with her, now. But say to Geri that if there's anything at all either of us can do, just let me know. Personally, I mean.'

Storm's smile was both sad and grateful. 'Aye, I'll do that. But all I'll ask is that you come and see her buried.'

'Who does Geri Foster think she is?' said Ashleigh under her breath as they made their way from the stone circle back along the lane to the chapel.

The mixture of outrage and empathy in her voice amused him. 'It's how she rolls. She can't help herself.'

'I suppose I understand. Just because it was expected it doesn't mean it wasn't a shock.'

'Yes.' They'd reached the gate to the churchyard by then and he laid his hand on the rough wood of the gate. *Nothing to avenge*, Geri had said, but she was wrong. Justice for Roger Duncan, and the prevention of any further killing, was their priority.

THIRTY

'Poor Storm,' said Ashleigh as they paused for a moment by the gate to watch an ambulance trundle across the meadow to where Raven lay, saw Geri apparently challenging Tyrone about something and the police officer deflect it with a good-humoured shrug. 'It'll be a nightmare, getting her buried.'

'Yep.' Storm and Raven had kept themselves as far removed as possible from the tangled bureaucratic web of modern life. They had no bank accounts, no passports, no fixed address. The lack of a routine form of identity had caused them endless problems when those in authority found them incompetent or sinister, while the general public regarded them with suspicion and blamed them for every lost camera or dropped bank card. Storm would want to bury his wife where she lay, knowing that was the place where she felt she had belonged, but even he must know it was impossible. He would end up standing beside some grave in the cemetery at Penrith in a ceremony organised by Geri to be as efficient as possible, and with barely anyone in attendance but himself, Geri, her son and (now an obligation) Ashleigh and Jude himself. 'I wonder if Geri will give the funeral to Rose?'

'I wonder.' Jude turned to look over the low wall into the churchyard, with its scant graves sticking up from the long grass. Only Capel retainers and their families had the privilege of being buried there. 'It would be less of a challenge than Lady Frances, with all her eccentricities.' He put his hand to the gate, rusted but recently oiled.

'Do you think the book is in the crypt?'

'If it's in the crypt, as long as it's not actually in the coffin, I'm tempted to have a look.'

'What?' said Ashleigh, surprised at his impetuousness. 'Even if it's in the sarcophagus or whatever Rose called it?'

'There's nothing to stop us except courtesy to Emma Capel. It's a public place so we don't need a warrant. And it's not as if we're opening a grave.' That would have opened a whole new can of worms. Even if the book wasn't obvious, he might consider the grimmer option of applying to have the coffin opened, if he thought he could make enough of a connection to Roger's death, but he didn't think that would be necessary. If the book was a clue to the whereabouts of something valuable, it would need to be accessible.

'Right. And if we look, do you know what I think we'll find?'

'The Burne-Jones *Emperor*?'

'Yes.' Ashleigh preceded him along the tone-slabbed path. 'Irene's seen it. That's pretty clear. She must have done, if she described it in such detail and there's no copy of it. That means it survived the fire and that probably means Lady Frances had it.'

'And wanted Irene to have it?'

'It's not the most valuable or high-profile picture he ever painted, but yes. It would be enough to keep her in reasonable comfort for the rest of her days if she could get rid of it discreetly. I can see that Lady F would quite have enjoyed the joke, not to mention the fact it would have saved her doing anything with the painting herself, and risking either her own good name or her grandfather's.'

'And so you think…?'

'Didn't I say it was about the same size as a laptop screen? That makes it just a little smaller than one of those ledgers. And when I dug a little deeper I discovered that it was common practice to take paintings out of their frames for transport and protection.'

'Let's have a look, then.' Jude felt in his pocket for the heavy key. 'I'd love to have a look in the sarcophagus, but we're probably better clearing it with Emma Capel first. At least we can have a look at the place. Apart from anything else, if the clue is for Irene, there would have to be some way in which she could get it without help, so I'd like to check that. Remembering that she's over seventy and pretty frail.'

'Lady F might have expected that she would have help.'

'Good point.' And the obvious person, thought Jude as they walked up the path to the chapel and he fitted the heavy key into its stiff lock, was Roger himself. Had he died because someone wanted to stop him from giving away what he might know? 'I still haven't ruled out Irene, but if she did that then she must have someone else lined up to help her out.'

The lock, like the hinges of the gate, had been recently oiled and the key turned with a satisfying click. Jude pushed the heavy door open. Outside the chapel was built in the traditional style, with sandstone quoins and window frames and sills, its walls painted white but inside it was plain and simple, reflecting a severe Nonconformist influence in its clear windows and bare wood. It had, Jude thought, a beauty of its own despite its lack of ornamentation; the white walls were adorned with brass and wooden memorials to the Capels and their vicars, and to those of their employees who had died in battle — two world wars, the Boer War, the Crimea. He moved past them, mostly second sons for whom Capel Lodge had been a poor substitute for the castle, and widowed countesses who had long outlived their husbands and their usefulness, ceding precedence to their daughters-in-law and retiring to the country leaving senior members of the family to lord it over the castle in Wales.

'Lovely,' said Ashleigh, in a hushed voice, and they stood for a while and looked at the draped flags above the tomb of a particularly heroic Capel son, while motes of dust drifted downwards on angel slides of sunlight.

'Isn't it?' agreed Jude, but there was no time to stand and stare. 'Let's have a look around. I'll go this side, you take the other.'

The chapel rang with their footsteps as they proceeded in silence along the two sides. It was bereft of kneelers or cushions or tapestries to muffle an echo or behind which to conceal a book, a spartan place that was no longer a living church but only, it seemed, a monument to the Capels' long-diminished authority. It didn't take long to be sure there was no hiding place above ground, nothing newly-painted or plastered to cover a cache, no loose mortar in the flagged floor. 'Anything your side?'

'No,' said Ashleigh, from the pulpit where she was checking between the pages of the huge Bible on the lectern.

'Then let's try the crypt.'

At the side of the lectern a short flight of steps, perhaps ten of them, worn and uneven, led down to a closed door. Taking the second key, he fitted it to the lock while Ashleigh clattered down from the pulpit to join him, and opened the door. Darkness surged out to meet them, a smell of damp and dust and decay.

There was a switch on the wall and he flicked it downwards. A bare electric bulb swung above them, too close to the top of his head for comfort, and showed a narrow corridor to their right, perhaps ten feet long, heading back under the main body of the chapel. At its end a square, low-ceilinged room contained a series of stone chests, each with a small brass plate affixed bearing the names of the deceased. These, too. had been recently polished as if in anticipation of Lady Frances's arrival; her name was fixed to a chest at the far end of the room. A wilted floral wreath lay on the top. With Ashleigh close beside him, Jude crossed to the chest and read the name. No title: just a plain and simple record of her name, *Frances Elizabeth Capel*, and her dates.

'Not so much as a *rest in peace*,' said Ashleigh, with a sigh. 'I imagine that was what she wanted, but all the others have their titles and all the rest of it.'

All of the dozen or so stone chests looked as if they'd been carved at the same time, clearly waiting for generations of Capels. It was convenient that Frances, the last of the line, should occupy the final space in the crypt. He laid his hand upon its rough sandstone lid.

'The others are sealed,' he said, casting a quick glance and seeing the thin line of lead between chests and lids, 'but not this one. Perhaps they haven't had time.' Or perhaps it was unsealed for another reason. His skin prickled with excitement. The answer might be in there. He closed his hands on the edge of the lid and pushed it, feeling it give under its fingers.

'Are you tempted?' said Ashleigh, clearly itching to see what was inside.

'Yes.' The two of them between them could probably lift the slab, even if just to see what was inside, to see whether there was a reward in there, or another clue to follow in Frances Capel's macabre treasure hunt, or just a dead end, but he could imagine what would happen if he did. Emma Capel might or might not be put out by such a liberty but Faye, who did everything by the rules and who, when there were no protocols, wrote her own, would go ballistic. 'Better not. We know it's here. We know the lid isn't sealed. We know we can get access. I've got the only key.' But if they left it, a lot could go wrong and he was itching to move matters on. He reached for his phone. If they could get one of the officers currently dealing with the paperwork around Raven's death to come down from the stone circle when they'd finished, they could leave them there while they went back for the authorisation.

'I'll get Tyrone to pop down when he's finished up at Long Meg, shall I?' said Ashleigh, sharing the same thought.

'Yes, if you've got signal.' With the key in his pocket and Tyrone standing guard, Jude reckoned it would be easy enough to get clearance from both Emma and Faye to proceed.

'Enough to send a message, anyway.'

While she fired off the text, he strayed along the row of other chests, snatching a look to see if there was any other crevice in which the ledger could have been concealed, but there was nothing to see but dust and spiders, and the old, cold, stone walls were thick with crusted mortar; none of the stones there had been moved since the place was built, certainly not recently.

'Okay,' said Ashleigh, 'that's done. Let's get back to the

open air before the bats come out and turn us into vampires.'

The light bulb flickered and went out.

In the sudden darkness, Jude turned towards the shaft of light that came from the staircase and found it blocked by a figure whose shadow jumped to a giant size across the uneven flagged floor towards them. 'Who's there?'

'Never mind,' said a voice, a heavy Mancunian accent. It had been that immediately-recognisable accent, realised Jude, that Gil had described for one of his captors. After all, there was a link. 'I'm armed. If you know anything about your job you'll know I won't hesitate to shoot.'

Just like he hadn't hesitated to shoot Gil to prevent his escape, would have shot him in sheer fury at the failure of his quest, whatever that quest was. He said nothing, but inched himself a little closer towards Ashleigh, in an attempt to place himself between her and the gun, but his priority had to be to calm the man down. If it went off in that confined space it was unlikely there would be no casualty, even if it missed its intended target.

'Don't be an idiot,' he said, as amiably as he dared and, even as he did so, realising how foolish, how weak this made him sound. 'This gets you nowhere.'

'Oh, but it does. I think you and I are here for the same thing but unlike you, I'm not going to have a fit of conscience about proper process. I don't have any conscience at all. You and your colleague can open that grave for me, and the coffin if that's what it takes, and explain it to your superiors later.'

Jude cast a glance at Ashleigh. In the strange light he saw that she, like him, was thinking frantically and that she, like him, had concluded that their options were limited. They were too far away from the gunman to rush him and the risk of catching a bullet was far too great. And anyway, what would happen except that the task they wanted to undertake with proper authority would be undertaken without it? If there was something in the grave they would see what it was. They had only to hope that the man wasn't of a mind to dispose of the two of them afterwards.

Jude reckoned not. He could only fire at one of them at a time; the other would have a chance to tackle him. It made sense for them to do as he ordered and for him to leave them alive to tell the tale while he made his escape.

'Okay,' he said, 'but you'll need to put the light on.'

A torch flashed on, its bright light leaving him blinking. 'Lift the lid off that and if there's anything in there with the coffin, get it out.'

'You know there are police down at Long Meg?' And the whole area crawling with police, searching for this man. How had they missed him?

'Aye, I've seen them. And the quicker you do as you're told, the quicker I get out. Then I don't get caught and you don't get shot.'

Tyrone, coming up from the field in response to Ashleigh's text, would walk straight into this situation unawares — and God knew how that would end. All they could do was follow this man's instructions and get him out of the place as soon as possible. 'Okay. Come on, Ash. Let's get this done.'

Sweeping the wreath aside, he moved to one side of the sarcophagus and indicated that Ashleigh should go to the other. He daren't say anything but he could see her eyes darting from here to there, wondering the same as he was. Did the gunman realise he was at much as risk as they were, possibly more, if he fired and missed?

'I'm ready,' she said, her voice steady.

He flexed his fingers against the lid, managed to lever it

up. There was a gap there, as if it was meant for exactly that. 'Tilt it forwards,' he instructed her.

'Right.' She flashed him a grim look, but it was one of grateful understanding. If the worst came to the worst they could use it as a shield.

'On the count of three. One, two…'

On the word *three* they shifted the lid sharply enough for it to overbalance and tilt on its end, both offering them something to hide behind and protecting the contents of the chest from the gunman's view. If he lost his focus, if his curiosity overcame him enough to tempt him forwards and within Jude's reach then maybe — maybe — they had a chance.

But he didn't. The light remained steady. 'What's inside?'

Jude looked down on polished coffin of walnut wood, its brass plate engraved with exactly the same simple identification as on the chest itself. A second wreath, this time of lilies, brown and desiccated. A large, dusty ledger. One part of the mystery, at least, was solved.

'Well?'

'A book,' said Jude, with extreme caution.

'Pick it up.'

He leaned forward into the sarcophagus, taking the opportunity to shake the volume as he lifted it, but nothing fell out. He had only a second to flick through its pages, but there was no note, no obvious clue, no recent interruption to the old and long-unopened pages where someone might have inserted a written word or comment, and certainly no Burne-Jones painting. Satisfied of that, at least, he vanquished the last of his queasiness about handing a vital clue over to a villain. Let the man make of it what he would. They would find him.

'Okay. Now what?' The next step, too, was fraught with

danger. He was under no illusions of how dangerous this man might be. 'You realise someone could be here any moment?'

'They aren't here yet,' said the man, calmly. 'Put it on the floor.'

Without taking his eyes off the light, Jude did as he was told.

'Now, give it a good push towards me. Don't be half-hearted about it. I don't want to have to come and get it. If I do I'll have to shoot you.'

Remembering the callousness this man and his associate had showed towards Gil, Jude had no doubt about that. He gave the book a good shove across the floor of the crypt so that it skidded over the uneven slates, slowed as it reached the man's feet.

This, he knew, was their best chance. He braced himself for a swift leap towards their assailant but the man must have thought it through. He fired, a second time and then twice more in rapid succession, at the low roof of the crypt.

Aware of the danger of the ricochet, Jude dived for Ashleigh and the two of them crashed down into the cold stone floor. The light went out. Fleetingly he thought of Becca and how he might never have the chance to explain to him how all this had come about. In the enclosed space the bullets pinged off the walls and it seemed an age, rather than a few seconds, before their energy was spent and there was silence. By that time the doorway was empty and the man was gone.

Jude jumped to his feet and raced down the narrow passageway and up the steps into the serene brightness of the church. It was empty. 'Are you okay, Ash?' he called, over his shoulder.

'I'm fine. I thought for a moment we were going to

have to hide in the coffin there,' said Ashleigh. Her voice was shaking. 'Where the hell did he come from? The whole place is crawling with police looking for him. Do you think he's been waiting all this time for someone to come?'

'Who knows? We'll get him, though.' Reaching for his phone he strode to the door and flung it open, but there was no sign of their assailant in the churchyard or the lane or the woods — only Tyrone Garner, sauntering up the path with a cheerful smile.

'Sorry it took me so long,' he said. 'The paperwork took forever. Always does when folk can't prove who they are. Now, did you say there was something about opening a crypt?'

THIRTY-ONE

'Dogs,' said Faye, sitting at the table in the incident room with her fingers pressed hard on the laminated top and a spectacular scowl on her face, 'drones, helicopter, God knows how many officers, and he was within walking distance the whole time. The whole time.'

Internalising his sigh, Jude pulled ups chair and sat down. He'd called in in search of Ashleigh, with the intention of heading home early after Faye had subjected the two of them to a fearsome and detailed debrief of the incident in the chapel, and instead he'd walked into what looked like a discussion on the matter that was going on without him. Faye was in the seat he usually occupied by the whiteboard, and Ashleigh and Doddsy were sitting there and listening to her tirade.

Ashleigh was looking tired, he noted. He didn't imagine he looked too great, either.

'We don't know he was,' said Doddsy, mildly.

'If he wasn't you'll need to explain to me how he got

there, because he'd have had to get past a lot of officers who were looking for him.'

'I imagine he was at Capel Lodge,' said Jude, resigning himself to a delayed escape, another session of going over and over things he'd never stopped thinking about.

'Didn't we look there?'

'We looked in the outbuildings but we didn't search the place. I'm pretty sure Irene said she hadn't seen anyone or anything. But it's a big place and very little of it is used. He could have hidden in there, for a while at least. It's not that far to the chapel from there.' And if he had, somehow he might have overheard Jude's conversation with Irene and followed him down to the chapel.

'You don't seem terribly concerned about that,' she challenged him, 'given there's an elderly lady living there on her own.'

Emma Capel was still in London. 'She wasn't on her own. The housekeeper is there. She said she hadn't seen anything, either.'

'So it's two women in the place on their own, not one. And you aren't concerned?'

He pushed his chair back a little, as though to distance himself from the conversation, and stifled a yawn of exhaustion rather than boredom. 'Irene wants the picture.'

'And so does our man and so does Wilf Hamley. But the difference between Hamley and this man is that Hamley is all talk and we know this fellow isn't afraid to use his gun.'

'I don't think Irene will have been in danger. I'm assuming the man went there for somewhere to hide, rather than with murder in mind, so his best chance was to keep quiet and make his getaway when he could. He almost certainly knew Irene didn't have it. But it's also possible she knew about him and was working with him.'

Faye drew in a long deep breath and all four of them contemplated the possibility of Irene as accomplice to a murderer. 'We'll need to speak to her again. Could he be at the Lodge now, do you think?'

'No. I sent a constable straight up there and I don't see how he could have got there beforehand without passing Tyrone or the ambulance. He'd have had to go a long way around to do that.'

'Right. And so we still know nothing about this man.'

'Oh, we know plenty,' said Doddsy, cheerfully. 'We recovered the car, remember, and there's all sorts of stuff in there which will lead us right to him. Given time.' He gave the impression that he'd been trying to pass on this information for the previous ten minutes, but had been unable to stem the tide of Faye's irritation.

'You're optimistic today,' said Faye, who was rarely so and who had now resumed her normal pose, sitting a little back from the table and waiting for one of her junior officers to make an error, or say something inappropriate, or simply fail to pick up on something quickly enough.

'I'm very optimistic,' he said, cheerfully. A large part of his good humour, Jude judged, was down to the good fortune that both Jude and Ashleigh had emerged unscathed and Tyrone had arrived too late to meet up with a homicidal stranger. 'There's a whole richness of forensic evidence in that car.'

'You say we know who he is?' said Jude, with a sidelong look at Ashleigh. She'd been unusually quiet since they'd got back to the office, and he sensed it wasn't due to either the rigorous debriefing or their recent brush with death.

'We do. The service documents were in the car and they give us its real numberplate and owner. And some lovely things which will probably tell us who his partner in crime is, if we don't get to her first.' Doddsy looked smug.

But the two were still out there. There was an armed guard on Gil Foley and a discreet police presence at Capel Lodge — and Becca, thank God, was still safe in Keswick — but the wealth of forensic evidence Doddsy set such store by might take a long time to process. In the meantime, what would happen?

Faye's scowl, he noticed, made her look exactly like the print of the Dalí *Empress* on the library wall at Capel Lodge. 'It won't give us the answers we need right now. I only met Frances Capel once but I'm beginning to think she was even more of an autocrat than I took her for, and probably a little senile, too. There'll be nothing to find.' She looked at Jude and Ashleigh and her expression softened imperceptibly. 'You said there was nothing in the book.'

'Nothing I could see.' There might have been a clue, glued in, or scrawled in faint pencil deep in a margin, but he tended to think not. He was coming to the same conclusion as Faye — that the clock, and the book, had yielded nothing because there was nothing to find and that Frances Capel had taken great pleasure in sending everyone off on a wild goose chase over a painting which had long since been disposed of, if it had survived. He turned to Doddsy. 'Whose is the car?'

'It's registered to a man called Toby Weston, with an address in Llandudno. I've got Chris doing a search on Mr Weston, but the pictures we've got match Gil's description of him and what Becca Reid was able to tell us. That makes me think he's our man, rather than a case of identity theft.' He glanced down at his iPad, turning it to them to show a photograph of a man with thick dark hair and a surprisingly cheerful grin that hid his malicious streak. 'This is a picture from his driving licence. I don't have much on him yet, as I say, but Chris is working on it now.

Our man Toby is thirty-eight, born and brought up in Manchester, but relocated to North Wales a couple of years back. He has no criminal record. He works as a maintenance man in a large hotel there.'

'Llandudno,' said Jude, with interest. 'North Wales. Is that far from Castell Capel?' He looked across at Ashleigh.

'Twenty miles, maybe.' she said with a nod, and sipped her coffee. 'But Wales is like Cumbria. Twenty miles can be a hell of a long way on some roads.'

'Do we know of any connections to the Capels?'

'Nothing that I've come across so far.'

'You might want to see if you can find something, especially a link to Irene' said Faye, 'as I wonder if it's a casual criminal who heard a story about the missing Burne-Jones and decided to take a chance on finding it before anyone else did, taking out poor Roger Duncan on the way. But I don't know if I'm that convinced about it, even as I say it.'

Jude nodded. It was plausible enough at the superficial level, but it didn't address the wider context. It didn't explain how Toby Weston might have found out about the painting, or the clock, or the book, unless there had been some kind of gossip locally, but both Irene and the late Lady Frances gave every indication of having been both tight-lipped and extremely stand-offish. 'We can talk to Irene about it. I'll do that.'

'I'll come,' Ashleigh said, 'if you need me. And maybe we should go and see how Storm and Geri Foster are getting on. And see if they saw anything.'

'Do it tomorrow,' said Faye, as if either of them was seriously considering going down to Capel Lodge at after six in the evening. 'I know we're all working our backsides off and most of us will be here until late, but your union rep will be after me if I try and keep the pair of you here too late after what happened today.'

'Good excuse,' said Doddsy, genially, 'facing down a homicidal maniac. I'll make a note for future use.'

They survived on black humour but this was a little too near the bone. Either Jude or Ashleigh, or both of them, might not have made it out of that crypt. Faye's response was the inevitable scowl and Ashleigh's smile was weak. She wanted, he sensed, to get out of the office. Fair play. He felt the same. He switched his attention back to Doddsy, moved the conversation back to Toby Weston. 'Just before we go. He wasn't working alone. Did you get any clues about his partner?'

'I'm hoping there might be something we get from the forensics on the car. Nothing yet. He was married, but divorced ten years back and the wife and kids are still in Manchester. There's no record of any subsequent relationship.' Which wasn't to say there wasn't one — or more than one — or that any partnership wasn't a purely contractual one, based on a shared desire for the money that a Burne-Jones painting would bring.

'You say he's a maintenance man,' Jude said, with interest. 'If our man was after a painting I'd have expected someone who knew about the provenance of it, perhaps knew about art.'

Doddsy shook his head. 'There are no clues in his background. We've said it already. He could be working for someone else, perhaps. Irene, as you suggested.'

'Or Rose?' said Ashleigh. 'She knows about art. Remember what Becca said, that she'd wanted to study history of art? It's a fair bet she fell out with her father about it. And then there's all this business of Weston's unknown partner in crime. Gil said she didn't try too hard to conceal herself, which makes me think she was disguised, and Becca said there was a wig and that the girl reminded her a little of Rose.'

Faye stared at her, a hard, unforgiving stare. 'Really? You think Rose Duncan might have been involved in murdering her own father for the sake of a painting when she, of all people, not only knew that Lady Frances wanted the book buried with her but was in a position to get hold of it without anyone asking too many questions?'

'Someone might have questioned it,' said Doddsy, 'because opening a crypt is a pretty damned odd thing to do unless you've got a good reason.'

'She'd have come up with some story, I suppose,' said Jude, 'but that's not the problem I have. It's why Weston and his pal, whoever she was, went through all the trouble of kidnapping Gil if they were in league with Rose. I might buy into that if that had happened after they'd raided the crypt and found nothing, but not before. Why chase up a clue in the clock when you can go straight to the chapel?'

'That's what was troubling me, too,' confessed Ashleigh. 'But there's something odd about Rose Duncan, if you ask me.'

There was, and it wasn't just that she seemed so strangely attracted to Adam Fleetwood, because Adam, when he wanted, could turn on the charm and also reinterpret his criminal record as a grave injustice. 'We need to talk to her again, too.'

'Perhaps Ashleigh could do that herself,' said Faye, crisply, 'because while I get that as a senior officer you probably should show face at Capel Lodge, I also think you probably ought to spend more time in the office than you do.'

Out of the corner of his eye, Jude saw Doddsy stifling a grin. Even in this day and age, Faye couldn't help a respectful nod towards the aristocracy. 'Fair enough,' he said, 'but I'd like to go down and talk to Emma and Irene sooner rather than later.'

'Tomorrow, then' said Faye, and checked her watch once more.

THIRTY-TWO

'I can't help feeling we're swinging the lead a bit,' said Jude, opening his front door.

'I know. I feel exactly the same way. But I wasn't going to argue and we've both put in the hours.' Ashleigh went ahead of him into the kitchen and dropped two cardboard boxes on the table. 'Shall I put the pizzas in the oven?'

'If you're not bothered, I'm not. They'll be hot enough, I think, and I don't plan for mine to be hanging round long enough to get cold.'

'I'll get plates.'

'Let's go through to the living room. I'm knackered and it always makes me feel a bit better if I behave like a slob.'

'Nothing to do with keeping an eye out for Adam, then?' She'd seen him snatch a quick glance across the street to where Adam was very much in evidence in his living room.

He laughed, rather sheepishly. She knew he tried not to obsess about Adam in the way that Adam so obviously obsessed about him, but there were times when someone needed to tell him to step back. He opened the fridge and got out two bottles of beer. 'He's making himself very obvious, and while I don't like to stare I thought there was someone in there with him and I wonder if it was Rose.'

They went through to the living room and he stood for a second looking down towards Adam's flat while Adam stood in the window and looked towards him, and then the ridiculousness of the matter seemed to strike him and he sat down.

'I'm not going to promise to forget about him, because clearly I won't. But although I can't get my head around what's going on with Rose, on the face of it, I do think if there's anything fishy Adam is pretty much an innocent bystander.'

'I thought he was completely smitten with her at the funeral and that was the first time they'd met.'

'He can move quickly when he wants to. Izzy Ecclestone told Mikey the two of them were snogging in the street — her words, not mine — in Lazonby yesterday. She was pretty much outraged.'

'That's saying something.' Izzy, Mikey's girlfriend, was by any measure a very modern young woman and if she was scandalised a lot of other people in Lazonby and around would be reaching for the smelling salts.

'Adam doesn't always think things through. If Rose asked him to help her with something, would he do it? I don't like to call him a useful idiot but I think he has the potential to be.'

'Love's a strange beast, isn't it?'

Jude sat down on the sofa beside her and they applied themselves to the beer and the pizza. These days Ashleigh found herself increasingly wondering how this relationship was going to pan out, how the perfect partnership they had as friends had somehow failed to blossom into love when the initial infatuation was over, and she guessed he felt the same. There had been a time when he and Ashleigh had first been together when he seemed to find it easy to forget about Becca, just as Ashleigh herself had been happy to have her feelings for her ex-husband to be obscured by that white-hot passion, but the flames had died down. In the embers was a friendship and a trust that would last a lifetime, but there was something else: the feelings they each had for someone else.

Ashleigh would stay overnight, and the sex would be fine and satisfying, fulfilling a need they both felt for human contact when they had had too close a brush with death. But in the great scheme of things it meant nothing, was only a matter of time before one of them cracked and went back to the first flame to try again. She supposed, when it all went wrong for one the other would be there to pick up the pieces — on the surface an ideal relationship, but profoundly lacking in any permanence.

'Are you still in touch with Scott?' asked Jude, once he'd torn though a couple of slices of pizza.

'I've never really not been, apart from that period after I asked for the divorce.'

Scott Kirby had come dangerously close to getting in trouble for harassment at that point. Jude, who detested the type of man Scott personified — glamorous, charming, toxic, constantly straying and always penitent — bit back whatever he had decided not to say, but she could guess. He and Becca had always been friends and their fallout had been a judgment on her part that, he thought, she regretted but was too proud to admit. There had been no angry deterioration, no fights — just a line in the sand between his work and their relationship which she wouldn't cross. With Ashleigh and Scott it was different, always had been. He knew that.

'Still friends?' he asked, lightly.

'I think he's grown up over the last couple of years, but I'm not about to do anything stupid. I've had my fingers burned too often with him.' It was a story as old as time, easy enough to say when Scott wasn't there and she was sitting on the sofa eating pizza and listening to a different lover talking with dull common sense. Anyone could be persuaded, or persuade themselves, of the right thing to do and then do the opposite in a moment of madness.

Maybe Gil, with his notorious intolerance of other people and his fierce independence, had the right idea after all.

Jude applied himself to the rest of the pizza and the subject dropped, or almost. 'I can't believe Adam's involved, but if Rose is, I can see how he might be sucked in.'

'That would be after the fact, though. They hadn't met before the funeral. He can't have been involved in Roger's death.' But he might be involved in a cover-up.

'Another beer?'

'Oh, why the hell not?' Ashleigh got to her feet and began clearing up the remains of the pizza. 'It's Saturday night after all, though it doesn't feel like it.'

'Are you sure you're okay?'

'About this afternoon?' She tipped half a piece of pizza into the bin and then made an unnecessary business of folding up the boxes and sticking them into the recycling, washing her hands, wiping crumbs off the worktop. 'I've been worse. But I'm glad I'm here. I don't think I'd want to be on my own tonight, or even at home with Lisa.' Her housemate was sympathetic, but she wouldn't understand.

'I get that.'

'And we still don't have the bloody *Emperor*,' she said, in tones of frustration, taking the bottle he held out to her.

'If it is the *Emperor*.'

'Of course it is. What else is it going to be? Even if Irene hasn't actually done anything criminal yet, you can bet your life she's planning to, as soon as she gets her hands on it. Where's your tarot deck?'

He went to the side table and took it out, a pack of cards in a tatty paper pack. 'I bet Earl Capel never had a pack like this.' He handed them to her and she sat down, then slipped them out of the pack and fanned them out in her hands. He sat down beside her and leaned in to look. 'You don't read yours any more.'

'I told you. I tore one up. In a fit of temper over Scott, in fact. It was the Three of Swords.' It was a horrible card, one she'd never liked, redolent with loss and bitterness and betrayal. 'It kept coming up and it always reminds me of him, so one day I ripped it in half and put it on the fire.'

'Any regrets?'

Plenty. 'About Scott or the cards?' She laughed. 'Definitely the second. I miss them, and they belonged to my grandmother. But I lived most of my life without them so I daresay I can navigate my way through the rest of it.'

'You can take these, if you'd rather.'

In a strange way this set of cards, a gift from her to him, a cheap purchase in a flea market in Sri Lanka, provided a link between them. Accepting them would feel wrong, as though his tenuous acceptance of her eccentric pastime would be lost. She liked the fact that he kept them, even though he had no time for what they said. 'That's very kind, but it wouldn't feel right. I would like another set, one day, but you know how it is. The cards find you.'

She sorted through them until she found the one she was looking for. 'Here's the Emperor. There are thousands of different interpretations, of course, all different, and this card is unique. But they all have the same elements.'

'Gil would be the Hermit, of course.'

She'd chosen this deck because every card had a tiny drawing of a grey cat lurking knowingly in the image and it reminded her of Holmes. It hadn't struck her when she bought them that Holmes wasn't Jude's cat but Becca's, though for all the attention he paid the one when the other was present he might as well have been. That was another reason why it would be wrong to take them back. In the card, the cat lay curled up in the Emperor's lap, ostensibly fast asleep but with one eye open, gazing adoringly at its master while a tiny mouse crept along the hem of the Emperor's robe.

'Becca's cat looks at you like that,' she said. And so, now she thought about it, did Becca.

'He's an excellent judge of character.'

In the companion card, the Empress, (she sneaked a look with a smile) the cat was fast asleep on the Empress's lap on the sheaf of wheat she held, and the mouse was nibbling away at the grain. She turned the card over. 'I doubt this helps us much.'

'You know I don't believe in all this nonsense,' said Jude, taking the Emperor and looking at it with an expression that exactly matched the one of the figure in the card, 'and I'm the first person to admit it makes no sense to me, but it must mean something to someone.'

'Probably nothing,' said Ashleigh, with a sigh. 'If it did we might work it out. But if it's only what someone else thinks it means, or if it doesn't mean anything at all, this is rather a waste of time.'

'You're probably right.'

It felt good to have a complete deck in her hands again, but even a quick sift through was too full of ideas and echoes and memories, personal ones and nothing to do with Roger Duncan. The Emperor reminded her of Jude and the empress of Becca, and so she shuffled them back into the pack before she could think about it too much longer before, in a moment of weakness, she could seek out the Three of Swords.

THIRTY-THREE

'All right, my lover,' said Rose, taking away the breakfast plates, 'that's enough fun.'

'We can never have enough fun,' said Adam, and winked.

She giggled, and poked him in the ribs. 'I think you've had a very rewarding Sunday morning already, and I even cooked breakfast in your own house. But there's something I need to do.'

'And that is?'

'A little bird told me Wilf Hamley is planning to go up to Capel Lodge this morning, and I'd like to go up there too, and catch a word with him.'

Adam drank the last of his coffee and enjoyed looking at Rose's backside as she bent to load the dishwasher. 'Can't we speak to him at his house?'

'Violet will be there. That's Mrs Wilf. I was speaking to her yesterday, in a very roundabout way, and she mentioned it. Which is good, because whenever he's done what he plans to do, I'd like to have a word with him.'

By now Rose had filled Adam in with the gossip about

Wilf's financial situation. He had initially treated it with a degree of scepticism because he knew how rumours took wing — and had used the bush telegraph in exactly that way for his own purposes in the past — but it hadn't taken long to convince him. In any case, the source of her information seemed impeccable — her murdered father.

'Are you sure you shouldn't tell someone?' He couldn't quite bring himself to say *the police* because that would involve helping Jude and he had no intention of doing that.

'They'll probably find out for themselves, but you know how it is. You've told me yourself how these things get personal.'

He got to his feet, nodding, and wandered through to the living room to glance up the street. The curtains were open in Jude's bedroom and his car had gone. So, no long Sunday morning for Jude and his sexy blonde. And yes, he knew exactly how these things panned out. He might have tried harder to persuade Rose to leave everything in the hands of the police if it hadn't been for the thought of Jude solving the mystery with a flourish and taking all the credit for it. 'Your really do think he killed your dad, don't you?'

'I really think he had a very good reason to. But actually I think he's a coward.'

'So no, then?'

'Cowards can accidentally get very brave. Or accidentally fire a gun.' She picked up her bag from the hall table. 'Let's go.'

Outside the summer air was soft and fresh, cool for the time of year. The church bells rang from St Andrew's for the morning service, and reminded him. 'Isn't it a bit early for him to be at Capel Lodge?'

'We can wait if he isn't there.'

She had no intention of announcing herself, then, only

of lurking in the grounds to catch a word with the errant Wilf. Internally, Adam shrugged. There would be no harm in having a chat with the man, and his presence would be a comfort to Rose as it had been previously. He was desperate for her to think well of him, to believe he would be there for her when she needed him.

He opened the car door for her, something he'd never troubled to do for any other woman, then went round to the driver's side and got in. 'Capel Lodge, then, Ma'am,' he said and winked, touching an imaginary cap.

'Via Lazonby, if you don't mind, Driver.' She touched his knee and gave him a look full of fun and love and all the other things he'd never until then realised had been missing from his life.

'That's a bit of a long way round.'

'There's something I want to pick up.'

He drove slowly along Beacon Edge, taking his time and savouring the pleasure of being alone with her. After a few miles he dropped down through Great Salkeld, on the opposite bank of the River Eden from Capel Lodge. Here the river wound its way out of sight through a deep cleft, its steeply wooded bank rising towards Long Meg and offering a glimpse of the solid stone and old slate roof of Capel Lodge. From this angle the building showed its stern, northwards-looking aspect rather than its frivolous Victorian one, frowning at them from its vantage point on the hill.

'Your place?' he said, as they approached the village.

'Not just now. Wilf's.'

She gestured to the large villa and Adam, obedient, turned off on the side road and pulled up by the kerb. 'But I thought you wanted—'

'Yes, we'll go up to Capel Lodge in a bit. He and Violet are at church right now, so we've got a bit of time.'

'I think love's addled my brain,' he said, placing a hand on her knee, 'but I don't understand what you want.'

'I want to have a look in his desk.' Rose opened the car door, jumped out and walked briskly up the side of the house. With a nervous look around for any twitching curtains, Adam followed her, trying to look as if he had every right to be where he was. When he reached the back door Rose had her hand on the door handle of the back door.

'I feel a bit bad about this,' she said, 'because Violet is such a lovely woman, really nice and far too good for Wilf. But she has this complete faith in human nature and she loves the fact that she lives in a rural area and can leave the back door open so the neighbours can drop any parcels off inside. Dad always used to tell her, everyone always used to tell her, but she always used to say *I've never been burgled yet.*'

'And are we burgling her?' asked Adam, helplessly.

'No. I want to have a quick look in Wilf's desk and you can sit out here and have a smoke, and if anybody comes — which they won't, because the only place that overlooks it is the Foxes' and they'll be at church too — then we'll tell them I'm dropping off some papers for Wilf that I found in Dad's office. Which I will, if I have to, but only if I have to because I'd rather he didn't know I was looking in his desk.'

She put her hand to the door and it opened, noiselessly. Adam sat on the step in the shade and fiddled with the packet of cigarettes in his pocket, though he hoped they wouldn't be there long enough for him to have a smoke and certainly not long enough for someone to turn up and demand an explanation. And it turned out to be even swifter than he'd thought. It took less than two minutes before Rose's slim figure reappeared in the kitchen.

'That's that, then,' she said, as he got up. 'Job done.'

'Won't they notice?' he asked, with a trace of nerves as he watched her close the door behind her and then set off down towards the car. 'What if they call the police?' Fingerprints would be the first thing they'd look at and and he didn't need Jude or one of his smug detective sergeants coming round to quiz him about whether or not he knew where Rose had been on Sunday morning.

'They won't. I didn't take anything. Violet's peace of mind can remain undisturbed.'

'Then why were you here?' he asked, again opening the car door for her.

'I just wanted to check something in his desk.'

'And did you find it?'

'Oh yes,' she said, with a satisfied smile, 'I most certainly did.'

THIRTY-FOUR

Doddsy called as Jude and Ashleigh were chewing the fat, literally and metaphorically, over a bacon roll in the one cafe that was open at an ungodly hour on a godly day of the week.

'Some good news for you at last,' he said cheerfully as Jude picked up the phone and, aware of the fact that the only other occupants of the cafe who seemed far more interested in planning their upcoming holiday might eavesdrop, kept it off speaker but held it away from him so Ashleigh could hear.

'About time, too,' she said, darkly, and sipped her coffee.

'Have we got our man, or is that too much to hope for?' asked Jude.

'We have.' Even at that time on a Sunday morning Doddsy sounded smugly satisfied. 'He got picked up at Penrith station about an hour or so. One of the station staff thought he looked a bit suspicious, hanging around the vending machine and looking like a down-and-out, so called us to check. It's him all right. Toby Weston.'

Thank God. If the man was in custody then the immediate threat to both Becca and Gil was pretty much removed. True, there was still his co-conspirator to think about but both of them had been much less concerned about her and identified him as the real danger. 'Anything useful from him yet?'

'Give a man a chance. I'm heading down to ask him a few penetrating questions about what the hell he thinks he was playing at, while you're taking tea with the aristocracy.'

'Mind and ask him where he was hiding.' Jude thought again of Irene, and of the narrow back corridors and cupboards that burrowed behind and underneath Capel Lodge. 'We've a few questions for Irene, too.'

'Faye said. You surely don't think she was hiding him?'

'I don't know. But I'll ask.'

He ended the call and finished his coffee, abandoning the remnants of the bacon roll, thick with pale fat, on the plate. Ashleigh had barely touched hers, he noted. 'Let's go. Irene's expecting us?'

'I texted her to confirm,' she said, getting up and picking up her bag.

'Are you sure you're okay?' he asked, when her silence had persisted from Penrith all the way to Capel Lodge. She had been efficient and businesslike over breakfast but he was left with a niggling feeling that something was very wrong.

'Of course.'

'We both had a bit of a shock yesterday,' he said, understating it, 'and I know I've said it before but I'm going to check again. Are you sure you're fine? If necessary I can handle this myself—'

'I told you yesterday. I'm fine and I want to get this dealt with. Irene might come at me with a silver-plated fish knife, I suppose, but I reckon I can handle that, even if I don't know which hand to hold it in.' They were approaching the gates of Capel Lodge as she spoke, but she made a point of looking out of the car window. 'There's no need to go on about your duty of care. It takes way more than yesterday to knock the stuffing out of me.'

'But something's bothering you.'

'This is what happens when you work with someone who knows you too well,' she said, and forced a laugh. 'Yes, there is, but it isn't work. Now don't worry. I'm a grown up girl and I've got a job to do. Let's get on with it. '

It wasn't professional it was personal, and if it was personal and she wasn't telling him, after all they'd talked about the previous evening and the night they'd spent together, he should keep out of it. But somehow they were still together, or he thought they were, and so he dared to ask. 'Scott, then.' He'd seen her stealing a look at the Three of Swords, with its triple knives spearing a bleeding heart and the tiny grey cat snarling ferociously as it spread three savage claws, before sliding it back into the deck.

'We can talk about it later.'

He stopped for a quick word with the policeman on the gate and crunched over the broken cattle grid and up the long stretch of gravel to the Lodge. He'd always sensed this moment would come, that Ashleigh would start thinking fondly once more of the ex-husband who was her one true love. Scott Kirby had proved cruel, coercive and manipulative until she'd had no option but to find the courage to leave him, but time healed wounds and eventually pain became memories, and even the worst of those faded. The only question was what had triggered it. That moment in the crypt, perhaps, when she must have sensed the presence of death as clearly as he had, and her thoughts, like his, must have fled to the people they cared about.

'Right,' he said, unable to let it go. 'We can go for a drink this evening and talk about it then.'

'We can. If we ever get off duty.' She fussed with something on her sleeve as the car drew up.

'Good point.'

They got out of the car, and Irene was at the door even before they reached it. 'Chief Inspector, Sergeant. I meant to tell you. Miss Capel got back from London late last night. She's in the library, waiting for you. I'll get Carly to make us some tea.'

Jude and Ashleigh exchanged a quick glance. This routine call was in danger of becoming a circus. Irene must have heard about the drama at the chapel — the whole neighbourhood would be buzzing with some version or other — and her anxiety was obvious.

'It's very kind of you, but this is just a quick visit for information purposes.'

'Lady Frances would never have allowed—'

'Please,' said Ashleigh, pulling herself together and smiling at Irene until the elderly lady calmed down. 'That's very kind, and of course you and Miss Capel must have tea if you feel you normally would, but we really wouldn't like you to put yourself to any trouble for us.'

Irene, he saw, was relieved. Spared the social elements, she thought she could escape the place. 'I'll take you through to the library.'

It would be useful to speak to Emma and see if any echo of the family scandal had reached her distant branch of the family, but he wasn't going to let Irene escape the interview. 'Yourself, too, Miss Jenkins.'

She deflated, and led them into the study with her head drooping slightly, but she remembered herself enough to hide it when in the presence of her boss. It wouldn't do, thought Jude with a sudden surge of sympathy for her, to give Emma Capel any reason to think she wasn't up to the job and could be justifiably eased out of it. Poor Irene, unwittingly a problem for her employer.

'I've been hearing such terrible stories about what's been happening,' said Emma, getting up to greet them, 'and I'm so glad to hear that everyone is all right.'

'Yes, I'm afraid there was an incident,' Jude reassured her, 'and a man is under arrest.' He kept an eye on Irene as they sat, with Emma in Lady Frances's armchair, the two detectives on either side and Irene perched on a stool by the door, but the older woman's face showed no flicker of either anxiety or relief. 'The main reason for our visit is to ask if you can help us with any information about this man. His name is Toby Weston.'

Emma frowned and shook her head. 'I've never heard the name. Have you, Irene?'

Irene pulled her thin cashmere cardigan (slightly faded but definitely good quality, something that might have been a hand-me-down from her late employer) around her thin body as if to ward off a sudden draught. 'I've never heard of a Toby Weston, but there was a Thomas Weston who used to work for the seventh Earl. Twm, we always called him. But dear me, he left after the Earl died and we never heard any more of him. He was of an age with him. Twm must have been dead for years.'

Jude did the maths in his head. It was most likely that Toby, if he was related, would be a grandson or a great-nephew. 'Did Twm have a family?'

'I'm sure he must have done, but I didn't really know him well. He was very much one of the servants.' Irene blushed slightly, acknowledging the awkwardness of her own situation, and surely she couldn't have missed Emma's roll of the eyes at such blatant class distinction. 'But the Earl was very fond of him, and Twm was very capable, very clever, but not educated. The Earl always turned to him when there was a problem, as well as when he needed manpower. I know Lady Frances's father, the eighth Earl, asked him to stay on after the seventh Earl died, but he declined.' She paused.

Jude picked up on her hesitation. 'Was there a disagreement?'

Irene folded her lips. 'There were strong words spoken. The eighth Earl was always reclusive — he had a bad war — and intended that Lady Frances should play a significant part in overseeing the estate. Twm said he would never take instructions from a woman. As you can imagine, that did *not* make a good impression on Lady Frances, and her father took her side.'

Quite right too!' said Emma. 'Outrageous!'

'You don't know where Twm Weston went?'

'Llandudno, I believe. I think that was where he came from originally and so it would make sense that he went back there.' Irene was looking anxious again. 'But goodness me, surely if this man you've arrested is somehow related to Twm — that's what you're implying, I think — what could he want? Why would he kill Roger? That must be what he's been arrested for?'

'He's been arrested in connection with a number of counts of theft, kidnapping and attempted murder,' said Jude, matter-of-factly. 'What we're trying to establish is how he came to be in this area and why. Can you tell us anything about Twm? Was he at Castell Capel during the War, for example?'

'Yes, he was there all the time. He never left the seventh Earl. I think he must have been too old for military service, or else he somehow got an exemption or managed to persuade them he was engaged in important work. Or perhaps the Earl couldn't manage without him and pulled strings to keep him.'

'And as the Earl's trusted man,' went on Jude, 'would he have been associated with the storage of the paintings and was he involved in the rescue of them?'

'I'm quite sure he would have been. I fact I think I heard that it was he who went into the burning building to bring the Earl out that final time. The story is that the Earl was furious with him because it was his intervention that prevented the painting of the Emperor being saved.'

'My word!' said Emma. 'Is that old story really true, then?'

Jude looked across at Ashleigh and caught her eye. She was thinking the same as he was, that this was the link that brought Toby Weston and his partner in crime to the Eden Valley. A tale told by a grandfather, perhaps on his death bed and not taken seriously, might have taken root in a young Toby's head — a tale of treasure that hadn't been destroyed, but was hidden. And something — pure chance, perhaps, or a memory triggered by the news that Lady Frances was dying — had led the younger Weston to seek this missing painting while no-one was looking for it. But how had he heard about the book and the clock?

He dithered, wondering whether to challenge Irene on the spot or whether to leave and go back and make sure Doddsy, who had the task of questioning Toby Weston, was fully briefed. The decision was made for him by a knock on the door and the appearance of Carly, the cook.

'I'm terribly sorry to bother you,' she said, looking anxious, 'but Mr Hamley's just arrived, and in a bit of a dither.'

'Oh dear,' said Emma, rather helplessly. 'Is it urgent? Could you tell him we have visitors and ask him to come back later? Would you mind?'

'I did say that, Miss Capel, and I did explain that the police were here, but it isn't actually you he wants to speak to. It's Miss Jenkins.'

Irene's head jerked upwards, and the look on her face shifted in an instant from one of dutiful respect to one of anxiety. She said: 'Oh, but I don't think—' and looked across at Jude as if for help.

'You can ask him to wait, perhaps?' suggested Emma, obviously unaware of his earlier visit.

Irene stared at Jude, eyes wide, twisting her fingers together. He came to a snap decision. If, as he suspected, Wilf Hamley was both a bully and a coward, the last thing he would react well to was a direct challenge.

'Just send him in,' he said cheerfully. 'I'd quite like to listen to what he has to say. Assuming you don't mind, Miss Jenkins.'

For a second he thought Irene Jenkins looked almost amused. 'I don't mind at all. I'd be quite happy for you to hear what he has to say.'

'Goodness me, Irene,' said Emma, rather testily. 'Don't tell me you're involved with the police. Any more than the rest of us, I mean.'

Carly closed the door behind her and there were voices in the hall outside. A moment later the door reopened and Wilf Hamley, neat in a suit and tie, popped his head in.

'Oh,' he said, in some surprise. 'Your housekeeper didn't say… I was hoping for a private word with Irene.' His gaze flicked across the room at Jude and Ashleigh. 'Perhaps I could…'

Jude got to his feet and introduced himself. 'There's no need for you to go, Mr Hamley. We were hoping for a word with you later and this is as good a time as any.'

'Really?' He swallowed, nervously, and looked round for a seat, but there were none to spare. Emma Capel wasn't for moving so the two men stood in the centre of the room.

'Yes. I believe you've been looking for a book that was left to Miss Jenkins.'

In the small silence, Wilf took a long sigh and loosened his tie. 'She told you, then.'

'Rightly so. May I ask you why you were so keen to get hold of it?'

'Oh God,' said Wilf, miserably. 'Oh God. You know, don't you? You know about the money. You know about the...' He stuttered to a halt and didn't meet Jude's eye.

Ashleigh, too, was on her feet. Like Jude, she would be all too aware that the person who had known where the book was was Roger and that the gun that had killed him had never been found.

'About the what?' said Jude, into the deadly stillness.

He licked his lips. 'About the business take-over. About the small technical problem with the money.'

'What we would call fraud, I think,' said Jude, dryly.

'Yes, but...but I didn't kill him.'

Another silence. 'Did I suggest you did?'

A dry croak rose from Wilf's throat. 'I didn't. I didn't.'

'But you had a row?'

'I asked him about the book and he wouldn't give it to me. He wouldn't help me. I tried to explain why it mattered. I tried to explain why I needed the money. But he wouldn't listen. He didn't understand. He told me I'd go to prison and I deserved to. God, I did like him, but he was a bit too upright, a bit too judgmental of other people's opinions. So unbearably smug and pious!'

'And what happened then?' asked Jude.

What happened then was that the door opened and Rose Duncan walked through it.

THIRTY-FIVE

Rose was dressed casually, in jeans and trainers with a light sweatshirt and a shoulder bag slung across her body, and looked absurdly young. Her face was fresh and make-up free and her hair tied back; as she turned sideways, she flicked it away from her eyes. She took in the assembled company, looking past Irene and Emma and dwelling a little more thoughtfully on the two detectives, but it was on Wilf Hamley that she concentrated. 'Wilf. Good morning.'

'What are you doing here, Rose?' he said, and his voice quavered.

'I came out for a walk,' she said, 'and saw your car.'

'There was a police officer at the gate,' said Jude, fascinated. 'Didn't he stop you?'

'No, I came up through the woods. I walked up with Adam and he doesn't like the police, or rather they don't like him, so we avoided them. But don't worry, he won't come in. I mean, there are enough people here already, aren't there?'

There was a bright hardness to her voice that Jude

recognised as indicating that she'd been caught unawares. To avoid the policeman at the gate had required deliberate effort, and the knowledge that Adam was somewhere around didn't cheer him. He could see Ashleigh sending a sly text, no doubt to whoever was at the gate. He waited for Rose to give herself away.

'I was so upset to hear about what happened up at Long Meg,' she said, looking round the circle of people staring at her. 'That poor woman, Raven. And so close to your chapel, Miss Capel.'

'Who is Raven?' asked Emma, bewildered.

'Are you all right, Rose?' asked Irene. 'Perhaps all the strain of what happened to your poor father…'

'Exactly right.' Rose's voice snapped with sudden resolve. 'I'm sure you're almost there, Chief Inspector, but just in case you aren't, I'd better tell you. It was Wilf who murdered my father.'

'Now, Rose, you really mustn't rush to conclusions,' he said, beginning strongly but soon deteriorating into a desperate bleat. 'I was just explaining what happened. We had words in the garden, Roger and I, but words between friends are soon forgotten and soon forgiven.'

The word *forgiven* was a mistake. Rose's expression hardened. 'I know what you wanted from my father. I don't know why you wanted it but it was important enough to you for you to kill him.'

'No.' Sweat prickled on Wilf's top lip. 'I swear it. He was alive when I left him in the garden. That housekeeper of yours saw me, Miss Capel. I'm sure she did. Surely she mentioned it, officer?' He looked pleadingly at Jude.

She hadn't, as far as he was aware. Maybe she hadn't seen him. Either way Wilf had made himself the prime suspect for a murder, if not for a kidnapping. 'What exactly did you say to Mr Duncan when he refused to tell you about the book?'

'Nothing. I...I walked away. A funeral isn't the right place for that sort of thing. I thought I'd talk to him again and persuade him. And as for killing him...I'm not a violent man. And I don't have a gun.'

'Liar,' said Rose, calmly. She gestured to the wall behind her. 'Lady Frances gave you a gun. She gave my father a gun, too. I think she even gave the vicar a gun. God knows why. The one she gave us didn't work, though, and my father gave it to the amateur dramatic society.'

'Lady Frances never liked the guns,' said Irene, in a small voice. 'I told the police that. I expect she wanted to get rid of them so she just gave them away.'

'I remember, now.' Wilf's face was pale. He plucked at the knot of his tie again and looked at Jude, pleadingly. 'It must have been a couple of years ago. I'd quite forgotten about it.'

'Forgotten?' said Jude, 'in the circumstances? When we knew a murder was committed by an historic weapon and you had just such a one in your possession,?' He nodded at Rose. 'Allegedly.'

'It was quite put out of my mind. I never thought of it. It was just a toy, just a curiosity. I don't think I could even tell you where it is now.'

'More lies. I know where you kept the gun, Wilf. You kept it in your desk. Because I've just been at your house and I went in and took it.' Her hand went to the bag.

Jude, the closest to her, found himself staring at a gun for the second time in two days, but this time it was different. He was within easy reach of it and it wasn't pointed at him. In a second, he had closed his hand on Rose's and forced it down. The soft little click from the weapon led to no explosion, no screams, no ricochet, no deaths. The gun didn't work.

'Help! Police!' With great presence of mind, Emma Capel jumped from her chair, and shouted through the open window.

Rose let go of the gun and it dropped to the floor where Ashleigh swooped to pick it up.

'In here!' From the hallway, Carly's voice, high-pitched in panic, was followed almost immediately by footsteps and the entrance of the uniformed officer whom Ashleigh had summoned from outside. In the middle of the commotion, in that packed room, Jude held Rose's wrist and the two of them stared at each other.

'I would have done it,' she said to him. 'I would have done. Because of what he did. I would have enjoyed it.'

'Rose Duncan,' he said to her, unheeding. 'You're under arrest for the attempted murder of Wilf Hamley.'

The officer detached handcuffs from his belt and clasped them on her wrist. Jude followed as they led her out of the room and into the dim, panelled hallway.

'Rose! Are you all right?' Adam Fleetwood, who had been sitting in the hallway, erupted to his feet, saw the two officers and the handcuffs, erupted in fury. 'What the hell are you doing, Judas? Take your hands off her!' He shoved his way past the two officers and squared up. 'This is your idea of revenge, isn't it, your vendetta against me? As soon as I find someone I care about you're there, aren't you? Making trouble for me by making trouble for her.'

Jude shoved him away. 'Keep right out of this, Adam. It's nothing to do with you.'

'You haven't heard the last of it. Rose, I'll make damned sure they let you go. You can trust me.'

'But I did it,' said Rose, her composure finally cracking. 'I did try and kill him. I wanted him to die, just like my father died, and I wanted him to see me.' She turned to Adam and her nostrils flared in contempt. 'You talk. It's all you ever do. I didn't want to be eaten up like you, my heart black and corrupted. You only ever talk about how miserable you are. At least I tried to change things.'

Adam's expression was dark with fury and he turned it towards Jude just as another couple of uniformed police officers appeared. Charlie Fry, the more experienced of them, and always remarkably cheerful when physical violence had been avoided and no blood spilt, glared at Adam.

'Enough, lad,' he said, and looked quizzically at Jude.

'Attempted murder,' said Jude wearily. 'Can you get her booked into custody? Ashleigh and I'll get witness statements sorted here.' He turned his back on Adam and Rose to head back into the study. Ashleigh came out as he did so, handling the gun very gingerly and passing it on to another of the officers.

'Everything okay in there?' he asked her.

'Yes.' She paused and lowered her voice. 'We need to go back in and talk to them. Now.'

She wasn't, he sensed, talking about the humdrum business of notes and statements. 'Has something else happened?' He racked his brain. What had he missed?

'No, but there's something going on and I can't put my finger on it.'

'What do you mean?'

'Irene. I mean, she's just watched all that drama and she thought Wilf was here to threaten her so she must have been terrified, and yet when I looked at her just as I came out she looked so relaxed. So smug she was almost triumphant. She knows something, and I sure as hell want to find out what it is before she gets a chance to cover up for herself.'

'About the painting?'

'Maybe that, but maybe about Gil, too, and even about Roger. I know it's impossible for her to have done it, because she was in the ballroom the whole time, but maybe she knows who did.'

'Make sure you arrest that man, too,' called out Rose, as Charlie led her away. 'Make sure you do. Because he killed my father. I know he did.'

Jude stared after her. If the gun Rose had turned on Wilf Hamley was the one she'd taken from his home, she was wrong about his guilt. It didn't work. If he had killed Roger it would surely have been with the gun he thought no-one knew about — and there wasn't a shred of evidence that Wilf's version of events was anything but the truth.

'You're right,' he said, turning to the door. 'We need to deal with Irene.'

'Is everything all right?' asked Emma when they returned to the library. 'Irene, you'd better ask Carly to fetch poor Mr Hamley a brandy or something.'

'You look quite faint, Mr Hamley,' said Irene, warmly, heading for the door, 'and I'm not surprised. What a terrible thing to happen. Poor Rose must have quite taken leave of her senses, though that's hardly a surprise after what the poor girl has been through.'

Emma Capel was rather more cynical, thought Jude, watching her watching Wilf, who had sunk into one of the chairs, through narrowed eyes.

'It's just as well for you the gun wasn't working, Mr Hamley,' she said and turned back to Jude. 'And for you, too. I wonder how many of these dangerous little toys my cousin distributed across the countryside?'

'I don't suppose we'll ever know.'

'I do hope they don't keep coming back to haunt you.'

They surely would, given they had no idea how many had gone and how many of those were usable. The one that had killed Roger Duncan had been; the one that had gone to Wilf had not. There could be any number, anywhere, and the game of roulette could roll on through the years.

'Carly is getting you a drink, Mr Hamley,' said Irene, coming back in and resuming her seat with a benevolent smile.

Ashleigh was right. She looked as if the weight of the world had been lifted from her shoulders. Trying not to arouse too much interest, he looked away from all three of them and left the vacant seat to Ashleigh, going instead to take his place at the window. The police van was driving off with Rose inside, and a uniformed officer wasescorting Adam to a patrol car and off to give a statement at the police station.

Adam's humiliation when Rose had turned on him had seemed total, but his fury took the channel it always did. He looked back towards the Lodge to shout an obscenity and waved two fingers at his old adversary.

Jude turned back to the matter in hand. 'We haven't finished what we came here for. I want to ask you more about the book and the ledger and the history of the Burne-Jones *Emperor*. You, in particular, Miss Jenkins.'

'It does strike me,' said Emma, thoughtfully, 'that my cousin Frances was a dangerous woman as well as an extraordinary and eccentric one. This wild and irresponsible distribution of weapons is another example of this. There was no reason to what she did, abut she did like causing consternation.'

She'd certainly done that. 'I'm sure I've asked you this before, Miss Jenkins, but I want to go over it again. There must be a reason why Lady Frances didn't just give you the book and the clock, or indeed give you whatever it was she wanted you to have.'

Her smile was almost a smirk. She fought to control it and failed. 'That was Lady Frances for you. As Miss Capel says, she was an eccentric.'

'It was the Burne-Jone *Emperor*, wasn't it?'

'The painting was destroyed,' she reminded him.

'But you described it in detail. There's no record of it other than the preliminary sketch, so you must have seen it. It wasn't destroyed. Lady Frances gave it to you, didn't she?' The clock and the book had been a wild goose chase to keep anyone else off the scent, to protect Irene and to make sure she received adequate payment for her service. He would have felt admiration for her if it hadn't been for Roger Duncan's death and all that he himself, that Gil and Becca and Rose and even Ashleigh, had had to endure as a result. 'We never found anything because there was nothing to find.' But Toby had thought there was, and someone had killed for it.

'I can't comment on what Lady Frances intended and clearly we can't ask her now,' said Irene, with spirit.

'She told me something about a treasure,' said Wilf, his voice a deep growl that showed he'd recovered enough from being threatened by Rose to be angry at being taken in by his client.

'I'm sure she did. I'm equally sure she had no idea you'd act on it in quite the way you did. Where is the painting, Miss Jenkins?'

'A brandy for Mr Hamley,' said Carly, coming in through the door and setting it down beside him.

'Miss Jenkins?'

'I—' Her eyes flicked round the room in panic, at the dusty bookshelves, at the wall empty of its weapons, at the strange collection of dingy oil paintings.

At the print of the Dalí *Empress*.

Ashleigh was already on her feet, crossing the room to lift it down. 'It's here, isn't it?'

Silence. She turned the picture over and tore away the masking tape that held a sheet of cardboard over the back. Inside, the colours of the Burne-Jones *Emperor* danced and gleamed in the daylight, fresh as the green and vermilion and indigo in the garden outside.

'My word!' said Emma Capel. 'Isn't that the dreadful print you said you wanted as a memento, Irene? May I see what was behind it?'

Jude nodded, and as Ashleigh went to hand it over to her, Carly stepped in to take it from her. 'Goodness me,' she said, forgetting her station. 'how extraordinary. Such a beautiful thing.'

Jude looked at her and his memory jarred by what Wilf had said. Carly was in the garden and had seen him but she hadn't said. Why not? She was the same height as Rose Duncan, the same build. Who had had access to the wall of death? Who could have hidden Toby Weston at Capel Lodge? 'Beautiful enough to kill for, Ms Weston?'

It was a guess, as lucky as Ashleigh's had been. Carly's movements hadn't after all, reminded him of Rose but of the man who had kidnapped Gil and Becca and trapped himself and Ashleigh in the crypt.

'What?' she said, and took a step backwards.

'You were in the garden when Roger Duncan died. Mr Hamley here saw you, and neither of you mentioned it. He didn't because he knew it would implicate him in the murder and I imagine you didn't for the same reason. You must have overheard their argument. What happened then? Did you wait until Wilf had left, ask Roger about the book, and shoot him when he refused to tell you?'

'But it's ours,' she said, her fingers tightening on it. 'It belongs to the family. The seventh Earl promised it to my grandfather and he told Toby and me that we could get it when the old woman died.'

'Toby is…who?'

'My cousin.' Her voice tightened. 'This is mine, not hers.' She looked at Irene with fury. 'I want it.'

'I think you'll find it belongs to the nation,' Jude said. 'Hand it over to DS O'Halloran. I'm placing you under arrest, Carly Weston, for the murder of Roger Duncan, for the abduction of Gilbert Foley and—'

Carla turned like a cat and made for the door, but she reached into her pocket as she did so and Jude saw, too late, that another of Lady Frances's unwanted weapons had found its way into circulation. The gun flashed and the shot, thank God, missed him; he crashed into Carly and forced her to the ground, twisting her arm behind her back and sending the gun spiralling away.

'Hey! What's happening?' From outside Charlie Fry, anxious now, called out his heavy footsteps thudded towards the door.

'Get the gun, Ash,' called Jude, as Charlie burst into the room.

'Sergeant, are you hurt?' said Emma, her voice pitched high with concern.

Jude left Carly Weston to Charlie's less-than-tender ministrations and struggled to his feet, turning with dread. Ashleigh, stood leaning against the wall with a hand on her chest and blood seeping between her fingers.

'Fine, Jude,' she said. 'I'm just fine.'

THIRTY-SIX

'It was obvious,' Ashleigh said, 'really obvious. I don't know how I didn't spot it earlier. That one print when everything else was quirky and original, and the print itself was the direct opposite of the *Emperor* and yet a pair to it. The two cards are very different but they belong together. But we got there in the end.'

They had, but at a price. Briefly, Jude remembered that moment in the library when he'd feared Ashleigh had avoided the ricocheting bullet in the crypt only to fall victim to it in the study, but he blanked it out. She'd survived. You didn't dare dwell on what might have been. 'Smart work, Ash. Really smart.'

She was sitting up in bed in the hospital in Carlisle, looking remarkably cheerful. A flesh wound was all she had to show for the adventure, and Jude thought he might be in more discomfort from a thumping headache. 'Irene did rather give herself away, though. They often do. Did Carly confess?'

'Yes. Killing was never in her plan, so she says, but she overheard Roger talking to Wilf and thought she could get him to tell her where the painting was. He refused and told her he would speak to Emma Capel about it, and she felt she had no alternative but to kill him and hope the blame fell on Wilf.'

He'd pushed his chair a little further back from the bed than he might have done if they hadn't shared that conversation the previous night. Before then he would have pulled it right up and sat holding her hand, but her confession had changed their relationship, so subtly that he couldn't understand. It didn't matter how much she denied that she was thinking of going back to Scott, or how much she really meant it; her ex-husband was her weak spot and all three of them knew it. Jude would always be second best, even though they were still lovers — a strange situation, one he didn't know how to handle, so he kept it cool and professional and talked about Carly Weston, her confession, about how she and her cousin Toby had hatched their plans to get hold of a picture they believed was theirs and would bring them enough money to make them comfortable and satisfy their late grandfather's sense of honour.

'Toby was the leader,' he said, watching as she laid her hand on the blanket. 'He was the brains man, which isn't to say he didn't make mistakes or fail to think things through properly. He was the ruthless one. It wasn't hard for Carly to get a job at Capel Lodge. She bigged up a North Wales connection and she was a shoo-in. She did the listening and asked the questions and — crucially — acquired a gun, though eventually Toby got a rather more reliable one of his own. Lady Frances had been laying a trail about the missing picture and Carly had been listening in and fell right into the trap. She was able to acquire the clock but Frances had already passed the book on to Roger Duncan. And she hid Toby after we rescued Gil.'

'And the picture was there in plain sight, all the time,' said Ashleigh, ruefully. 'I should have guessed. I noticed it the first time I was there. It's so striking, and I've always had a fondness for that card. I always aspired to be The Empress but of course I never will be. She represents someone much more controlled and sensible than I'll ever be. But she's the partner card for the Emperor. It makes perfect sense that Lady Frances would have left that kind of clue as well.'

'I'm not altogether sure I would have got on with her but from what I hear I think she might have grudgingly accepted being beaten, given the way you spotted it.' He heard his own voice sounding clipped and distant.

'I don't know. At that point I was feeling very negative about the cards. Nothing seems to have been quite right in my personal life since I stopped reading them. I don't know whether I just took confidence from them last night or what,'

'But you know it's all nonsense,' he couldn't stop himself saying.

'Up to a point.' She twitched her hand a little further away from his, even though he hadn't moved. 'What happens to the Burne-Jones *Emperor* now? My goodness, it was beautiful.'

The glimpse he'd had of it, its colours shimmering like a dragonfly's wing, had shown him why it was so highly valued. 'It's on its way to London to be verified. If we want to see it again we'll have to go down to the National Gallery.'

'And everyone else? they're all fine? Is Gil still in hospital?'

'No. They let him go home this morning, fighting fit and very grumpy.'

'And Becca?'

'I imagine she's fine.'

'You imagine?' she said, with the slightest edge to her voice.

So she thought the same about him and Becca as he did about her and Scott. He hadn't wanted the conversation to go this way. It was early evening and he hadn't stopped for more than ten minutes, or eaten more than a sub-standard petrol station sandwich. Now he had a roaring headache and hadn't had time to process his thoughts. 'I'm going on to pick her up from Keswick and drop her home. I'll be visiting my mum anyway.'

The silence that came between them on the rare occasions when Ashleigh tried to remind him of his feelings for Becca as a means of cooling down their already on-off relationship, was broken by a tap at the door and the unlikely appearance of — of all people — Geri Foster.

'I'm on a mission,' she said, by way of greeting. 'I'm sorry to hear what happened to you, Sergeant O'Halloran.' That was her one concession to courtesy, a dip of the head to respectability and convention before she went back to her irreverent self. 'Good to see not all the police hide in their offices when there's danger about, though.'

Knowing she was fishing for a contentious reply, Jude let it pass and Ashleigh, who had never got on with her, did the same.

'Is your dad all right?' he asked her, to move the conversation on and because he did care. Without Raven, Storm would be lost, and he wasn't the only one. Mikey's goth girlfriend, Izzy, had been very close to her and even Jude himself would miss her gentle, slightly exasperated presence on the occasions he found himself up near the New Agers' field at Long Meg.

She shrugged. 'No. Which is ridiculous, because he knew it was coming. We all did. So all he's done since is sit in the sun and weep and talk about how he won't manage without her, while completely ignoring any practical suggestions as to how he can move on.'

'He'll find that hard.'

'Very. Although I had a call from Emma Capel just as I arrived and she's offered to let us bury Mum in the grounds of the chapel. At least Dad won't have to go trailing up to Penrith cemetery if he wants to have a chat with her. That's one less thing for me to tick off my to-do list. Which is how I find myself here.'

Her brisk brand of common sense was the last thing Storm would need. Jude always found it odd that Geri had turned out so brutally practical when both her parents had been much more attuned to feelings and thoughts.

'I almost daren't ask,' said Ashleigh, and she did look a little apprehensive, as if she expected Geri to deliver some kind of complaint about how they'd handled Raven's death.

'Oh, don't worry. I'm not here to weep at your sick bed or anything. But there's something my mother wanted you to have.'

'Me?' said Ashleigh, in some surprise.

'Yes. I've told you she liked you, God knows why. Not that I mean that personally, but she really didn't like the police and she'd had plenty of reason not to. However. She did like you and so before she died she told my father she wanted you to have her tarot cards.' She fished in her bag and brought out a packet wrapped in purple silk. 'They're pretty tattered and I don't know why she thought you'd want them, being a policewoman and as hard-headed as the rest, but there you have it. She said to take very great care over how you read them and what they're trying to tell you.' She handed the packet over. 'She didn't leave anything for you, Chief Inspector, except kind words, but they have a value of their own.'

'Thank you.' Ashleigh took the packet and turned it over in her hands, slowly.

'I can see by the way you're smiling that you and she had a secret I'm not in on. Never mind. I'm only the messenger. I wish you joy of them. And I will say that they always seemed to have a very calming effect on my mum.' She checked her watch. 'I can't stop. I have to go and worry about an undertaker, now, since obviously using Duncans is out of the question.'

'On a Sunday evening?' asked Jude.

'You can worry and plan any day of the week, as no doubt you're aware. I want to get this sorted as soon as possible, preferably by lunchtime tomorrow. So, if you don't mind, I'll be off.'

'I was just leaving, too.' Jude saw Ashleigh looking down at the cards, saw what she was thinking. Raven had somehow validated this notion that the tarot cards could give her better guidance than her own common sense and bitter experience. He was too tired to have that discussion with her, and he was already going to be late picking up Becca.

'I'll see you later then.' Ashleigh held out her hand to him and he touched it gently where he would once have leaned in and kissed her. 'I'll be discharged tomorrow, they say, though I don't expect you'll see me back in the office for a few days.'

He held the door open for Geri, who preceded him out into the corridor and almost collided with a tall, good-looking man bearing a bunch of red roses.

'Sorry!' he said, cheerfully, then surged past them and into the room. 'Ash! What have you been up to now?

Determined to die in the line of duty or something? Well, I'm not having that.'

The door swung shut. Turning to stare through the glass panel, Jude saw Scott Kirby place the bunch of roses on the locker and lean in to kiss his ex-wife on the cheek.

'Who's that?' asked Geri.

'An old friend. Now, if you don't mind, I've had a hell of a day and I need to get on.'

'Old friend, eh?' said Geri, not without malice, keeping pace with him as he strode towards the door, 'I'm sure you don't need my opinion but it looks to me as if your personal life just got a whole lot more complicated.'

'You reckon?' he said, and laughed, because it struck him that in fact the opposite was true and that his life had just got a whole lot simpler.

THIRTY-SEVEN

Becca couldn't wait to get home. She must have been waiting in reception at the B&B for him, because she appeared at the door before he could get out of the car.

'Thanks for coming to get me,' she said, as he turned the car up towards the A66. 'I know you've got a lot to do. And wasn't today supposed to be your day off?'

He smiled at that, because Becca always seemed to know his working patterns just as he always knew hers, doubtless from the same source — his mother and Mikey. 'No rest for the wicked, as they say.'

'I appreciate it. I feel like I've been in prison. I never realised how much I like to be outside.' She pulled down the mirror and fussed unnecessarily at her hair. He sensed she was snatching sideways glances at him. 'And I do miss poor old Holmes.'

'I'm sure Mikey's keeping tabs on him.'

'Gil called me to say thank you, bless him. He was very gruff. He hates the phone.'

Jude chuckled. 'He's a tough old lad, is Gil.'

'I expect he'll be on my list for next week. That wound will need the dressing changed.' She flipped the mirror back up. 'I'm glad everything turned out all right. Can you tell me what happened?'

He was happy enough to eat up the journey with as much of the detail as he could — Gil's rescue as they drove along the A66, Raven's death as they dropped down into the steep dip through Dacre, the tale of the seventh Earl Capel as they headed for Pooley Bridge, and the events in the crypt and Rose's dramatic intervention as they breasted the side of Askham Fall and looked down on the ruins of Lowther Castle, rosy in the evening light. The detail of Ashleigh's injury, too complicated to deal with because it brought with it the spectre of her past, was something he left out.

'So, mostly all right,' concluded Becca as he finished. 'Except for Rose, poor thing.'

Jude spared Rose a thought, but he wasn't as kindly disposed towards her as Becca seemed. He'd come across a lot of people in his time who hid a ruthless, self-serving streak behind a deep veneer of good-nature and respectability and Rose fell into that class. The great majority of those who could kill would never find the need to do so but Rose, her mind made up, would have been more than happy to have pulled the trigger on Wilf Hamley in revenge for her father's death and watched him die.

But Wilf hadn't done it. This thirst for baseless revenge could have brought a further senseless death and both Wilf and Rose were fortunate that it hadn't. 'Rose will reap what she sowed.' As Wilf would do, though his crime was fraud rather than murder.

'That's harsh. The poor woman had just lost her father.'

'That's not an excuse for turning a gun on an innocent man.'

'She didn't know he was innocent.'

'She had no proof that he was guilty. We can't go round executing vigilante justice just because we've convinced ourselves someone did something.'

Becca huffed a little. He could sense she was as tired as he, probably from too many sleepless nights worrying about what would happen to her, and so he tried to cut her some slack, but he was on edge himself after the events of the past few days and he wasn't sure he had the emotional energy to deal with that. With any other person he would have engaged his professionalism, but he knew Becca too well and cared too much.

'Adam said she was distraught,' she said, fiddling with the strap of her handbag.

'I'm sure he did.' She ought to know better than to give too much credence to what Adam said about him.

'She did what she thought was right.'

'She can't possibly have thought killing him was right.'

'Can't you learn to be a bit more forgiving?'

He guided the car along a twisty downhill stretch, already regretting having offered to pick her up, wishing the journey away. 'It's nothing to do with being forgiving. It's about—'

'Doing the right thing. I've heard that before.'

He felt the row developing, powerless to prevent it. If it had been anyone else he would have let it go but with Becca years of shared living and thinking had left him in a grip of a need to explain himself. It mattered. 'What's wrong with doing the right thing?'

DEATH IN GOOD TIME

'People have different ideas of the right thing. You aren't the judge of it.'

'Okay.' He slowed as they went through Askham, passing the pub where the green was full of carefree drinkers. Maybe he should offer an olive branch. 'Look, it's been difficult for both of us.'

'I know you think I did the wrong thing about Gil.'

He did think that, and he knew he shouldn't say anything, but he couldn't help himself. 'Okay. Since you ask. I thought you knew enough about these things. I thought you knew how it worked. If you know anything you tell the police and you leave it to us to sort it out.'

'It turned out fine,' she said, and he saw the stubborn set of her lips.

'Luckily. But I thought you trusted me, at least. And Gil wanted you to talk.'

'He didn't say that.'

'Because he couldn't. But that was what he wanted you to do, and he thought you had.'

'It isn't a question of trust,' she said, got out her handkerchief and blew her nose. 'I wanted to explain. That's all. I know where you're coming from. But I wouldn't have been able to live with myself if something had happened to him. I thought you'd understand that, but you don't.'

'But it isn't about that. It wasn't just about Gil. It was about your safety, too.' He sighed as he turned into Wasby. 'Do we have to have this argument? I don't know why you had to bring this up.'

'It's because, just for a moment, I thought you cared,' she said, and fiddled about with her phone.

He brought the car to an over-sudden stop outside her cottage. 'Just for a moment, maybe I did.'

She got out. 'I'm sorry I put you out.'

'You didn't. Not one bit.' He got out, too, and looked around. Mikey was on Becca's front step and Holmes, beside him, was rearing up on his back legs and pawing at the door.

'You're back!' said Mikey, and stepped away. 'You can feed this horrible animal yourself, then, Becca. I don't think I pass the staff test. He's not pining for you, though. I know for a fact he's been getting fed down the street.' He grinned. 'And here's Inspector Poirot, too, fresh from exercising those little grey cells. It's been a busy time for you, Jude, or so I hear. Hunting down the villains and rescuing your beloved from certain death.'

'What's this?' Becca had been getting her bag out of the boot.

'Ash ended up in hospital.' Jude bent down to make a fuss of Holmes, who had forgotten about food and come racing joyfully down the path to greet him. 'A stray bullet.'

'Oh, goodness! Is she all right?'

'Just a flesh wound. She'll be fine.'

'Give her my best.' Becca picked her bag up and headed up the path. 'I'd better go and feed his lordship. Thanks again for your help, Jude.' The door banged behind her.

'Thanks, pal,' said Jude.

'Why?' Mikey looked after Becca in bewilderment. 'Did I say something wrong?'

'No.' Apart from calling Ashleigh his beloved, but Mikey hadn't been serious and Becca ought to have known that. 'It's my fault. I'm tired and I was a bit sharp with her.'

'I was only joking.' Mikey looked up the path. 'I didn't think she'd take that the wrong way. Wow. Women are complicated, aren't they?'

More than Jude had thought possible, and way too complicated to worry about just then.

'Right,' he said. 'I'm done. I've had a busy day. Let's go and find a drink.'

THE END

ALSO BY JO ALLEN

Death by Dark Waters

DCI Jude Satterthwaite #1

It's high summer, and the Lakes are in the midst of an unrelenting heatwave. Uncontrollable fell fires are breaking out across the moors faster than they can be extinguished. When firefighters uncover the body of a dead child at the heart of the latest blaze, Detective Chief Inspector Jude Satterthwaite's arson investigation turns to one of murder. Jude was born and bred in the Lake District. He knows everyone — and everyone knows him. Except his intriguing new Detective Sergeant, Ashleigh O'Halloran, who is running from a dangerous past and has secrets of her own to hide. Temperatures — and tensions — are increasing, and with the body count rising Jude and his team race against the clock to catch the killer before it's too late…

The first in the gripping, Lake District-set, DCI Jude Satterthwaite series.

Death at Eden's End

DCI Jude Satterthwaite #2

When one-hundred-year-old Violet Ross is found dead at Eden's End, a luxury care home hidden in a secluded nook of Cumbria's Eden Valley, it's not unexpected. Except for the instantly recognisable look in her lifeless eyes — that of pure terror. DCI Jude Satterthwaite heads up the investigation, but as the deaths start to mount up it's clear that he and DS Ashleigh O'Halloran need to uncover a long-buried secret before the killer strikes again…

The second in the unmissable, Lake District-set, DCI Jude Satterthwaite series.

Death on Coffin Lane

DCI Jude Satterthwaite #3

DCI Jude Satterthwaite doesn't get off to a great start with resentful Cody Wilder, who's visiting Grasmere to present her latest research on Wordsworth. With some of the villagers unhappy about her visit, it's up to DCI Satterthwaite to protect her — especially when her assistant is found hanging in the kitchen of their shared cottage.

With a constant flock of tourists and the local hippies welcoming in all who cross their paths, Jude's home in the Lake District isn't short of strangers. But with the ability to make enemies wherever she goes, the violence that follows in Cody's wake leads DCI Satterthwaite's investigation down the hidden paths of those he knows, and those he never knew even existed.

A third mystery for DCI Jude Satterthwaite to solve, in this gripping novel by best-seller Jo Allen.

Death at Rainbow Cottage

DCI Jude Satterthwaite #4

At the end of the rainbow, a man lies dead.

The apparently motiveless murder of a man outside the home of controversial equalities activist Claud Blackwell and his neurotic wife, Natalie, is shocking enough for a peaceful local community. When it's followed by another apparently random killing immediately outside Claud's office, DCI Jude Satterthwaite has his work cut out. Is Claud the killer, or the intended victim?

To add to Jude's problems, the arrival of a hostile new boss causes complications at work, and when a threatening note arrives at the police headquarters, he has real cause to fear for the safety of his friends and colleagues…

A traditional British detective novel set in Cumbria.

Death on the Lake

DCI Jude Satterthwaite #5

Three youngsters, out for a good time. Vodka and the wrong sort of coke. What could possibly go wrong?

When a young woman, Summer Raine, is found drowned, apparently accidentally, after an afternoon spent drinking on a boat on Ullswater, DCI Jude Satterthwaite is deeply concerned — more so when his boss refuses to let him investigate the matter any further to avoid compromising a fraud case.

But a sinister shadow lingers over the dale and one accidental death is followed by another and then by a violent murder. Jude's life is complicated enough but the latest series of murders are personal to him as they involve his former partner, Becca Reid, who has family connections in the area. His determination to uncover the killer brings him into direct conflict with his boss — and ultimately places both him and his colleague and girlfriend, Ashleigh O'Halloran, in danger...

Death in the Woods

DCI Jude Satterthwaite #6

A series of copycat suicides, prompted by a mysterious online blogger, causes DCI Jude Satterthwaite more problems than usual, intensifying his concerns about his troublesome younger brother, Mikey. Along with his partner, Ashleigh O'Halloran, and a local psychiatrist, Vanessa Wood, Jude struggles to find the identity of the malicious troll gaslighting young people to their deaths.

The investigation stirs grievances both old and new. What is the connection with the hippies camped near the Long Meg stone circle? Could these suicides have any connection with a decades-old cold case? And, for Jude, the most crucial question of all: is it personal, and could Mikey be the final target?

Death in the Mist

DCI Jude Satterthwaite #7

A drowned man. A missing teenager. A deadly secret.

When Emmy Leach discovers the body of a drug addict,

wrapped in a tent and submerged in the icy waters of a Cumbrian tarn, she causes more than one problem for investigating officer DCI Jude Satterthwaite. Not only does the discovery revive his first, unsolved, case, but it reveals Emmy's complicated past and opens old wounds on the personal front, regarding Jude's relationship with his colleague and former partner, Ashleigh O'Halloran.

As Jude and his team unpick an old story, it becomes increasingly clear that Emmy is in danger. What secrets are she and her controlling husband hiding, from the police and from each other? What connection does the dead man have with a recently-busted network of drug dealers? And, as the net closes in on the killer, can Jude and Ashleigh solve a murder — and prevent another?

Death on a Monday Night

DCI Jude Satterthwaite #8

An ex-convict. A dead body. A Women's Institute meeting like no other…

It's an unusually challenging meeting at the Wasby Women's Institute, with local resident and former drug-dealer Adam Fleetwood talking about his crimes and subsequent rehabilitation…but events take a gruesome turn when prospective member Grace Thoresby is discovered murdered in the kitchen.

The case is particularly unwelcome for investigating officer DCI Jude Satterthwaite. Adam was once his close friend and now holds a bitter grudge, blaming Jude for landing him in jail in the first place. To complicate things further, the only thing keeping Adam from arrest is the testimony of Jude's former girlfriend, Becca Reid, for whom he still cares deeply.

As Jude and his colleague and current partner, Ashleigh O'Halloran, try to pick apart the complicated tapestry of Grace's life, they uncover a web of fantasy, bitterness and deceit. Adam is deeply implicated, but is he guilty or is someone determined to frame him for Grace's murder? And as they close in on the truth, Jude falls foul of Adam's desire for revenge, with near-fatal consequences…

A traditional detective mystery set in Cumbria.

Death on the Crags

DCI Jude Satterthwaite #9

Everybody loves Thomas Davies. Don't they?

When policeman Thomas falls from a crag on a visit to the Lake District in full view of his partner, Mia, it looks for all the world like a terrible but unfortunate accident — until a second witness comes forward with a different story.

Alerted to the incident, DCI Jude Satterthwaite is inclined to take it seriously — not least because of Mia's reluctance to speak to the police about the incident. As Jude and his colleagues, including his on-off partner DS Ashleigh O'Halloran, tackle the case, they're astonished by how many people seem to have a reason to want all-round good guy Thomas out of the way.

With the arrival of one of Thomas's colleagues to assist the local force, the investigation intensifies. As the team unpick the complicated lives of those who claim to care for Thomas but have good reasons to want him dead, they find themselves digging deeper and deeper into a web of blackmail and cruelty … and investigating a second death.

A traditional British police procedural mystery set in Cumbria.

Death at the Three Sisters

DCI Satterthwaite #10

Three feuding sisters. A faded spa. And a woman, dead in the water…

As they head towards retirement, Suzanne, Hazel and Tessa Walsh are locked in bitter disagreement about the future of the lakeside beauty spa they jointly own. Should they keep The Three Sisters going as their parents wished, or should they sell to a neighbouring hotelier who seems determined to acquire the failing business, even at a preposterously high cost?

When their employee, Sophie Hayes, is found drowned close to the spa one cold January morning it rapidly becomes clear that it's no accident: Sophie has been murdered. But who could possibly want to kill her — or was she mistaken for someone else? As DCI Jude Satterthwaite seeks the answers he and his team dig ever deeper into the complicated and embittered relationships between the sisters and their neighbours.

As the investigation proceeds Jude becomes convinced that Sophie's murder may only be the beginning and it's not long before a shocking and tragic turn of events proves him correct and he and his team find themselves in a race to prevent a further, final tragedy overtaking the Three Sisters. Can he uncover what deadly secrets the sisters are prepared to die — or kill — for, or will he be too late?

Written as Jennifer Young

Jo writes romance and romantic suspense under the name of Jennifer Young.

Blank Space

Dangerous Friends Book 1

He's made a lot of enemies. She has some dangerous friends.

Bronte O'Hara is trying to move on from her ex-boyfriend, Eden Mayhew, but when she finds an injured man in her kitchen in the run-up to an international political summit in Edinburgh, a world she thought she'd left behind catches up with her with a vengeance.

Eden's an anarchist, up to his neck in any trouble around — and he's missing. The police are keen to find him, certain that he'll come back, and that when he does, he'll have Bronte in his sights. What does he want from her — and does she dare trust a handsome stranger with her life?

With danger and romance in equal measure, Blank Space is a

contemporary take on the romantic suspense tradition pioneered by Mary Stewart.

After Eden

Dangerous Friends Book 2

In the aftermath of a violent G8 summit when she almost lost her life, Bronte O'Hara finds herself fighting against her feelings for Marcus Fleming, the policeman who saved her. When Marcus is cleared of any wrongdoing over the deaths of three people during the undercover police operation, Bronte isn't the only one who struggles to come to terms with the outcome. The friends and relatives of those who died are determined not to let the matter rest, whatever the cost. Some are looking for closure; some want justice. And someone is determined to use Bronte in a bid to gain revenge…

Storm Child

Dangerous Friends Book 3

Scotland can be a dangerous place.

When their car comes off the road in a blizzard, Bronte O'Hara and her boyfriend, detective Marcus Fleming, stumble across an unconscious teenager in the snow. After he's rescued by two passing strangers, the boy simply disappears, and even Marcus's police colleagues don't believe their story — until the youth's body is found.

It looks like the accidental death of a young criminal, but Bronte and Marcus are convinced that things aren't as straightforward as they seem. Who was he? What was he doing out in the storm? Who else might be in danger?

And who will stop at nothing to make sure that Bronte and Marcus never find out?

Looking For Charlotte

Divorced and lonely, Flora Wilson is distraught when she hears news of the death of little Charlotte Anderson. Charlotte's father killed her and then himself, and although he left a letter with clues to the whereabouts of her grave, his three-year-old daughter still hasn't been found.

Flora embarks on a quest to find Charlotte's body to give the child's mother closure, believing that by doing so she can somehow atone for her own failings as a mother. As she hunts in winter through the remote moors of the Scottish Highlands, her obsession comes to threaten everything that's important to her — her job, her friendship with her colleague Philip Metcalfe and her relationships with her three grown up children.

ACKNOWLEDGMENTS

An author doesn't work alone. In writing this series I have had help and support from too many people to name.

I must, however, give a name-check to the usual suspects: Graham Bartlett, who kindly advised me on aspects of police procedure; Mary Jayne Baker delivered, as always, a stunning cover; to Caroline Shenton, whose book *National Treasures* helped me out with my plot as well as being a rip-roaring read; and finally, as always, I owe a huge debt of gratitude to the eagle-eyed Keith Sutherland, for proofreading.

Thank you to you all!

Printed in Great Britain
by Amazon